THE PERFECT MOMENT

ALIX KELSO

Happy Reading!

Alix Kelso

Lake Falls
Publishing

Published by Lake Falls Publishing, Glasgow, Scotland UK.

JOIN MY READER'S CLUB

Reader's Club members enjoy lots of lovely goodies including a free Fairhill book, exclusive content, and a regular newsletter packed with fun stuff straight from my writing desk.

Don't miss out! See the back of the book for details about how to sign up.

For my husband, David.

Thanks for believing in me, even when I didn't.

CHAPTER 1

Laura set the plate of scrambled eggs and toast down for Mr Davidson, offered him her best smile and braced herself. "Enjoy your breakfast. Would you like more tea?"

"No, but don't go anywhere yet."

The other waitresses would've rolled their eyes at this command, but Laura only smiled again and watched the old man dig into the eggs. He chewed thoughtfully for a moment, before tossing his fork on to the plate and shaking his head.

"Has the chef heard of seasoning? Salt? Pepper?"

"There's salt and pepper on the table, Mr Davidson."

"What next? You want me to cook the eggs myself too?" He waved a hand in the air. "Take them away. Tell the chef to make them again. She needs to whisk before she cooks. She needs to add cream, salt, pepper. She needs to warm the pan. And please God don't tell me she microwaves them or I won't be held responsible for my actions."

"No problem, Mr Davidson." Laura removed the

offending plate of eggs and headed for the kitchen, where she could already see the chef, Tanya, peering through the door pane, her eyebrows beetling.

"What's the old fart's problem today?" Tanya asked.

"Not enough seasoning. Not enough cream. He hopes you aren't microwaving them."

"*Microwaving* them! He drives me up the wall. Why do we let him in here anyway?"

"Because he's a lonely old man who likes our company, although he'd never admit it. And you know he only sends the food back to wind you up."

Tanya tasted the eggs and shrugged. "There's nothing wrong with these. But if he wants more seasoning, that's what he'll get. I'll give him enough salt to pop an artery."

"Don't you dare!" Laura tore a sheet from her order pad and pinned it to the pick-up station. "Four full Scottish breakfasts for table seven, which means you don't have time for a stand-off."

Tanya scowled and began breaking eggs into a bowl. "You're too nice to that old codger. In case you hadn't noticed, he never tips you."

"I don't do this for the tips. I do this for the sheer fun of it."

"Then there's something seriously wrong with you," Tanya called out as Laura disappeared from the kitchen.

Laura was only half joking, too. She loved her job, loved waitressing, and loved Valentino's, the gorgeous Italian cafe and restaurant run by the Fachini family for more than eighty years. From its corner spot on Shaw Street, in Glasgow's Fairhill area, the banks of windows offered views of the busy road outside, and most of the booths were usually occupied from mid-morning with people-watchers looking for a prime spot to observe the comings and goings, of which there were plenty.

Glancing through the windows as she wiped a table, Laura saw the usual Fairhill bustle and activity. The greengrocer was stacking crates of onions and peppers beneath the striped canopy of his pavement display. The hairdresser was dashing from her salon into the minimarket where she bought her gossip magazines and chocolate bars. A couple of volunteers in the charity shop were dressing a window mannequin in a summer dress and sunhat. In the window of a tenement flat above the pharmacy, a young woman rocked a baby on her hip while she talked on the phone cradled at her ear. And on a tree-lined road that spurred off Shaw Street, a man stood on the wide stone steps of a sandstone townhouse, tending to pots of lush red geraniums that crowded the doorway.

In a beat, Laura took it all in. There was always something going on in Fairhill. And everyone knew the best spot from which to watch this busy little world go by was inside the jewel in the Shaw Street crown – Valentino's.

Laura loved everything about the wonderful old restaurant. She loved the age-speckled mirror that hung behind the beautiful bar, reflecting the spirits and liqueurs that lined the shelves. She loved the framed photographs on the walls depicting various members of the Fachini clan over the years. She loved the smell of bolognaise sauce and red wine, the oohs and ahhs over Valentino's legendary ice cream sundaes, the easy-listening music that played all day, the rush inside the kitchen, and the buzz of a busy service.

On a day like today, with the summer sunshine

warming the flower-decked outdoor seating area, it was easy to find something to smile about while working. But even in the depths of a cold Scottish winter, the restaurant still managed to fill Laura with joy, with its old-fashioned bronze chandeliers glowing warmly while the aroma of hot soup and stew lured diners from the dark, damp streets beyond.

Working at Valentino's made her happy, and being in the restaurant felt like home.

In her apron pocket her phone vibrated, and she saw a message from her boyfriend, John: *Pick you up tonight at seven for the cinema.*

She'd forgotten they were going out, and for the tiniest moment felt a stab of disappointment. Her flatmate, Yvonne, would be out tonight, and Laura was looking forward to the solitude of her little flat above the laundrette. She'd planned to pour a glass of wine and heat up whatever scraps might be lurking in the fridge. Maybe she'd stretch out on the sofa and watch television for a while.

Immediately, she felt guilty. Instead of anticipating a night of warmed-up leftovers and getting into her pyjamas by eight o'clock, she ought to be excited about seeing John.

She *was* excited about seeing John. Of course she was. He was a nice guy, and she liked him, quite a bit. When they were together, she could just switch off her brain, because they spent most of their time at the cinema, which was John's favourite place in the entire world. Being with him was a lot like being alone, which suited her just fine.

She typed a quick reply confirming the plans and slipped her phone back into her pocket. As she headed for the server station, Paul, the restaurant's assistant manager, signalled to her from behind the bar, where he was working the coffee machine.

"Natalie wants to speak to you," he said, frothing a jug of milk.

Laura's eyes widened. "I didn't know she was here already."

Paul poured the milk into two coffee cups. "She came in while you were dealing with Mr Davidson's eggs."

She frowned. Natalie Fachini, the owner of Valentino's, didn't usually arrive until late morning. But something had been off with her for a while. She wasn't keeping her normal routines and didn't seem her normal self.

"Did she look okay?"

Paul appeared confused. "I don't know. I'm just telling you what she told me to tell you." He picked up the tray of coffees and left the bar to serve them.

Laura glanced towards Natalie's office at the back of the restaurant. Not for the first time, she thought about her boss and all she'd gone through recently and wished there was something she could do to help her and make everything alright again.

And, also not for the first time, she reminded herself that life just wasn't that simple.

Laura walked down the narrow little corridor towards the office at the other end. When she knocked on the door, she felt a strange flutter in her stomach, as if things that had been in balance for the longest time were about to be upended.

Which, it turned out, they were.

. . .

LAURA OPENED the office door and saw Natalie on the other side of the desk, staring at a montage of photographs that hung on the wall. A sweetly sad Italian aria played on the little stereo in the corner. Opera was the only music ever heard inside the office. Out in the restaurant, it was easy-listening music, but in here, it was opera. The arrangement, she knew, dated to when Natalie and Angelo had taken over the restaurant after Angelo's father retired. Angelo, the showman, had run the front of house and liked his music fun and romantic. Natalie, the businesswoman, had run the back and liked her music serious and contemplative. For decades, their arrangement had worked and made both of them very happy.

Anyone who wanted evidence of that happiness only had to look at the photographs Natalie was gazing at on the wall. The largest of the group, in the centre, told the entire story. It was a black-and-white shot of Natalie and Angelo in a loose ballroom pose in the restaurant, laughing as they gazed into one another's eyes and twirled around the empty tables. It was a beautiful shot, one their son had taken late one night after the restaurant had closed, and which he'd later had framed for their anniversary. Laura knew that Natalie treasured the photograph. It was the one that best captured the brilliant twinkle in Angelo's eyes.

There had always been dancing and fun and laughter whenever Angelo was around. Laura missed him still. She could scarcely imagine how much Natalie must miss him.

"Natalie?" she said quietly, so as not to startle her.

Turning, Natalie cleared her throat and smiled. "I was a million miles away. Come in, have a seat."

Laura took one of the tub chairs on the other side of the

desk and studied her boss, who looked elegant today, as usual, in crisp linen trousers and a lemon shirt, with one of her signature silk scarves draped around her neck. Natalie always looked immaculate and graceful, a skill she wished she possessed herself. Laura tucked a few stray hairs behind her ear and smoothed her apron over her lap.

"How are you this morning?" Natalie asked, sliding into the leather desk chair and picking up a pen, with which she began to fidget.

"I'm good, Natalie. How are you?"

"Oh, yes, I'm just fine." She tilted her head towards the little stereo. "Listen to this part of the music, Laura. Tell me it isn't beautiful."

Laura listened to the soaring orchestra and the rising voices. Yes, it *was* beautiful. Natalie had probably played the piece for her before, and probably said the same thing about the beauty of the music. She waited a beat before speaking. "Is everything okay, Natalie?"

The older woman's eyes snapped back into focus and exhaustion swept her face. "No, Laura, everything's not okay. Nothing's been okay since Angelo died." She let out a sound that was half laugh, half sigh.

"It's been hard for you. You need to give yourself time."

Natalie shook her head. "You are a sweet girl, but too polite. It's been two years since Angelo died. Instead of telling me I need to give myself time, you ought to be telling me to pull myself together."

Laura was appalled. "I'd never say something like that."

"Well, in that case, you're not as good a friend as I thought you were."

Stung, Laura dropped her gaze. In the ten years she'd

worked at Valentino's, she'd come to adore Natalie, and although the woman was her boss first and foremost, she treasured the friendship that had bloomed between them. In the terrible weeks and months following Angelo's sudden death from a heart attack, she'd done everything possible to lessen Natalie's load where Valentino's was concerned. But she'd also been a shoulder for Natalie to cry on once her children had returned to their own lives. After the shock had passed, she had tried to offer Natalie kindness and understanding as she began to navigate the world with her husband no longer in it. Natalie's accusation therefore hurt, a great deal.

"I'm sorry, Laura," Natalie said. "That was a terrible thing to say. It was wrong, and it was untrue. Of course you've been a good friend to me." She fidgeted with the pen for a moment. "But I've been drifting since Angelo died, and I can't keep on drifting. I'm only sixty-two, for God's sake. I thought we'd have our old age together, retire together and travel a little. We were planning a trip to Naples just before he died."

"Maybe you should still take that trip. Maybe your daughter might want to go with you, or one of your friends from your exercise class."

"Perhaps." Natalie looked thoughtful. "But I need something more than a few weeks' holiday somewhere."

She tossed the pen on to the desk and her thoughtful expression turned apprehensive. Laura watched, waited, and a sinking feeling began in her stomach.

"The thing is," Natalie continued, "whenever I walk in through Valentino's door, I think of Angelo, smiling and laughing with the customers, and it breaks my heart all over again. For a while, I hoped our memories here would be a comfort. But they aren't, and I've come to accept that. And I've made a decision. I'm going to sell Valentino's."

Laura sat frozen. Her brain would not process what she'd just heard.

"I wanted you to be the first of the staff to know. You've been here the longest and I consider you a friend, of course, not only an employee. Valentino's is a solid, profitable business, and I don't expect it will be hard to sell. I intend to select a buyer carefully, but ultimately whoever comes in here will want to change things. And so I want you to know what's happening so that you can think about your own future too."

But Laura wasn't listening. Natalie's words simply floated over her head.

"Laura Evans, you are gaping like a goldfish and it is most unbecoming." Natalie laughed, but after a moment a concerned expression crossed her face. "Oh Laura, I do wish you'd say something."

It took another few seconds, but Laura finally got her mouth working. "You can't sell this place. It's your life."

"It *was* my life. But every day I come here, I'm living in the past. I want to move on. I *need* to move on. You understand that, don't you?"

Laura shook her head. "But it's so drastic! You'd be giving up everything you and Angelo worked for. You can't walk away from Valentino's. What if you sell it and regret it?"

"I won't regret it, and—"

"You need to do something else, make some other

changes in life, before you do something so huge. Natalie, please. Don't rush into this."

"It only seems like I'm rushing because you just heard about it. But I've been thinking about this for a long time."

Laura hunched forward, practically leaning over Natalie's desk. "Take that holiday to Naples. Take a whole tour of Italy! Enjoy yourself and catch up with all those relatives of Angelo's you're always talking about. Or maybe you could swap your aerobics class for something new. Or start a new hobby. Anything! But *selling Valentino's?* Please don't do it."

"Laura, I—"

"Maybe you need to make some new friends. Maybe it's even time for you to start thinking about seeing men again."

Natalie opened her mouth, then plopped it closed again. "Well, I'd be lying if I said I hadn't thought it might be nice to go out with some man or other sometime. I loved Angelo, but I can't say I like being a widow. Women have needs, even heartbroken ones. Maybe especially heartbroken ones."

"See! There you go! You don't need to sell Valentino's. You just need to find a man."

But Natalie waved a hand. "I probably *do* need to find a man, and maybe I will. But that's entirely separate from the restaurant. I'm sorry, Laura, but my mind's made up." She glanced at her watch and rose from her chair. "Look, you joined us at the restaurant after a horrible, difficult time in your own life, and I know how much this place has come to mean to you. I know it was hard for you when Angelo died, and it will be hard for you when I leave here too.

Don't think I don't know that, because I do. But things change. Life goes on, whether we want it to or not. I'm ready to move on with my life. Maybe it's time for you to move on with yours too."

"But I don't want to move on! I love Valentino's!"

"In which case, I have no doubt the new owners, whoever they turn out to be, will be happy to keep you on."

"But it won't be the same here without you, Natalie."

She smiled sadly. "Just as I think it's not the same here without Angelo."

Laura felt tears brim at her eyes and blinked them away. Furious embarrassment flushed her cheeks. At twenty-nine, she was too old to start blubbering in the boss's office. But Natalie, noticing the tears, came around the desk and put her hands on Laura's shoulders.

"We'll always be friends, you and I. Don't cry, I feel bad enough as it is." She pulled her into a hug. "Everything will turn out fine. You'll see."

But Laura didn't see how things could possibly turn out fine. Angelo was gone, and now Natalie would soon be gone too. The people she loved kept leaving her.

It was turning into the story of her life.

She hugged Natalie hard, wishing it didn't have to be this way, and wishing she could find some way to change it.

"I'M NOT SURPRISED she wants to sell the place. I'm surprised that *you're* surprised."

Laura and John were standing in line for popcorn. The little girl ahead of them couldn't decide which snacks she wanted, and John had begun nervously glancing at the clock above the hot-dog warmer. Laura knew he hated to miss the movie trailers. He even enjoyed watching the advertisements that preceded the movie trailers, which she found bizarre.

"Why are you surprised that I'm surprised?"

He shrugged and selected an enormous bag of Minstrels from a display. "You must have known something like this was coming."

"Why must I have known? I'm not a mind reader."

"You don't have to be a mind reader to guess that when a husband and wife run a restaurant together for forty years and one of them dies, the other might find it too hard to keep the place going."

"I thought the restaurant would've been a comfort to her. I thought she'd want to hold on to all those memories."

"Did you want to hold on to all the memories when your parents died? I mean, isn't that why you sold the house, because it hurt too much to be there? Natalie's just doing the same thing you did."

She found herself staring, hard. They'd only had the briefest of conversations about her parents' death and everything that had happened afterwards, and it had never gone as far as any serious discussion about how she'd actually *felt* about any of it. The truth was, she'd never talked to anyone about how she'd felt. It had just been too painful. And by the time the pain had begun to soften, she'd found she didn't want to risk reopening the wounds by discussing it.

John had jumped to conclusions based on a few casual

conversations they'd had. He didn't know her well enough to make those kinds of observations, and it rankled.

"Look, I'm just worried Natalie's making a mistake. Valentino's is her livelihood, and it's her life. If she sells it, she can't get it back again if she decides she did the wrong thing."

"She's a grown woman. She's probably talked with her kids about this and with her friends."

"I'm her friend."

He glanced up from the sweets. "You know what I mean. She can look after herself. Maybe you ought to leave her to it and think about yourself."

"And wouldn't it be a nice world to live in, if we ignored everyone else and only thought about ourselves?"

John held up some sweets. "Revels or M&Ms?"

She glanced at the other two bags he'd already tucked under his arm. "You're going to eat three bags of sweets during the film?"

"I floss. Anyway, one of these is for you. Which do you want?"

She pointed to the Revels. The little girl ahead in the line had finally chosen her snacks, and her mother herded her away. John moved forward, stacked the sweets on the counter, and ordered drinks and a bucket of popcorn. Laura wondered if he'd really be able to eat so much junk in the next two hours or if he'd end up hauling half the sweets back home with him, like he did last time. And the time before that.

She studied his face while he pulled out his wallet and paid. Four months into their relationship and she still didn't really get him. She wondered if that was good or bad.

They left the snack lobby and headed to their cinema screen.

"Natalie said she might be interested in starting to see men again," she said. "You know, romantically. Maybe if she found someone new, someone to share things with, she'd see things differently about selling Valentino's."

"It's probably hard to find someone when she's working all hours at the restaurant. Once she's rid of the place, she'll have all the time she needs to get loved up again."

Laura gave him a look, but he was oblivious, checking their tickets to see where their seats were and grumbling appreciatively when he saw advertisements still playing on the screen.

"What I'm saying is that if she found someone new, maybe she wouldn't want to sell Valentino's at all. Maybe the memories wouldn't hurt so much."

John settled into his seat, slotted their drinks into the cupholders, and organised the snacks. "I'm looking forward to this movie. I heard there's a really great chase scene."

She turned and looked at him. "You want me to shut up."

"I wouldn't put it like that. But I came here to watch the movie."

She glanced at the screen. "This isn't the movie. This is an ad for a mobile phone you already own."

"Here, have some popcorn."

She got it. She did. This was the most in-depth conversation the two of them had had in weeks, and she'd gone and bored him with her story of Natalie. They were her concerns, after all, not his. He just wanted a night of fun at the movies. There was no harm in that.

But she wondered if he truly had no idea how much her heart was breaking after what Natalie had told her, or if he knew and just didn't want to get into it any more than he already had.

Settling back in the seat, she ate some popcorn before handing the box back to John. She wasn't hungry. She tried to concentrate on the movie, but soon lost the thread of it.

Her mind wandered to Valentino's and to Natalie, and just wouldn't come back to the here and now, no matter how much she told it to.

CHAPTER 2

Bruce was enjoying the late morning quiet while cleaning the counter in The Crooked Thistle pub, when the peace was shattered by a blood-curdling howl from his Uncle Keith who, by the sounds of things, had just fallen down the back stairs.

Not all the stairs, though. Bruce had already heard his uncle's footsteps come down most of them. Although with Keith's mood currently being what it was, that wouldn't stop him making a noise consistent with a gruesome fall from fifty feet above.

Bruce stuck his head through the back. Keith sat awkwardly on the bottom stair riser, a look of shock and fury spreading over his face.

"Okay through there, Uncle Keith?"

"No, I'm not bloody okay! Who left these stacks of paperwork sitting on the stairs?"

"You did, Uncle Keith. You said you wanted to take them up and look through them."

"Well, for God's sake." Keith propelled himself upright

and gestured to the spread of papers that now lay over the stairs and on the floor. "If you realised I'd forgotten, why didn't *you* take them up?"

Bruce began gathering the spilled invoices and accounts and stuffed them back into the foolscap folders. "Did you hurt yourself?"

Keith scowled and raked a hand through the mad tufts of grey hair that sprouted from the top of his head. "I'll have a bloody great bruise on my backside tomorrow, no doubt."

Bruce suppressed a grin and laid the stack of paperwork on the hallway table. "Want me to fetch you a couple of painkillers?"

"No, I bloody don't. Have you changed the Tennent's barrel yet?"

"Yes."

"And have you cleaned the bar?"

"I was just doing it."

"Well get back to it then, for God's sake. We open in five minutes."

Amused, Bruce returned to polishing the lager taps while Keith roamed through the public area, still scowling as he aligned the bar stools and set out fresh beer mats. Watching him carefully, Bruce decided that as his uncle's mood couldn't possibly get any worse, he might as well ask about the woman he'd been seeing, since he suspected she was at the root of his grumpiness.

"How was your big date last night with Tracy?"

Keith's scowl deepened. "She didn't turn up. I sat on my own like a fool for thirty minutes before she texted to say she couldn't make it."

"Sorry, Uncle Keith. That's rotten."

"Aye, it is."

"I know you liked her. Will the two of you arrange to see each other again?"

"Not bloody likely."

"There are other women out there, Uncle Keith. You're a good catch, and decent company when you're not in a foul mood."

"Hey, enough cheek from you, son."

Bruce laughed. "We'll find someone for you, Uncle Keith."

But he waved a hand. "I'm done. I'm not interested. I don't need women messing me around any more."

"They're not all like that."

"Aren't they?"

Keith arched an eyebrow, and Bruce automatically ran his thumb over the inside of his palm and felt the absence of the wedding ring he'd been wearing until just a few months ago. It still felt strange not having it on his finger. And it still hurt any time he thought of the reason it was no longer there.

He cleared his throat. "Don't be a pessimist, Uncle Keith. You have to have hope."

"I do have hope. I have hope that you'll get this place opened so we can make some money." Keith looked out the window. "Look, Jimmy Pearson's already out there waiting. Get a move on."

Keith marched off in the direction of the kitchen, where Bruce assumed he'd start harassing Marek, the pub cook, about bar food matters. And right on cue, as soon as the kitchen door swung closed behind him, he heard Keith complaining and arguing.

The man needed a woman, Bruce decided. A woman who'd be good to him, unlike the women he usually ran after.

Bruce unlocked the pub doors and said hello to Jimmy Pearson, who took his usual stool at the bar, ordered a pint, and turned to the sports pages in the newspaper he unfolded from his jacket pocket. As Bruce pulled the pint, he gazed again at the still pale strip of skin on his ring finger.

Maybe he needed a woman too.

Yeah, sure. Possibly in ten years he'd have recovered enough from the tornado that Heather had brought down on his head to consider having a cup of coffee with a woman sometime.

He sat Jimmy's pint in front of him, took his money, gave him change, and had just begun fiddling with the house music system when he glanced through the big glass window that overlooked Shaw Street and, on the other side of the road, saw the doors of Valentino's open and saw Laura dash out and head in the direction of The Crooked Thistle.

The smile was already on Bruce's face before he even knew it was coming.

LAURA SWUNG through the doors of the pub and smiled when she saw Bruce. "Mind if I have my lunch break here?" She held up a foil-covered dish.

"Pick a table. You want a drink?"

She waved the water bottle she'd brought. "I'm all set."

"Valentino's busy today?" He knew it must be. Laura usually took her lunch or dinner break in the restaurant at a spare table. Sometimes he saw her through the window, eating a sandwich or forking something from a plate while reading a book or flicking through a magazine. But if Valentino's was busy, she came to The Crooked Thistle, bringing with her whatever food Tanya the chef was laying on for the staff that day. Laura had told Bruce that she couldn't settle to eat her meal when the place was jammed, when her colleagues were run ragged and could use a hand. It was easier to step across the road, get out of the chaos for a short while, eat quickly and in peace, and then get back into the fray.

When Bruce had first come to work at The Crooked Thistle and was acclimatising to his uncle's unpredictable moods, he'd been gobsmacked to discover that the older man had a soft spot for Laura and didn't seem to mind her coming in to eat her lunch – and didn't mind that she didn't even buy a drink. But surprise had soon turned into understanding. Laura was someone a person could easily develop a soft spot for.

"We've got an early booking for a table of sixteen today," she said. "A big family birthday celebration. It's hectic." She looked down at her covered dish and pulled off the foil. "Where's Keith?"

"In the back shouting at Marek."

She laughed softly. "That man's all bark."

"Yeah, and Marek's all bite. He'll only put up with a few more minutes of what Uncle Keith's dishing out before he takes a chunk out of him."

The pub door swung open and another local, Big Kev, ambled in. He grunted a greeting at Jimmy Pearson, who grunted in return, and took a bar stool beside him. While Bruce prepared Big Kev's drink order, he watched Laura peer into her lunch bowl before poking unenthusiastically at the pasta it contained. He thought it looked delicious, and it certainly smelled delicious, but she ate only a few forkfuls before pushing the food around the inside of the bowl.

She had an odd look on her face. Whenever he saw her she wore a smile, and not just on her lips but in her eyes too. It made her glow in a way that few people did. Today, though, her expression seemed troubled. The fork had now been set aside completely and she was unhappily contemplating the mound of uneaten pasta.

Under the auspices of wiping down a nearby table, which he'd already wiped before opening up, Bruce strolled over, cloth in hand. "Everything okay?"

She glanced up and flashed a smile. "Of course. Why?"

"You look like you've got something on your mind."

She waved a hand. "Oh, I'm fine, really."

He folded the cloth a few times. "If there's something you want to unload, feel free. That's what barmen are for, you know. We get special training to turn us into good listeners. It's compulsory. We can't work without it."

Laura laughed, and he liked hearing the sound of it. He watched her consider whether to share the thing that was racing around inside her head.

"If I tell you something, can you keep it a secret?"

"Absolutely."

"You couldn't even tell your Uncle Keith."

"I understand the meaning of the word secret, Laura. Whatever you tell me goes no further."

She nodded, then glanced around the bar, and when she spoke her voice was quiet. "Natalie's planning to sell Valentino's."

Seeing the sadness sweep over her face, he pulled out a chair at her table. "I'm sorry to hear that. Not as sorry as you must be."

She fidgeted with her pasta fork for a moment. "Natalie says she wants to move on. I know losing Angelo hit her hard, but I never imagined she'd want to leave Valentino's."

Bruce shifted in his seat. He could understand Natalie's reasons only too well. Natalie's bereavement was quite obviously in a league of its own. But in his own life, his wife's betrayal of their marriage had left him stunned and floundering, and once he'd finally got his wits back, the only thing he'd wanted was to get away, to somewhere, anywhere. That was what had brought him to The Crooked Thistle – that desire to leave the past behind.

Still, he could see that her boss's decision had left Laura surprised and shocked. "I know you think a lot of Natalie. It'll be hard for you to see her leave."

"I've worked there for ten years, Bruce. Natalie feels like family to me. Angelo felt like family to me too. Losing one of them was bad. Losing them both—" She glanced up and shrugged. "I know how crazy that must sound. Employees aren't supposed to feel this way about their bosses. But it's just the way it is."

"Will you keep working there once new owners arrive?"

"I don't know. It'll be strange having new people come

in. Maybe I'd have to move on. But I don't want to. I love it there."

"A sale won't happen right away. There'll be time to think about what you want to do."

"It's not just me, though. I'm worried about Natalie. Her whole life is in that place. What if she sells up and then wishes she hadn't?"

He watched Laura twist her hands together and saw the trouble that clouded her eyes. It touched him to know she cared so much about her boss. "It's sweet of you to worry about her."

Laura laughed, but it was filled with melancholy. "My boyfriend doesn't think so. He says I ought to leave her to make her own decisions and just think about myself."

"I'd hate to imagine the state we'd be in if everyone thought only about themselves."

She looked up in surprise. "That's exactly what I said."

Just then, there was a great clatter of pots from the kitchen. The door was thrown open and Keith was propelled through it, with Marek shoving at his back. Bruce and Laura looked over at the commotion.

"Stay out of my kitchen!" Marek yelled. "I'm the chef. I decide what's on the menu. Today, the special is chicken paprika. End of discussion! If you don't like chicken paprika, then don't eat it! Now leave me alone!"

Marek stuck out his chin and marched back into the kitchen. As the doors swung behind him, cooking smells wafted out into the bar. Jimmy Pearson and Big Kev sniffed the air.

"Smells good," Jimmy said. "If that's the chicken paprika, I'll take a plate."

"Me too," said Big Kev, chuckling.

"Oh, shut up, the pair of you," Keith shouted. "Neither one of you could tell paprika from parkin."

The two men chortled. Keith scowled around the pub and spied Bruce sitting at the table with Laura. "Laura, nice to see you," he said, and pointed at Bruce. "You, get up and get some work done. I'm not paying you to sit around chatting to the punters."

"You're not paying me at all, Uncle Keith."

But Keith just ignored this. "I'm off to the baker's for a sausage roll for my lunch, since Marek's decided to try to starve me to death with this new-fangled cooking of his."

Keith stomped out of the pub.

"Your Uncle Keith thinks chicken paprika's new-fangled?" Laura asked.

Bruce shook his head. "No, he doesn't. He loves Marek's cooking. He's just being difficult and trying to pick a fight."

She looked puzzled. "Why?"

"He needs a woman," he said, his tone quiet, "and can't seem to find one who doesn't mess him around."

She considered this. "Maybe we should set him up with Natalie. She needs a man to show her some fun and distract her from making the worst decision of her life by selling Valentino's."

Bruce looked at Laura. She looked straight back. Finally, they broke into laughter.

"Yeah, really bad idea," Laura said.

"He's too bad-tempered."

"And she's too nice to be expected to put up with him."

Still, they stared at one another, the thought swirling between them. Laura's phone began beeping. "That's my alarm," she said, silencing the noise. "Break's over." She covered her uneaten pasta with the foil and picked up the bowl. "See you later, Bruce. And thanks for listening, I appreciate it."

"Any time."

She disappeared out the door, and Bruce watched her dart across the road, her ponytail bouncing over her shoulders. Once she was back inside Valentino's, he saw her grab a tray of drinks waiting to be delivered to a table and pull out her pad to take down an order.

She was a whirlwind.

"Any chance of some service?" Jimmy Pearson said, turning on his bar stool and gesturing with his empty pint glass.

"Hope you're not so loved up you'll leave your punters to die of thirst," Big Kev said.

Coming around the counter, Bruce's eyebrows shot up. "What are you talking about?"

"You've got your heart set on Wee Blondie over there." Jimmy chuckled. "We've got eyes."

"Well, you must need them checked at the opticians," Bruce said, pulling the fresh pint.

"If you say so," Jimmy said, chuckling again with Big Kev.

But Bruce wasn't listening. Instead, he was focusing very hard on not peering out the window towards Valentino's and on not thinking about how pretty Laura's ponytail had looked as she ran across the road.

Just don't go there, he thought. The last thing he needed was to start slobbering over some girl. His heart had already been broken once this year. And she had a boyfriend, anyway. It was a non-starter on every conceivable level.

He'd come here to work, get his head sorted, and think about what direction to take next. He'd come here to get over Heather and the detonation of their marriage. He had no bandwidth for anything other than that.

He set down Jimmy's fresh pint and decided it was time the shelves behind the bar were cleared and scrubbed. Mindless, physical work – that's what he'd come to The Crooked Thistle for. And so that's what he'd do.

THAT EVENING, Bruce drove to his brother's house for dinner. The lovely summer's day had turned into a pretty summer's evening, and it felt good to get into his car, roll down the window, and just drive.

His brother, Jack, lived on the south-west edge of Glasgow with his wife, Claire, and their children, Chloe and Isla. The two girls barrelled out the front door as soon as he pulled on to the driveway, and Bruce smiled to see them. During the years he'd spent living in London, he'd missed watching the girls grow up. The opportunity to enjoy more time with his nieces had been one of the few upsides of the disintegration of his marriage.

"Uncle Bruce!" Chloe yelled as he got out of the car. "We've got a paddling pool in the garden!"

He took in their brightly coloured swimming costumes and the pool toy that little Isla was clutching. "I hope you're watching out for sharks."

The girls screamed with laughter. "You don't get *sharks* in *paddling pools*, Uncle Bruce!"

"I'll remember you said that when I have to dive in and haul you out from between the teeth of a great white."

More screaming laughter.

"Do you like hamburgers, Uncle Bruce?" Chloe wanted to know.

"Love 'em."

"That's what Dad's cooking on the barbeque for dinner."

"Uh-oh, has he set fire to the garden yet?"

The girls darted around as they all walked through the house and out to the garden at the rear. There, Bruce found his brother hunched over an enormous gas barbeque, and his sister-in-law, Claire, spooning salad on to plates.

"New toy?" he said, clapping his brother on the back and gesturing to the shiny barbeque.

Jack beamed. "I bought it at the weekend. Still haven't worked out what all these dials and whatnot are for. But she's pretty cool, don't you think?"

"He's already referring to that thing as a *she,* which I find disturbing," Claire said, giving Bruce a kiss on the cheek. "Last night he cooked some chicken, and then spent an hour cleaning it afterwards, pouting at the splashes the marinade sauce had made."

Bruce grinned. "You've truly entered the realms of middle age, Jack. My condolences."

"It'd be a shame if your burger happened to fall to the ground while I'm bringing these over to the table," Jack said.

Bruce peered at the burgers. "If one of those hit the

ground, it'd likely crack your paving stones. Should they be as charred as that?"

Jack snorted. "They look delicious and you know it."

They did, and tasted even better. The hamburger recipe was Jack's own and fiercely guarded, the result of much tinkering and tweaking of ingredients and seasonings. The girls chatted while they ate, regaling Bruce with tales of what they'd been up to that week, and when they grew bored of eating, were allowed to return to the paddling pool.

"How's Uncle Keith?" Jack asked, popping the last of his burger in his mouth.

"Grumpy, but otherwise fine."

"The man's been in a bad mood for as long as I can remember."

"Why's he grumpy?" Claire asked. "I don't know that side of your family. He's not even a full uncle, is he?"

"He's our dad's cousin," Jack said, and drank from his bottle of beer. "And he's had three failed marriages. I guess that'd probably leave a person in a bad mood."

"That's a shame. Is he with anyone now?"

Bruce shook his head. "He had a few nights out with a woman but it fizzled out. I feel bad for him. I think he'd like to have someone in his life, but he keeps picking the absolutely worst women to hook up with."

"The women he married were no good?" Claire asked.

"That's an understatement." Jack plucked a fresh beer from an ice cooler. "The first wife I don't remember because we were just kids at the time, but she ran up a lot of debt, then hoofed it and left him to pay it all off. Nearly ruined him, financially. The second wife ditched him to go back to her first husband. The third wife was already having affairs before they even got married. Dad tried to tell him, but Uncle Keith insisted he had her all wrong. Two years later, she ran off with one of the men she'd been sleeping with behind his back. That was, what, three, four years ago, Bruce?"

"Sounds about right."

"I feel bad for him," Claire said, spearing some leftover salad from the bowl on the table. "He's had bad luck to end up with three women who treated him that way."

"And that doesn't include the women he's gone out with in between the wives," Jack said. "A few of them have been hair-raising according to my mother. Considering what a good businessman he is, running that pub of his, it's odd he's got such bad judgement when it comes to women."

Reaching for his glass of lemonade, Bruce caught his brother's eye. "Being good at making business decisions doesn't automatically make you good at making life decisions."

Jack opened his mouth to respond, but apparently realised the blind alley down which he was stumbling. He laid a hand on Bruce's arm. "Sorry, I wasn't thinking. And it was a stupid thing to say anyway."

He waved a hand. "Forget about it."

Claire laid down her salad fork. "You still haven't heard from Heather since you moved back?"

"No."

"She really did a number on you," she added, anger flushing her cheeks. "It makes me fume any time I think about it."

"Then don't think about. That's the only strategy that's been working for me so far."

But she had the bit between her teeth. "She was so sneaky about it. Running around behind your back, cheating on you with whatever-his-name-was, and then dropping that *bombshell*."

Bruce loved Claire for the righteous fury he saw in her eyes. It felt good to have people on his side. In London, he'd had no one, not really. He'd been too busy building up his business to make the sort of friends upon whom he could rely in moments of personal crisis.

He'd had big dreams when he'd moved to London and had worked around the clock to make them come true. Risking every penny he had, and every penny he'd convinced the bank to lend him, he'd bought and restored an unloved, tumbledown pub on the edges of west London and turned it into a lucrative, and much-admired, business. All his time had been ploughed into running it, and it had made him proud to accomplish something meaningful, to take a wreck and transform it into a livelihood.

Meeting Heather, and falling for her and marrying her, had been the icing on the cake. What spare moments he managed to carve out from running his pub he'd happily spent with her.

When it turned out she'd been spending her own free time rather more creatively than he could ever have imagined, he'd discovered there was literally no one in London he was close enough to talk to about any of it.

That his beautiful new wife had been cheating, while bad enough, was only half the story. When he'd heard the rest of it, explained to him by a sobbing Heather late one night as he sat dumbstruck at the kitchen table, it'd hit him like a juggernaut.

And so he'd come home, back to where there were people he could be comfortable with, while he put himself back together again. As much as he ever could put himself back together. He suspected he would always remain scarred by what Heather had done. But spending time with Jack and Claire and their girls, with his parents, and with his grumpy Uncle Keith – maybe, bizarrely, *especially* with his grumpy Uncle Keith – had kept him going. The separation of their lives from the one he'd tried to build in London with Heather had helped him get his arms over the ropes and begin hauling himself up from the canvas.

Still, hearing his sister-in-law grow angry as she spoke of Heather only reminded him of all the punches he'd taken in the ring before he'd gone down for the count.

"Let's not waste a beautiful summer's evening talking about her," Bruce said, and gave Claire a squeeze on the arm.

Her expression softened. "I suppose it doesn't exactly help you to hear me let off steam. It doesn't change anything, does it?"

"I've discovered that letting off steam makes you feel better for about two seconds, but that it absolutely does not change anything whatsoever."

She smiled and glanced at her watch. "Okay, I'm off to load the dishwasher, and then I need to get ready for tomorrow. I've got surgery scheduled from eight and medical journal reading to do before I have an early night."

"Surgery? Medical journals? How'd you manage to get such a smart woman to marry you, Jack?"

"I tricked her."

Claire grinned, kissed Bruce on the cheek, then her husband. "Don't gossip too long, boys."

"Men don't gossip."

"Of course they don't." Claire looked over to her daughters, still splashing in the paddling pool. "Five more minutes girls, then it's bath time."

"Why do we need a bath?" Chloe yelled, feigning puzzlement. "We're already wet."

"Being wet doesn't make you clean. Five minutes."

Claire disappeared into the house, and Bruce soon heard her through the open window humming along to the radio as she dealt with her kitchen chores. Jack stretched out in his chair, beer cradled against his belly. The girls splashed around in the pool, the last of the evening sunshine slanting through the trees at the bottom of the garden.

"This is a nice life you've got here, Jack."

"I know. Beats me what I did to deserve it."

"Me too." Bruce grinned at his brother. "How's the business doing?"

Jack, an enthusiastic car fan ever since they'd been kids, had turned his passion into a living by setting up his own luxury limousine service. His fleet now encompassed more than a dozen high-end vehicles – Mercedes, Jaguars, Range Rovers – and Bruce knew his brother had worked tirelessly to grab a slice of the corporate market and attract business from those with the wallets to pay for such indulgences.

"Things are good," Jack said. "I won a contract for one of the big golf tournaments. There's a lot of work there, driving VIPs between the airports and the hotels and the venue."

"You've always had an eye for a lucrative business opportunity."

"So have you." Jack slid a glance at his brother. "Still can't believe you walked away from that gold mine you made for yourself down in London."

"I didn't walk away. I sold up."

"As if Heather didn't hurt you enough, you let her drive the blade in even deeper by selling off your livelihood."

Bruce sipped his lemonade. "Tell me, Jack. All that work you put into your limo company. Why do you do it?"

Looking confused, Jack shrugged. "For my wife. My girls. For me too, sure, but it's for them."

"At the start, when I first bought that old place and refurbished it, it was for me. It was my baby, and I wanted to see if I could pull it off. But after I met Heather, it was for her too. For my wife and the kids I thought we'd have. When all that was gone, I couldn't face going back to that place I'd built, knowing the thing I'd built it for didn't exist any more."

Jack frowned and sipped his beer. "Still don't think you should've sold it."

"I made a good profit."

"Yeah, and what are you doing with it? Nothing. You're the only thirty-two-year-old self-made millionaire I know who'd end up living in his uncle's spare room and working for free in his pub."

Bruce laughed. "The Crooked Thistle's a nice place and I like it there."

"You've been there four months. When are you planning on getting back into the saddle?"

"Just as soon as I stop feeling sick at the idea that I had this great life and I lost it."

"You didn't lose it. Heather destroyed it. Stop blaming yourself."

"Easier said than done."

Just then, Claire shouted through the open kitchen window to the girls, telling them their five minutes were up. Chloe and Isla got out the paddling pool and began running towards the house. But Isla, her feet wet and uncoordinated, slipped and tumbled to the grass. Bruce was preparing to leap from his chair to help her, but no sooner had his little niece hit the ground than she was bouncing back up again, brushing grass from her legs and running to catch up with her sister, throwing a huge grin to her father and Bruce as she sped past.

"That's what it's time for you to do, Bruce," Jack said. "Get up, brush yourself off, and keep going. Simple."

Sure, Bruce thought. Simple.

CHAPTER 3

Laura woke with the dawn, just after four thirty. Outside all was quiet, the red sandstone of the tenements just beginning to catch the first colour of the rising sun. The sky above the rooftops was the perfect blue of a midsummer morning.

It was going to be a beautiful day.

Laura pulled on her running gear and bundled her hair into a ponytail. Across the tiny hallway, her flatmate's bedroom door was open. Yvonne had not come home last night. For days, she'd been talking non-stop about her new guy, Olly, and how she couldn't wait to spend the night with him. Clearly, last night had been the night. Good for them, Laura thought. No doubt she'd hear all the lurid details soon enough.

Jogging down the tenement stairs, she stepped outside and breathed the sweet summer air. The conditions were perfect for an early morning run.

She set off east, along the blocks of streets lined from one end to the other with four-storey tenements, taking in the colourful flowerpots that dotted the stepped entrances. Passing the Salvation Army centre and the old Fairhill parish church, she crossed Shaw Street jogging past shuttered shops and cafes and scattering pigeons pecking at discarded takeaway food. When she reached the grand gates of Mungo Park and veered inside, she slowed her pace to enjoy the tree-lined walkways and flowerbeds, before pressing on around the small pond where ducks quacked happily and then up the incline around the municipal golf course.

She'd only recently got into running after seeing a poster advertising a ten-kilometre city race in the late summer. She had liked the sound of the challenge. It had begun with a lot of hard work to improve her endurance and strength, pounding the pavements and wondering if she'd ever manage to run without getting an agonising stitch in her side.

Now, though, there were a couple of months of hard work under her belt. While she'd never be mistaken for a skilled athlete, she enjoyed the simple pleasure of feeling her feet propel her over the ground. Early morning runs were best, when the city was still. Sometimes as she ran, she felt like the only person who was awake in the world.

This was her quiet time before the rush of her shift at Valentino's, when she let her body test its strength and let her mind wander where it would. No kilometre markers, no finish lines – not yet, anyway. Just the peace that came with the physical rush of the run.

Yet even as her legs protested at the steepening incline of the hill around the golf course, she sensed her usual tranquillity was eluding her, as it had done ever since Natalie's shock news about her plans to sell Valentino's.

Laura wasn't stupid. She understood the world and understood the logic of her boss's motivations. But none of the other staff had reacted the way she had when Natalie told them her plans. There had been sadness, yes. Surprise too, perhaps. But not shock, not the sort that she had felt. The staff had, to a person, told Natalie they'd be sorry to see her go, wished her well for whatever lay ahead, and had then simply got back to work.

In the days since, Laura had wondered where she was in her life, exactly, that news about the impending departure of an employer should shake her so, especially when her own job was not in danger. Whoever ran Valentino's would still need waitresses. And she would be one of them.

It was the loss of Natalie that would hurt the most. That and the certainty that Natalie was doing the wrong thing by selling up.

At the summit of the hill that rose above the small golf course, she paused to catch her breath and look out over the city. From here, she could see straight across to the Campsie Hills that hugged Glasgow to the north. She saw motorways snaking through town and across the River Clyde, saw the jumble of streets and buildings that stretched for miles in either direction.

Years earlier when she'd first arrived in Glasgow, she'd thought she'd never really get to know the city, its character, its way of life. But she had. It was home now.

And the home she'd had before, with her parents in their lovely house out in the rolling countryside, fifty miles to the south, felt more and more like a half-remembered dream with each passing year.

Things changed. The death of her parents when she was nineteen had forced her to set aside the dreams she'd had in life to find work and support herself. She'd found Valentino's and begun to recover from the grief. In Angelo and Natalie Fachini, she had found not family, but as close an approximation as she could get. She hadn't expected to be there still, a decade later, and there was no doubt that the Fachinis were part of the reason she had remained. And if she was happy and content, why move on?

Valentino's had changed after Angelo died, his absence keenly felt. But Laura had thought that time would heal the place and everyone closely associated with it. If Natalie was gone, too, what sort of place would Valentino's become? Would it still be the place she had grown to love if neither of the people who'd made her love it belonged there any more?

Sighing, she began running again, heading down the incline and towards the park exit.

If there were answers to these questions, she couldn't find them.

VALENTINO'S OPENED for breakfast at seven, and the assistant manager, Paul, was already behind the bar when Laura knocked on the locked door just after six thirty.

"Coffee machine's warming," he said, unbolting the door to let her inside. "Would you set napkins on those booths by the window when you're ready? Looks like the late shift forgot."

In these moments before service started, Valentino's always looked perfect. The tables were set and neat, the floor scrubbed, and the bar counter gleamed. The place smelled of old polished wood and of the flowers in the bud vases, overlaid with the hints of bacon and sausage being prepared by Tanya in the kitchen and the glorious smell of freshly ground coffee.

Laura laid out the napkins on the tables that had been overlooked the night before and accepted the mug of coffee Paul prepared for her. She was leaning back against the bar counter to take her first sip when someone began banging at the restaurant doors.

Looking up, she saw the grinning face of her flatmate, Yvonne, framed in the glass panels. Her curly hair was a mess of untamed corkscrews, her mascara was smeared, and her cheeks were flushed. Laura couldn't be entirely sure, but it looked like the shirt she wore beneath her light summer jacket might be inside out.

"Open up!" Yvonne shouted. "I'm starving!"

Paul rolled his eyes and turned back to the coffee machine. Laura unbolted the door and let Yvonne inside. "We're not supposed to open until seven," she said.

Yvonne threw herself into a booth. "I've just had the most amazing night of my life, Laura. Opening times, other routine constraints, those don't apply to me right now." She picked up a menu and tossed it back down after barely a glance. "Tell Tanya I need a full Scottish breakfast. Extra potato scones, and no scrimping on the black pudding. I must've burned off ten thousand calories last night."

Laura curled a lip. "Spare me."

"Spare us all," Paul called out from behind the bar.

"And I need coffee, lots of it," Yvonne shouted in Paul's direction. "Grande. Venti. Whatever it is, give me the biggest you've got. I'm exhausted."

Once she'd delivered the breakfast order to the kitchen, Laura slid into the booth opposite Yvonne. "I'm working, so just give me the edited highlights."

Yvonne's smile was somehow both serene and smug. "It was amazing. He's amazing. Imagine the best sex you've ever had, and then imagine it to the power of ten."

Laura just stared.

"Maybe even the power of twenty." Yvonne's smile grew wider. She gazed at Laura, and then the smile suddenly disappeared. "Oh no, wait. You're not imagining it with John, are you?"

"Who else am I going to imagine it with?"

She frowned. "He's not the best sex you've ever had."

"Well, no. But before him, it'd been so long since the last time, I hardly remember anything else to compare it to."

"That's just sad. Why are you even going out with that guy?"

"He's okay."

"Okay."

"Okay is something, Yvonne. We don't all have your sparkling personality and yogic flexibility in the bedroom. Some of us just have to take what we can find."

"Don't talk rubbish. You could have anyone you wanted. Take a look at yourself in the mirror. You're a knockout."

"I don't have time for pouting at myself in the mirror."

"Of course, I forgot, you're the busiest woman in the Western hemisphere. Between your shifts here, and your weekly cinema trips with John, and – oh let's see, what else? – your completely non-existent social life otherwise, it's amazing you can find time even to get dressed in the mornings."

"You're mean."

"Not mean enough where you're concerned."

The kitchen bell pinged. Laura brought out Yvonne's breakfast and watched her dive into it like someone who'd just spent a week lost and starving in the wilderness.

"You need to find a man who excites you," Yvonne said around a mouthful of fried egg. "Someone who gets your blood running. Last night Olly got my blood running so hot I thought I'd catch on fire."

"Jesus," Laura said and went off to refill her coffee.

The restaurant doors swung open and Natalie breezed in. She pushed her sunglasses up on to the top of her head and looked around the restaurant.

"Good morning, Paul. Morning, Laura. Morning, Yvonne. Yvonne, are you aware that you have mascara gloop running out of one eye?"

Yvonne pulled a compact mirror from her bag and rubbed at the offending make-up. "You might've mentioned this, Laura."

"You were too busy telling me about all the sex you'd just had."

Natalie brewed herself an espresso. "Please keep all sex discussions for the privacy of your own flat, girls. No need to make us old people jealous. Paul, the commercial estate agents will be here this morning at eight. I thought it best to have them visit early, before the rush of the rest of the day. Just come and get me in my office when they arrive."

"No problem," Paul said as Natalie disappeared down the back corridor.

Laura gazed at her retreating figure before looking over at Paul. "It's really happening."

"Of course it is," he replied, looking puzzled, before opening a fresh bag of coffee beans and turning back to the machine.

"You don't still think she'll change her mind?" Yvonne said, slicing into a strip of crispy bacon.

"No, just hoping. I wish she'd give it more thought before she does this."

"Any luck fobbing her off with other diversions?"

"I'm not fobbing her off. And they aren't diversions. They're activities she might enjoy."

"You really thought you could convince her not to sell Valentino's by signing her up for a salsa class?" Yvonne could barely conceal her grin. "Did she even go to the salsa class?"

Laura pouted. "No."

"You're a meddler."

"If I was about to make a huge life mistake, I'd hope someone would care for me enough to meddle too."

"Hence my suggestion that you ditch Movie Boy and find someone who's actually right for you."

"I don't have time for silly nonsense like that right now, Yvonne. I'm trying to help Natalie."

"Yeah, help her stay here forever just so you don't have to accept that things change."

Laura stared at her friend. "That's not fair."

"Probably not. Sorry." Yvonne laid down her fork. "Listen, if you're really so fixed on getting her to change her mind, you need to give her something to stick around for. And she's not going to stick around for a salsa class, that's for sure. You need to find her a man."

"That was my first instinct. She's open to the idea, she said as much. I've been trying to think of guys she'd like to go out with. What do you think about Harry Nairn?"

Yvonne frowned. "The man who spends all his time at the allotments? Won't he just bore her to death about carrot mites and soil additives?"

"Hmm, maybe. How about Jim from our building?"

"He's okay, I suppose, but he's not exactly someone who's going to knock her socks off, is he?"

"That's all I've come up with so far."

"You're trying to give her vanilla. But Natalie doesn't need vanilla, not at this point in her life. What she needs is chunky monkey."

Laura sprayed a mouthful of coffee across the table. "Jesus, Yvonne."

"It's true! She needs someone who's going to surprise her and show her a really good time. And, yeah, I do mean in bed."

"You're obsessed."

"Look, I'll tell you a story. Last year, someone I know at work came out of a long relationship. It ended badly, her heart was broken, all that stuff. Said she'd never be able to face going out with a man ever again, blah blah. For a few months, this continued. Then, her friend – not me, someone else – sets her up on a date with this guy she knew. He was in the same situation, just out of a long-term thing, not sure what to do next. We all laughed when we heard about it, because this guy was totally the opposite of the long-term boyfriend she'd just been with. I mean, just completely different."

Yvonne scooped up some eggs and took a slurp of coffee before continuing. "Anyway, her pal talks her into going along on this date, just to get the muscles moving again, you know? She ends up seeing him for six weeks. Has a great time. They're completely wrong for each other, not compatible in the slightest. But for those few weeks, they had fun and surprised each other, if you know what I mean."

Laura rolled her eyes.

Grinning, Yvonne spread her hands. "And then they both happily went their separate ways. No grief, no drama. They'd enjoyed one another for a few weeks and they were ready to move one. Straight away, she starts seeing someone new. She got married to him just last month. How's that for a happy ending?"

She leaned back in the booth. "The point is, if you want to set Natalie up with someone who'll get her interested in romance again, you need to think of the least likely person for her. Not some gruesome horror show of a man. Just someone you wouldn't expect her to be with. Maybe that's all it'll take to get the men juices flowing again."

"Men juices. That's gross."

"But you get my meaning. You need to find someone who's completely off the radar of possibilities, someone who's about as unlike Angelo as it's possible to get. But also someone who isn't likely to bore her senseless, like either of those guys you already thought of. Can you think of anyone that fits that bill?"

Gazing out the bank of windows across Shaw Street,

Laura looked at The Crooked Thistle on the other side. "Actually, maybe I can."

"Good, so set it up." Yvonne checked her watch, then pulled money from her purse and laid it down on the table to cover her meal. "I'm going out again tonight with Olly. Don't wait up. And get moving on fixing someone up with Natalie, before it's too late."

Laura unlocked the restaurant doors. Yvonne dashed out, and a few waiting customers stepped in. The morning service began, but as Laura served coffees and breakfasts her head swirled with one idea and one idea only.

Natalie. And Keith. Natalie and Keith *together*. Was it crazy? Or a stroke of genius?

At eight o'clock when the commercial estate agents turned up – two shark-faced men in expensive suits who reeked of aftershave – she watched them move around the restaurant with speculative looks on their faces, and her stomach rolled.

She decided she not only should take drastic action; she *would*.

CHAPTER 4

When her shift finished at one, Laura crossed over Shaw Street and into The Crooked Thistle. It was busy inside, the lunchtime crowd tucking into pub lunches and enjoying their pints. On the big screen that hung on the far wall, a golf tournament was playing on mute, while the house system boomed out old rock tracks. Laura noticed Jimmy Pearson and Big Kev in their usual spots on the bar stools, drinks in hand. She wondered if the pair of them ever spent time anywhere else.

She saw Bruce working behind the bar filling drinks orders. Another of the bar staff, Sophie, was clearing tables. There was no sign of Keith anywhere.

"Hey, Bruce," she said, leaning over the bar to get his attention.

He turned from the whisky optic where he was adding a measure to a glass and smiled. "Hey yourself." He set the drink on the counter, took money from the customer, and gave change. Seeing no one else waiting to be served, he moved down the bar towards Laura.

"Do you have five minutes to spare?" she asked.

"Sure." He gestured to a free table in a quiet corner of the pub.

"Where's your Uncle Keith?"

"He's off at some whisky lunch junket laid on by one of the distilleries."

"Sounds like fun."

"Four-course meal with paired whisky tastings. He'll be in a great mood when he gets back."

She arched an eyebrow. "In that case, I've come at the perfect time. Remember the other day when I told you Natalie was selling Valentino's, and I was worried she was making a mistake and maybe she needed to start doing other things in her life instead of spending so much time at the restaurant?"

"Sure."

"And remember I said she ought to go on a few dates with a man, someone who could show her a good time?"

"Sure."

"And we joked about setting up Natalie with your Uncle Keith."

"Sure."

"Do you really not see where I'm going with this?"

Bruce laughed and raked a hand through his hair. "I *do* see where you're going with it. But it's so nutty, I thought you must just be having a laugh."

Shaking her head, she leaned over the table. "I know it's a mad idea. They're completely wrong for each other.

Natalie is a lovely, smart, beautiful, capable woman. Your Uncle Keith is ... well, he's ..."

"A grumpy old sod."

"I was aiming for words more diplomatic than that."

"There aren't any. He is what he is and doesn't make any apologies for it."

"And he shouldn't. But listen, here's the thing. I'm not trying to marry Natalie off, for God's sake. She just needs to get out and have fun. Since Angelo died, she hasn't done much of anything. She has a few close girlfriends, but mostly she spends her time at Valentino's. It's not healthy. No wonder she wants to sell the place. But maybe she *won't* want to sell if she spent time doing other things. Maybe she'd want to hold on to it, cut back her hours, hire someone to take on more of the managerial stuff."

"That all sounds terrific. But what's it got to do with my Uncle Keith? You said yourself, they're completely wrong for one another."

But she was smiling, almost rocking in her seat. "That's precisely it! My friend got me thinking about it, she said ... well, I won't bore you with the story. But just because they're wrong for each other on paper doesn't mean they wouldn't have some fun together. Like I said, it's not like I want her to get married to him. And I'm guessing your Uncle Keith must know a thing or two about women. He's been married, what, three times? And he's gone out with plenty of women in between."

She took in his raised eyebrows. "Okay on the face of things, this might not make him the best candidate," she said. "But on the positive side, surely it means he knows how to show a woman a good time?"

He looked thoughtful. "Actually that's true, as far as I can tell anyway. He was seeing a woman recently and took her to some nice restaurants, and she seemed to enjoy herself. She came by here one time and he was really sweet with her."

"Great! Oh, but is he still seeing this woman?"

"No. She dumped him. He was pretty upset about it. In fact, he says he's not interested in women, or dating, or anything like that any more."

Laura beamed. "This is perfect!"

"It is?"

"Of course! Here's what we do. You tell your Uncle Keith that as Natalie's getting ready to sell Valentino's, maybe it'd be a nice gesture for him to take her out to dinner. Just one local businessperson to another, in honour of all the time they've both run their businesses here. And that he should do it now, rather than later, because ..."

She searched for an excuse and clicked her fingers when she found one. "Because once a sale starts to go through, Natalie might not have time."

Bruce scratched his head. "He's so annoyed after being dumped, I don't see him wanting to do this any time soon. He'll say that Natalie won't be leaving for a while, the *For Sale* sign isn't even up yet, so what's the hurry?"

"Okay, tell him that you heard me mention how Natalie was finding it all a bit emotional, starting the sale process, and how she could use a friend right now."

"But you're still relying on him doing all the running and on me manipulating him into it. This is *your* set-up. What exactly are you contributing?"

"I'll tell Natalie that Keith's faith in women has been

crushed ever since he got dumped and wouldn't it be nice if she went out with him to show him that not all women are like that."

"This all sounds really complicated," Bruce said, glancing up at the golf tournament on the television.

She could see he was losing interest, for good reason. It *was* too complicated. If this was going to work, it had to be simpler.

Suddenly, the solution appeared and she grinned. "I've got it!"

He turned back from the big screen. "Spill it, then."

"We set it up so they both think that the other one asked them out," she said, moving closer. "They've known each other so long, neither will want to offend the other by not going. So you tell your Uncle Keith that Natalie dropped by while he was at his whisky lunch thing and said that she'd heard from me that it hadn't worked out with this woman he was seeing, and she wanted to treat him to dinner to cheer him up. Meanwhile, I'll tell Natalie that Keith did the same thing, popped into Valentino's while she was elsewhere, said he'd heard that the place was going on sale, and that he wanted to take her out to dinner for old times' sake."

She paused and squinted as she considered. "Today's Friday. We set it up for tomorrow night, which reduces the chances that they happen across each other in the meantime and rumble us. I heard Natalie say she was taking the day off to go shopping tomorrow and then spending the night at home. Is your Uncle Keith free tomorrow night?"

Bruce had a look on his face as he watched her, a look

she couldn't decipher. But a second later, he began nodding. "He normally enjoys working the Saturday night shift, but I'll cover for him and ask Sophie to come in for a few extra hours."

"Perfect!" Pleased that it seemed to be coming together, Laura rose to leave. "There's a lovely steak restaurant in the city centre. I'll book a table. And a taxi. Tell your Uncle Keith it'll be there for him at seven. Here, give me your mobile number and I'll give you mine, and we can text to confirm it's all on."

They swapped numbers and she headed for the door, Bruce following.

"Laura, aren't you worried that once they're out together, they'll realise that neither of them were behind this and that we were?"

She gave a crafty smile. "Of course they'll realise it. But by then, they'll already be on the date, won't they?"

He laughed and shook his head, but then looked at her with a serious expression. "Listen," he said, his tone soft. "It's a sweet idea, setting up the two of them. Maybe they'll even have a good time together. But you don't really think any of this is going to change Natalie's mind about selling Valentino's, do you?"

The smile slid from her face. "Maybe it won't. But I have to try." She had no idea if he understood what she was talking about. He probably thought she was crazy, running around like this, hatching foolish plans.

But then that warm smile returned to his face. "Okay," he said. "You have to try. So let's get them on this date and see what happens."

Reaching out, she squeezed his arm. "Thanks, Bruce." She left The Crooked Thistle, and headed out into the afternoon sunshine of Shaw Street and towards home. But Bruce's words kept running through her head as she walked.

You don't really think any of this is going to change Natalie's mind about selling Valentino's, do you?

What she was attempting was absurd. Some half-baked set-up with the guy who ran the pub across the road would never make Natalie change her mind about the decision she'd already made, would it?

Of course not. It was ridiculous, and the more she thought about, the more ridiculous it sounded. Natalie was a smart woman, unlikely to be swayed by some silly meddling, even if that meddling was motivated by the best of intentions.

She pushed away the negative thoughts. Yes, her plan was silly. Yes, her plan was absurd.

But it was the only plan she had.

BRUCE WAS REFILLING the bottle fridges beneath the bar when Keith rolled into The Crooked Thistle just after four o'clock that afternoon with a flushed grin on his face. As the doors swung closed behind him, Keith paused to look around the pub, swaying on his feet a little and nodding in satisfaction.

"Thanks for holding the fort, son."

"No problem, Uncle Keith."

"I see the Gruesome Twosome have vacated their usual

places." He indicated the bar stools normally occupied by Jimmy Pearson and Big Kev.

"It's happy hour over at The Duchess. They'll be back."

Keith hoisted himself on to a stool, looked around at the scattering of customers nursing drinks and nodded again. "Good lunch shift?"

"Not too bad. How was your whisky junket?"

"Aye, it was good. It's quite a function room they have in that hotel. And we must've tasted a dozen whiskies."

"I'll make you a coffee in that case," Bruce said, and began fiddling with the automatic coffee machine behind the bar.

"I plan to buy in a few of the whiskies they let us try." Keith fished a crumpled piece of notepaper from his pocket and squinted at what was written there. "Got the names here. I'd like to expand our range. We've got a good base stock, but people like to try new things and don't mind paying a bit extra for something different."

Bruce set a cup of black coffee down in front of his uncle. "No one around here knows their whiskies like you do. You should make it a feature, offer yourself as the expert who can guide customers to something they might enjoy. You could make up a little whisky menu, describing the single malts and the flavours. People like that kind of thing."

Keith tapped his temple. "Good thinking, kid."

Bruce cleared his throat and shoved his hands in his pockets. "Um, you know Natalie from Valentino's? She came over while you were out."

Keith slurped his coffee. "And?"

Bruce hated this. Technically this was lying, and he

hated lying. He couldn't lie to save himself. He'd rehearsed and tried to locate a breezy tone, but now that he was actually doing it, it just felt awkward, especially with Keith staring at him, waiting for him to continue.

"Well, she heard that things hadn't worked out between you and Tracy, and—"

"How on earth did she hear about that?" Keith boomed, his good mood gone in a flash.

"You know how people talk. Probably Jimmy Pearson and Big Kev – their lips flap about anything and everything."

Keith considered this. "Those two old fishwives, wait till I get a hold of them."

"Anyway, listen. Natalie said ... well, she said she'd like to take you out to dinner, as a pal, to cheer you up."

He scowled. "I don't need cheering up."

"Table's already booked for tomorrow night. Taxi's coming for you at seven."

Keith almost exploded off the seat. "Tomorrow night! What if I had plans?"

"Do you?"

"Yes! I'm working here tomorrow night. I can't just waltz off to some dinner."

"We coped fine without you this afternoon. Look, Natalie's an old friend of yours and she's just trying to be nice. And once she sells her restaurant, you probably won't see her much, maybe never. Maybe it'd be nice to get together while you've got the chance. You're not going to tell her you don't want to go, are you? That'd hurt her feelings."

Keith's expression softened. "Of course I wouldn't hurt her feelings. No, I can see it's a nice thing she's suggesting."

"So, you'll go?"

"I suppose so."

Bruce breathed a quiet sigh of relief.

"I'll be sad to see her leave that restaurant," Keith said. "I should've tried to spend more time with her after Angelo died. We were always on good terms, the three of us. It's a brave thing she's doing, moving on. She and Angelo devoted their lives to that place."

Bruce stacked clean glasses on to shelves as he eyed his uncle. "You think she's doing the wrong thing, selling up?"

"No, she's a smart woman, she knows what's best. Anyway, where's this restaurant she booked?"

"Some steak place in the city, I don't have the details."

"I'll just run across the road and ask her."

"No!" Bruce yelled, drawing looks from the scattering of drinkers and a raised eyebrow from Keith. "What I mean is that she said she wouldn't be in the restaurant this afternoon."

Keith watched him carefully and drained his coffee cup. "I suppose I'd be wearing my suit wherever we're going. I'll just go upstairs and make sure I've got a pressed shirt." Moving off the bar stool, he narrowed his eyes. "You're acting strange."

"Me? No, I'm not."

"Hmm," Keith murmured and headed for the back stairs.

Pulling his phone from his jeans pocket, Bruce wasn't surprised to find his palms sweaty and scolded himself for getting dragged into this nonsense. But he'd known he'd been hooked from the moment Laura had begun laying it out.

He sent her a message, confirming that Keith was signed up. Then, to distract himself from thinking about her any further, or the mad scheme into which she'd conscripted him, he began unloading clean glasses behind the bar and prepping for Friday night service.

It was torture, Laura thought, waiting until the last possible moment to go and speak to Natalie at Valentino's. The hours dragged after she heard from Bruce, confirming he'd got his Uncle Keith to cooperate. By the time nine forty finally rolled around, she was almost losing her mind. The restaurant closed at ten and would've already stopped taking dinner orders at nine fifteen. Natalie would be front of house, overseeing the final few minutes of service and clean up.

It was time to strike.

She locked her flat and jogged down the street. Inside Valentino's the last of the dinner customers were swirling what remained of the wine in their glasses, or finishing coffee and dessert, while the staff laid out settings for breakfast service the following morning.

"What are you doing here?" Natalie said from behind the till, peering over the top of her spectacles when Laura came through the door.

"Oh um, I forgot I left my scarf here earlier."

"Well go and fetch it quickly, unless you want to be commandeered into some task or other."

Laura made as if to head towards the small staff closet

at the back, and then paused. Natalie looked back up from the till receipt she was examining. "What is it?"

Laura hadn't realised it was going to be so difficult to tell her boss a lie. It was a little white lie, sure, and designed only with Natalie's best interests in mind, but a lie was a lie. She wondered if Bruce had had the same trouble when he was setting up his Uncle Keith.

"Laura, are you quite alright?" Natalie said, now frowning at her.

"I'm fine. I just remembered something I forgot to tell you."

Natalie stared. "And that something would be?"

"Oh. Well after you left this morning, Keith from The Crooked Thistle came over."

"And what did he want?"

"He said he's sorry you're selling the restaurant and he wants to take you out to dinner, for old times' sake, before you leave."

Natalie frowned and looked back at the till receipt. "That's very nice of him. I'll pop over in the next week or so and see when he wants to do it."

"But he's already organised it for tomorrow night."

Natalie's head shot up. "What? Well, for goodness sake, that's not much notice, is it?"

"He said he knows you'll soon be busy getting ready to move on, and he doesn't want to miss the chance to take you out."

"Well he'll have to reorganise it. I can't make it tomorrow."

"I already told him that you *could* make it."

Natalie narrowed her eyes. "Laura Evans, what on earth would possess you to do a thing like that?"

Laura shuffled on the spot, trying to avoid Natalie's thunderous expression. "You said you were taking tomorrow evening off at home."

Balling her hand on her hip, Natalie's eyes blazed. "Yes, that's what I wanted. To be at home and have a little quiet time to myself."

Laura sensed she was losing control of things, if she'd ever been in control in the first place. What had made her think she could trick this woman – who, in all honesty, did scare her just a little – into going on a date with a man she'd most likely never have thought twice about otherwise?

Be brave, she told herself. *This whole idea is crazy, yes, but you started it so now you have to finish it.*

And Bruce had already talked his Uncle Keith into this thing. Was she just going to back out and leave Bruce to untangle the mess she'd made? Force him to come up with some excuse to feed to his uncle? How would it make the man feel to be told Natalie had set up a dinner date for them, only for it to be cancelled a few hours later?

Laura cleared her throat. "Once you've sold the restaurant, you'll have all the quiet time you want. And it'd be a shame to postpone this dinner when Keith has already gone to the trouble to organise it."

Natalie's expression changed. "Well, Keith is a strange old goat, but essentially harmless. I suppose he's being very thoughtful, surprising me with a dinner treat like this."

"Exactly! So, you'll go?"

Natalie sighed. "I really was looking forward to an

evening at home on my own, Laura. Do you know how many hours I work in this place?"

"Yes, too many. Which is why you need to get out and do something fun."

She waved a hand in the air. "Fine, I'll go, if it means you'll stop badgering me."

"Terrific!"

"I'll pop by the pub tomorrow to check the details."

"You can't!" Laura shouted. "What I mean is that Keith said he won't be in the pub tomorrow, he's got errands to run."

Natalie peered over the top of her spectacles. "Errands?"

"Yes, errands. Which is why he wanted me to give you the details. The taxi will collect you at seven. He's booked a table at some fancy steak house."

Natalie gave an exasperated sigh. "Fine. Now, I've got work to do if it's all the same to you."

"No problem," Laura said, and turned for the door.

"Haven't you forgotten something?" Natalie called out.

"What?"

"Your scarf? Isn't that why you came back here in the first place?"

"Oh, of course."

Shaking her head again, Natalie looked back down at her paperwork. Laura walked to the staff cupboard, but inside her peg was empty, as she knew it would be. Muttering under her breath, she tried to leave without her boss noticing she was empty-handed.

"No scarf?" Natalie said, arching an eyebrow as she passed.

"I must have left it somewhere else."

"Mmm."

"Have fun tomorrow night!" Laura shouted as she headed for the door.

But she could feel Natalie's eyes burning into her back all the way out onto the street.

CHAPTER 5

The two taxis arrived outside the restaurant at the same time, and when Keith and Natalie got out and looked at one another, they laughed.

"Don't we scrub up well?" Natalie said, taking in Keith's smart suit, glinting cuff links, and perfectly chosen tie in deep blue. Even his hair, normally a mad fountain of wild tufts, had been wrangled under control.

Keith walked over and kissed her cheek. "You look beautiful Natalie, as always."

She was glad she'd made the effort, now that she'd seen that Keith had too. She wore a green silk summer dress, simple silver jewellery, and a pair of heeled sandals that would in all likelihood have her ankles screaming within the hour, but which made her feel glamorous and young. It had been a long time since she'd got dressed up for a night out, and she'd enjoyed the ritual.

"This was a nice idea, Natalie," Keith said, looking up at the grand building in which the restaurant was located.

Glancing his way, she realised he remained apparently

clueless about the machinations that had brought them together. Laughing quietly to herself, she decided there was no harm in him remaining in the dark until they were comfortably seated. It would be fun comparing notes on how the two of them had ended up together on this date.

"How about a drink before dinner?" Keith said, opening the door of the restaurant.

"I like the sound of that. I went shopping this afternoon and could use a nice glass of something to recover."

The bar was tucked below the steak restaurant, which was located on the first floor. A waitress showed them to a small table by a window overlooking the city streets. Tall palms in glazed pots and enormous mirrors on the walls added art deco glamour to the space. Natalie chose white wine, while Keith studied the drinks menu before opting for a single malt.

"I forgot you were a great Scotch lover," she said when the waitress departed.

"It's the water of life," he replied. "I'm planning on expanding the range we carry at the pub, actually. Make it more of a feature."

"That's a wonderful idea. In our business, we have to keep things fresh for the customers. They come first."

"You won't miss it when you sell the restaurant? Looking after your customers?"

Her smile wavered for a second before she shook her head. "Forty years in this business is long enough for me."

"I'll be sorry to see you go, Natalie."

"And I'll be sorry to leave, in many ways. But it's time to move on."

The waitress returned with their drinks and a little bowl of fancy nuts. Keith raised his glass in a toast.

"I wish you the very best for the future, Natalie. No one deserves happiness more than you."

They touched glasses. "Thank you, Keith. That's very kind."

He tasted his whisky and nodded appreciatively. "What do you plan to do after the restaurant's sold?"

She relished a few sips of her perfectly chilled wine before answering. "Well, I'd like to travel. As you know, when you own a restaurant, it's not easy to just disappear off somewhere. You either have to close for a few weeks or trust your business to a manager. Angelo and I always preferred the former to the latter, which meant we didn't travel as much as we would have liked, because you cannot simply close your business whenever you feel like some time away. So I plan to make up for that with a good, long spell of travelling."

"Where are you thinking of going?"

She paused and sipped more wine. "Angelo and I planned on travelling to Italy when we retired, to take a grand tour and see some of his relatives. But I can't imagine going there alone, it would simply be too sad."

"I can understand that."

"So, I've drawn up a new list of destinations."

Keith smiled. "Good for you. What's on the list?"

"Well, I've never been to Ireland. Can you believe that? I'd like to go to the south-west coast, maybe start in Galway and hire a car and drive wherever takes my fancy. Then I'd like to visit Seville. I want to see the flamenco and eat tapas and drink sherry."

"I'm sold. Any space for two on this trip?"

She laughed. "And after that, I want to visit Bordeaux. Tour the vineyards, drink some wonderful wine and see a little of the French countryside."

"You're making me jealous, Natalie. Keep talking and yours won't be the only business on Shaw Street being put up for sale." Keith laughed before looking at Natalie more soberly. "Seriously, though. You deserve to take those trips and enjoy them. It can't be easy, letting go of the plans you and Angelo made and deciding to start again."

"What's the alternative? Keep running the restaurant until I simply die of exhaustion? No thanks. I've been in limbo since Angelo died, but it's time to move on. I need new things in my life." She paused and sipped more wine. "Which is why I suspect Laura set up this little date for us tonight."

Keith continued smiling for a beat. Then confusion clouded his expression, and a second later his eyes flew wide in sudden understanding. Natalie laughed gently and nodded at his questioning look.

"I thought there was something fishy about this whole thing," he finally said. "*Laura* set this up?"

"I'm afraid so. That said, I'm very happy to be here with you, Keith."

"Oh aye, me too. When I heard you were selling the restaurant, I planned to take you out somewhere nice, for old times' sake, to say goodbye and wish you well."

"Laura put it to me in just those words."

"That's sneaky."

"What story did she feed you to get you here?"

"Well, actually she didn't. It was Bruce."

"So, Laura engaged him as a confederate."

"He said you'd heard I'd recently had some bad luck with a woman, and you wanted to take me to dinner to cheer me up. It struck me as a bit odd, if I'm honest. You and I have never really got into the nitty-gritty of one another's personal lives." He scratched his chin and looked sheepish. "But maybe I was feeling gloomy enough about things to treat it as a nice, and very welcome, surprise."

"What bad luck are you talking about?"

He drank some whisky before continuing. "I was seeing this woman for a while, and to tell you the truth, I quite liked her. I had a good feeling. Well I get that good feeling too often for my own good, and I build up my hopes, and then they come crashing back down. Anyway, she ended it. She sent me a text message while I was waiting for her in a restaurant."

Natalie gasped. "That's awful, Keith. What a terrible thing to do. She didn't deserve you."

Just like none of those appalling women you married deserved you either, she thought but didn't say.

"I'll learn my lesson some day," Keith said.

"You're a romantic. There's nothing wrong with that."

"You hit the jackpot with Angelo. Or, more accurately, he hit the jackpot with you."

"Now you're just flirting."

"Maybe a wee bit, aye."

They held one another's gaze for a moment. Natalie was the first to look away.

"So, why did Laura do this anyway?" he asked. "Does she really think we could get together?"

"I doubt it. She's upset I'm selling Valentino's. She

thinks that if I had things going on in my life again, I wouldn't want to sell. She's young, yet, I suppose. And while I have no doubt she cares for me and wants what's best for me, I suspect she can't face up to how things will be once I'm gone. You may remember she joined the restaurant staff not long after her parents died. I always assumed it was a temporary thing, a job with decent pay to get her through the first year after losing them while she thought about what to do next."

"Yet she's still there."

"Indeed she is. I wonder if Angelo and I didn't do her a disservice by not sitting her down a long time ago and telling her straight that it was time for her to move on and get her plans back in motion, whatever those plans had been before tragedy struck. Maybe the world scares her just a little more than it should. But when I'm gone from Valentino's, and things change there as they inevitably will, she'll have to start making decisions again in her life in order to become unstuck. I don't think she can face that. Hence why the two of us are here on this date together."

"Bruce is in the same situation. He's had a bad time since his marriage ended, and he's gone to ground to lick his wounds. If he doesn't pull himself back together soon, I'll have to give him a push. I can't have him still hanging around with me, ten years down the line, like poor Laura." He drained his whisky glass. "That said, Laura's meddling has got us here together tonight, so it can't all be bad. I'm enjoying myself."

"Me too."

"In that case, how about we get our table, order a

couple of big juicy steaks and a good bottle of red, and take it from there."

"Lead the way."

LAURA GLANCED AT HER WATCH, yet again. It was ten to midnight. Another day spent clock-watching. Sad. Very sad.

"Do you think they're back yet?"

Yvonne glanced up from the drawer she was rummaging through. "I have no idea. Probably. They're old. Old people don't stay out late."

Laura clicked her tongue. "They're not old, for God's sake."

"Have you seen my little vest? The red one with the lacy bits?"

Laura pointed at the clothes drier hooked over the radiator. "Is that it?"

"Yes! You're a star. What about my silky robe with the leopard print?"

Laura glanced around. "On the hook, next to your wardrobe."

Yvonne plucked the tiny robe from the crowded hook and tossed it into the overnight bag on the bed, beside the rest of the racy underwear she'd already packed.

"Anyone would think you're an actress auditioning for a part on *Dynasty*."

"I'd love a part on *Dynasty*."

"I meant the original 1980s series."

"Me too."

They grinned at one another.

"Olly won't know what hit him when he sees me in this stuff."

As if on cue, a car horn began honking out on the street. Yvonne ran to the window and threw it open. "I'm nearly finished!" she called down.

Peering out the window, Laura saw Olly's head pop out the driver's side. "Hurry up, Yvonne. How long can it take to pack a few things for a couple of nights away?"

Yvonne gave Laura a look. "Men. They have no idea."

Since she was at the window anyway, Laura looked down towards Shaw Street, where she could see part of The Crooked Thistle pub. There was still no sign of a taxi arriving with Keith inside, home from his big date with Natalie. Maybe she'd missed him coming back. It wasn't like she'd sat staring out the window for every single minute of the past hour and a half.

Just most of them.

"I thought Bruce was texting you when his uncle got home?" Yvonne said, choosing make-up from her dressing table.

"Maybe he was busy working in the pub when Keith got back and forgot."

Yvonne zipped up the cosmetics bag and added it to the overnighter. "You need to get out more, Laura."

"Probably."

"I'm surprised you're not out with Movie Boy tonight."

She shrugged. "Didn't feel like sitting through another superhero film."

"Thank God, she finally sees the light. Okay, I'm out of here. See you on Tuesday."

"Have fun."

"Count on it."

Yvonne slammed the front door behind her, as usual. A few seconds later, Laura saw her barrel out the tenement door into the street, throw her overnighter into the back of Olly's car, and get into the passenger seat. The car tore off, music blaring from the open windows, and turned the corner before disappearing. As relative quiet descended once more, Laura heard a dog barking somewhere, and faint laughter from a nearby flat, and the distant sound of the guy who played the saxophone further along the block.

Down on Shaw Street, a taxi pulled up outside The Crooked Thistle. She scrambled to press her face closer to the glass. Maybe Keith would emerge with Natalie in tow, invited upstairs for a nightcap.

But no one got out of the taxi. Instead, a couple emerged from the pub, veered drunkenly towards the vehicle, poured themselves inside and departed.

Sighing, Laura picked up her phone, and after a brief moment of debate, sent a message to Bruce.

Is your Uncle Keith back yet?

She waited for a reply, but none came. At the pub, a flurry of activity began as drinkers started leaving the premises in a swarm, ejected now that last orders had been served and consumed. Then Bruce appeared in the double doors of the entrance, throwing the deadbolt on one side and disappearing behind the other to do the same. The lights went out inside not long after.

And then her phone pinged. When she glanced at the screen, she saw a reply from Bruce: *Not yet.*

That had to be a good sign. Although Laura couldn't be sure if Natalie had already returned to her own place, leaving Keith to his own devices, she didn't think that was a likely scenario. They were both still out together, she just knew it.

She grabbed her phone again and dialled. Bruce answered after three rings.

"Hey," she said.

"Hey yourself."

"Your Uncle Keith and Natalie must be having a great time together."

"I guess so. He mentioned something about a jazz club he'd suggest if they had fun at dinner."

On the other end of the line, she heard the clinking of glasses. "Am I disturbing you while you're cleaning up in the bar?"

"I was just shifting a few empties. We don't clean up until morning. The last thing you want to do after working behind the bar until midnight is work for another hour scrubbing up."

"You must be tired. I'll let you go."

"No, don't go. It'd be nice to unwind for a bit. If you didn't mind talking."

Silence filled the line, a strangely comfortable silence. Leaving Yvonne's bedroom, Laura walked to the living room which overlooked the same view, and sank into the old armchair by the window.

"You know, I can see the pub from my flat," she said.

"I'll see if I can spot you."

A light came on in one of the rooms above The Crooked Thistle, then the blinds were opened, and she saw Bruce's outline in the window.

"Where should I be looking?" he asked.

"Bottom of Drygate Street, the main door past the laundrette, third floor. I'm waving to you."

A moment later, Bruce returned her wave. "You really do live close to work."

"Not as close as you."

"True. Although this isn't really work. More like a sabbatical."

"What do you mean?"

She could just make out his shrug, lit by the lamp he'd turned on in the room.

"It's a long story."

"Tell me."

"Maybe some other time."

The silence came again and she saw a grin spread over Bruce's face. "Hang on. Don't go anywhere, I'll be right back." He disappeared from the window and returned a few seconds later with a pair of binoculars, which he pointed in the direction of her flat.

"Hey, that's an invasion of privacy!"

"You're the one who invited me to look over. I have to tell you, that armchair you're sitting in is the ugliest piece of furniture I've seen in my life."

"That's a terrible thing to say!" She glanced down in mock outrage at the armchair she sat in. It was tatty and worn, with stuffing innards spewing from the back of the cushion, and the fabric was a shade of green that surely existed on no colour wheel. But she loved it. "There's nothing wrong with this chair."

"You ought to go furniture shopping. Where'd you find that thing? In a skip?"

"This was my father's chair."

"Let me guess, he made it seem like he was doing you a big favour by giving it to you, and he's now relaxing at home in an enormous leather recliner, chortling about how he finally managed to get rid of the armchair from hell."

Beats passed. Laura watched Bruce lower the binoculars. "And I just put my big fat foot into my big fat mouth, didn't I?" he finally said.

"No, it's just ... well, it happened a long time ago. But my parents died – in a car crash."

"God, Laura, I'm sorry. I had no idea."

She shook her head and smiled. "You weren't to know. But that image you gave me, of my father relaxing in a big recliner, I liked it." She paused, and thought for a moment, running her hand along the arm of the chair. "It's nice to think of him that way. He used to like watching golf on television, and he'd sit in this armchair, his feet propped up on the little stool, perfectly content. But I bet he would've loved one of those huge recliners. Yeah, I know he would've."

"I'm sorry, just the same."

"No more apologising, or I'll hang up."

"Okay." A long beat passed. "You must've been young when you lost them."

"I was. But let's not talk about sad stuff." She patted the armchair and grinned. "Let me just say that I love this armchair because my father loved it, and I'm never getting rid of it, and if you want to poke fun at my possessions, find something else."

"Fair enough. And you're not the only one with questionable stuff. Since I'm embarrassed that I made a fool of myself just now, I ought to try and make it up to you by letting you take a look at this."

He pulled the window blinds fully up, stepped aside and pointed. It wasn't easy to see details from so far away, but Laura realised that details weren't necessary.

He was pointing at a large framed painting that hung on the wall above the bed. The painting was dark grey and covered with jagged yellow brushstrokes. As soon as she saw it, she felt cold and on edge.

"What's it supposed to be?"

"It's not supposed to be anything. It just is. At least, that's what my ex-wife told me when I asked her the same question."

"You don't like the painting?"

"I hate it."

"So why is it hanging on your wall?"

"Because my ex-wife loved it, for reasons I couldn't understand. I bought it for her, even though it made my eyeballs ache. When we separated, I took it, just because I knew she loved it, and told her that if she wanted to fight me about it, she could instruct her solicitor." He gazed at the painting. "She hurt me, so I hurt her, or at least I tried to. I can't imagine there's anything I could've done to her that would've hurt as bad as what she did to me." He cleared his throat. "And I'm talking about sad stuff again, so I'll shut up."

"Talk about it if you'd like to."

"We hardly know each other.'

"Seems like we're starting to."

Bruce seemed to consider her across the expanse of the street before clearing his throat and waving a hand at the painting. "There's nothing else to say about it. I took her ugly painting just to spite her, end of story."

"Now it's hanging above your bed, so you see it every day even although you hate it."

"Yeah, that's twisted. I probably need help."

"Not help. Just time. They say time is a healer."

"They do say that, don't they? Although I can't say I feel like I'm healing yet."

"How long has it been since you separated?"

"My divorce just came through, but we split almost five months ago."

"God, that's nothing. You've got ages to go."

"Thanks, that makes me feel much better."

As they laughed a taxi pulled up outside The Crooked Thistle and they both craned their necks to see who would get out.

"It's Uncle Keith," Bruce said when the car door opened. "He looks ... yeah, he looks happy."

Keith got out the taxi, waved it off, then thrust his hands into his pockets and rocked on his heels for a minute, looking up and down Shaw Street, smiling to himself. When a couple of late-night revellers rolled past singing loudly and almost knocked into him, he only laughed.

"Definitely happy," Bruce said. "I guess the two of them had a good night."

"I won't see Natalie until tomorrow afternoon," Laura said. "Will you update me when your Uncle Keith tells you how it went?"

"Like I say, it looks like he enjoyed himself."

"I need details. Specifics."

"He won't like me sticking my nose in."

"But you'll do it anyway?"

Laura watched him shake his head, but thought she saw a smile on his face too.

"Okay, I'll text you."

"Thanks, Bruce. Goodnight."

"Goodnight, Laura."

AFTER THEY HUNG UP, Bruce watched for a moment longer as Laura pulled the curtains at her window and gave him a little wave before disappearing from view. His heart was thudding in his chest. Talking to her, he realised, was beginning to have that effect on him.

Bruce heard Keith come through the back door of the pub and head upstairs. If he heard his uncle switch on the television in the living room, he'd take it as a signal and go through. But Keith's footsteps turned towards his own bedroom at the other end of the landing. Bruce would have to wait to get the lowdown in the morning.

He looked back once more towards Laura's flat and found that he was still thinking about her.

What are you doing? he wondered, and lowered the window blinds.

The answer came quickly enough. *I have no idea.*

CHAPTER 6

Early the following afternoon, Laura was working in Valentino's, attempting to placate old Mr Davidson – who'd found fault with the cheese panini he'd ordered – while peering out of the restaurant windows for any sign of Natalie arriving. If she had to wait any longer for news on how the big date had gone, she'd burst.

Bruce had sent her a message early that morning, but it had been thin on details, saying only that Keith was still in bed. It was now after one, and he hadn't been back in touch.

The suspense was killing her. So was Mr Davidson.

"I said I didn't want tomato on my sandwich," he complained.

"There isn't any tomato on it."

"But there *has* been." He lifted the top of the panini and pointed. "Look, there are tomato seeds in here. The chef has put the tomatoes on, then remembered I ordered the panini *without* tomatoes, and taken them back off again."

"So what's the problem? No tomatoes, just like you said."

Mr Davidson looked appalled. "But the *essence* of the tomato is in there. I can see the evidence of tomato slime. I can't eat tomatoes, young lady. They give me the trots. Which means that I can't eat this sandwich." He pushed the plate away in disgust. "Tell the chef to make it again, from scratch. No tomatoes!"

She whisked the plate away to the kitchen. "Make another cheese panini for Mr Davidson," she told Tanya. "No tomatoes."

"There weren't any tomatoes on the one I sent out."

"He says he saw evidence of tomato slime."

"What the hell is tomato slime?"

But Laura was already heading back out to the restaurant, where Natalie was breezing through the doors with a big smile on her face.

"Good afternoon," Natalie said, offering a wave to the customers she recognised as she passed their tables before heading behind the bar to make herself an espresso. "Laura, how are you today?"

"I'm good. Um, so how did it go last night?"

Natalie turned, sipping her espresso. "How did what go last night?"

Laura stared. "Your dinner date, with Keith from the pub."

Natalie arched an eyebrow. "It was a very pleasant evening, thank you."

When Natalie added nothing further, Laura gaped. "Pleasant? That's all you've got to say about it?"

"Indeed, what more do you need to know? We enjoyed

our dinner together and went to a little club that Keith knew, where a very nice jazz trio was playing. All in all, I enjoyed myself." She sipped some more coffee. "In fact, Keith suggested we ought to do it again."

Laura's eyes widened. "That's terrific. I mean, that's a great idea."

"Hmm."

"So will you go out with him again, do you think?"

Natalie levelled her gaze. "Laura, I know."

"Know what?"

"I know that you set the whole thing up. You told me Keith had asked *me* out, and Bruce told Keith that I'd asked *him* out."

Laura raised her hands in a calming gesture. "Natalie, let me explain—"

"There's nothing to explain. What you did was sweet in a roundabout sort of way, and I understand your reasons for doing it." Natalie reached across the bar counter and patted Laura's hand. "But don't do it again. I'm perfectly capable of making my own decisions. Quite how you imagined packing me off on a date with Keith McGraw would make me change my mind about selling Valentino's is a mystery."

"That wasn't why—"

"Yes it was, and there's no need to pretend otherwise." Natalie drained her espresso. "Now, I might go out with Keith again as we had a lot of fun. And I must thank you for reminding me that I can have fun again with a man. But me seeing him, or not seeing him, will have absolutely nothing to do with my business decisions. I need your word that there'll be no more meddling."

Laura gulped. "I'm sorry."

"Don't be sorry. I don't expect it, nor am I asking for it. But I do expect you to stay out of my personal life. I'm a grown woman. I don't need a girl who's less than half my age meddling. So promise me, no more meddling."

Laura felt her cheeks burning with embarrassment. "No more meddling."

"Good." Natalie set down her espresso cup and squinted towards the window. "Ah, the sign man is here."

Laura turned as a van pulled up outside the restaurant. A man got out and began hauling a *For Sale* board from the cargo bay at the rear.

Laura's heart sank.

By the time she turned back, Natalie was already heading for the door to supervise the sign-hanging.

It had been a stupid plan and she'd known it all along, Laura thought as she watched Natalie step outside and begin talking with the man and gesturing to the front of the restaurant. Natalie simply wanted to move on with her life and there was nothing wrong with that. It was healthy.

Moving on was what you were supposed to do.

The kitchen bell rang. She delivered the fresh panini to Mr Davidson, but didn't wait to see if he approved. Her heart just wasn't in their little game today. Glancing at her watch, she was relieved to see there were only five more minutes before the end of her shift.

For the first time in a long time, she couldn't wait to get out of the place. She didn't want to see that *For Sale* sign being drilled into place above the door. That would just be too awful to watch.

. . .

When Bruce walked into The Crooked Thistle just after one o'clock, he found Keith behind the bar pulling drinks for Jimmy Pearson and Big Kev, who were already on their stools with the Sunday papers spread out on the countertop.

"Bruce," Keith said, "how'd it go?"

He shrugged. "A wasted journey. It wasn't what I'm looking for."

"There's no such thing as a wasted journey."

"That's philosophical." Bruce rested his hip against an empty bar stool and tossed down the paperwork tucked under his arm. Jimmy and Big Kev craned their necks to take a look.

"You're not thinking of buying that place?" Jimmy asked, pulling the paperwork closer and pointing at the photograph of the pub printed on it.

"No, I'm not thinking of buying it."

"That's not a good location to buy a pub," Big Kev said. "A bit rough and ready for the likes of you, son."

"The boy's just getting himself oriented, isn't that right?" Keith said. "Starting his research and thinking about where he might want to locate his next venture."

"Well, don't start it anywhere in that part of town." Jimmy pushed the paperwork back towards Bruce. "Not unless you want to lose all your money."

"This one's got a good head on his shoulders," Keith said. "He knows what he's doing."

Surprised by the compliment, so rare from his uncle, Bruce shrugged.

"Take a seat over there," Keith said, pointing towards the rear of the pub. "I had Marek make up a nice lunch plate for you." He ducked into the kitchen and reappeared with a tray bearing soup and a sandwich.

"I could've sorted myself something before I get to work," Bruce said.

"Nonsense." Keith sat down beside him once he'd checked there were no customers waiting to be served at the bar. "And anyway, I want you to take the day off."

"I don't mind working, Uncle Keith. I like working."

"A young man like you should be out enjoying the lovely afternoon instead of being stuck behind this bar working for free. Don't get me wrong, I don't mind the unpaid labour. But still, you should go out and do something."

Bruce studied his uncle and the smile on his face, and thought about his unusually good mood. "I take it you had a nice time last night with Natalie," he said, picking up the spoon and sampling Marek's soup.

Keith grinned. "We had a terrific night. In fact, I asked her out again and she said yes."

Bruce looked up from his soup. He wasn't surprised Keith had enjoyed the night out and wasn't surprised that he'd asked to see Natalie again. Keith had always been good in the romance department, at least to begin with. But unease snaked through him just the same, knowing the speed at which his uncle seemed to fall for women.

"Listen Uncle Keith, is that such a great idea? She's selling her business and moving away. What's the point in getting involved if—"

"We enjoyed one another's company. Why not go out again?"

"But, look, the thing is—"

But Keith was waving a hand. "Bruce, Natalie already worked out that you and Laura set us up."

Bruce laid down his soup spoon. "Are you angry?"

"A little bit to begin with. But I was out having a good dinner with a beautiful, interesting woman. How could I get upset? Plus, she wants to see me again. Who knows what might happen in the future?"

Bruce stared. "Oh God, you really like her."

"What's not to like? I don't know why I didn't think of asking her out before. Angelo's been gone two years, I ought to have made a move sooner. She's an amazing woman, Bruce. Amazing."

"But—"

"And who knows how quickly she'll find a buyer for that restaurant. Maybe she won't even go through with it. If we start spending time together, she might want to stay after all."

Bruce put his head in his hands. "You sound just like Laura. I knew this would end in tears."

But Keith just laughed. "Don't be such a pessimist, son. Nothing is ending in tears. I'm going to take Natalie out again, we're going to have fun, and maybe it'll lead somewhere good for both of us."

Grinning and rubbing his hands together, Keith rose from the table. "Natalie might just be the woman I've been looking for all these years. And there's no *For Sale* sign up yet. Maybe she's not as sure about selling as she claims to be."

Keith returned to the bar, whistling happily. Bruce felt sick inside. Natalie said she'd sell her business, and she would. Having gone through the process himself, he understood that once you took a decision like that, you didn't just suddenly change your mind.

As he watched his uncle wipe a cloth over the bar top and hum to himself, drawing amused expressions from Jimmy Pearson and Big Kev, Bruce glanced out of the pub windows and saw Natalie step out of Valentino's and begin talking to a man getting out of a van. Then the man moved a set of ladders into place and began shifting a large *For Sale* sign into place above the restaurant doors.

His appetite gone, Bruce once more laid down his spoon and sighed.

CHAPTER 7

The plan was to have a picnic in the park. Having begged off on seeing a movie with John the night before, Laura had suggested they get together after her shift, pick up some sandwiches, and enjoy the summer sunshine while it lasted. It would be nice to laze around on the grass beneath the shade of a tree. And it would be nice, too, to take her mind off Natalie, and off Valentino's, and to think about something else for a while.

As she changed out of her waitress uniform, she deliberately set her mind to thinking about John instead. The two of them ought to start doing things other than going to the cinema. John was a nice guy, but it was hard to get to know someone when the time you spent together only ever involved sitting in silence while staring at a huge movie screen. It was little wonder things felt flat between them. A picnic might be the perfect way to begin fixing things.

When the doorbell rang, she grabbed her sunglasses and the picnic blanket she'd dug out of the linen closet. But when she opened the door, she found John standing on the landing with a solemn expression on his face.

"Laura," he said, glancing at the blanket tucked under her arm. "I'm sorry, but I have to cancel the picnic."

"What?" Her good mood deflated like a burst balloon. "Why?"

"Jeff phoned this morning. He got tickets for *Raiders of the Lost Ark*. I didn't even know it was on. Can't believe I nearly missed it, actually." He shook his head in disbelief. "Anyway, it starts in an hour. So maybe we could do the picnic thing another time?"

She stared in disbelief. "You're ditching me for an Indiana Jones film you've already seen a hundred times?"

"Not a hundred times. Maybe Jeff's seen it a hundred times but I haven't. And I can't miss this. It's on the big screen! It'll be awesome."

"But I was looking forward to having a picnic with you."

He glanced at his watch. "Look, I'm picking up a couple of the guys, I have to go." Leaning over, he gave her a quick peck on the cheek. "I'll make it up to you, I promise. Thanks for understanding."

Astonished, she watched him rush down the stairs.

Dumped in favour of Indiana Jones. That hurt.

"I hope you choke on your gigantic bucket of popcorn!" she yelled down the empty stairwell. "Okay, I didn't really mean that." She closed her flat door. "And now I'm standing in my hallway talking to myself."

Sighing, she tossed the picnic blanket back into the linen closet and pulled the sunglasses from the top of her head.

And then paused.

"It's a beautiful day," she said, looking at the sunglasses. "What, I'm just going to sit around inside because some guy ditched me? And I'm still talking to myself."

Grabbing her bag, she pushed the sunglasses back on to her head and locked the front door behind her. She was halfway towards Shaw Street when she realised she had no actual idea what she planned to do next.

A bus was trundling away from the nearby bus stop. She could catch the next bus into the city centre, she thought. Maybe she'd head to Glasgow Green, buy a picnic lunch for her own damn self, and eat it by her own damn self. Why shouldn't she have a picnic on her own?

Reaching the bus stop, she glanced at the timetable and sat down on the metal bench to wait for the next bus.

She passed a minute scowling across the road at Valentino's, and at the *For Sale* sign now fixed firmly in place above the door. It hurt to see that sign up there. It just didn't look right. She hoped Natalie might be thinking the same thing.

A few minutes later as the heat of the mid-afternoon sun was beginning to bake her, a car speeding past tooted its horn and came to a halt a little further down the road. Squinting at the car, Laura wondered who it could be. She didn't recognise the vehicle.

The car horn tooted again. She walked over and looked through the open window.

"Bruce!"

He smiled. "Need a lift?"

"No, I'm waiting for the bus."

"Where are you headed? Hop in, I'll drop you."

"I'm happy to wait for the bus."

"Laura, let me give you a lift. It's no trouble."

He gestured for her to get in. Deciding that the air-conditioned car was a more attractive prospect than another ten minutes on the hot metal bus bench, she opened the door and got into the passenger seat.

"So where are you going?' Bruce asked as he pulled back into the traffic.

"Nowhere in particular, just heading into town for a wander." She glanced out the window, then back at Bruce. "I saw Natalie at Valentino's earlier. It sounds like she had a good time with your uncle. Did he say if he had fun with her?"

Bruce shifted in his seat. "He did. In fact, he's already talking about how maybe they'll end up with a great thing going on between them, and she won't want to leave after all."

She could tell from his tone that he was unhappy. "You think he's already falling for her?"

"When it comes to Uncle Keith, when he falls, he falls fast." He glanced her way. "Does Natalie happen to think the same thing?"

She closed her eyes and groaned. "She had fun, but I can't say she looked like someone on the cusp of love. In fact, she told me off for meddling. She said they'd see each other again, but it won't change her decisions about the restaurant. I feel bad for dragging your uncle into this thing."

Bruce shrugged. "He's a grown man. He gets caught up too easily with women. The problem is that the women he gets caught up with are always wrong for him. Natalie's different, she's a good person. But if he's going all mushy over her and she leaves anyway, it'll be an even worse romantic disaster than usual."

"I feel like an idiot."

He glanced at her. "Don't say that. You were trying to do a good thing. And nothing bad has happened yet, except that Uncle Keith's romance radar has been tweaked. Let's just see what happens. Okay?"

"Okay." But she sighed unhappily and turned towards the window. A thought occurred to her. "Maybe I'm looking at this all wrong. I wanted to set Natalie up to see if going out with a man might make her rethink selling up. Well it was never going to happen straight away, was it? And she had a good time with your uncle. She's planning on seeing him again. So who knows how this will turn out? Maybe Keith is right. Maybe a few more dates will get her seeing things differently."

When Bruce said nothing, she looked his way. "You think I'm delusional."

"Not delusional. Just optimistic. And that's not a bad thing."

She smiled and looked out the window. "We lit the blue touchpaper. Now maybe I ought to just stand back, keep my fingers crossed, and see what happens next." They'd had a good run of green lights and were now nearing the city centre. "Just let me out anywhere that's handy."

"I said it's no trouble to take you where you're going."

"I'm not really going anywhere."

When Bruce slowed for a set of traffic lights, she picked up her bag from the floor. "I can get out here. Thanks for the lift Bruce, I appreciate—"

"Wait, don't go," he said, turning towards her. "Listen, I don't really have big plans today either. But someone in the pub mentioned a food festival that's happening this afternoon, and I thought I'd drop by and check it out. Want to come?"

"Um, no, I don't think ..."

The light changed from red to green, and he returned his attention to the road. "I thought I'd have a look around, try some food, watch some cookery demonstrations. Come with me, keep me company."

"Um ..." She searched for a good reason not to go, but couldn't find one. It sounded like a nice way to spend the afternoon. Despite setting off for a solo picnic, the truth was she didn't really feel like being on her own.

"Okay, that sounds nice," she found herself saying. "Thanks."

He smiled. "Good. I didn't want to wander around by myself. I've been back in this city four months, and I'm still Johnny-no-mates."

"Hey, I'm your friend."

He looked at her and smiled. "That's good to hear."

The busy traffic of the city centre soon eased as they crossed the river and drove towards Queen's Park, where Bruce swooped on a parking space near the entrance gates. An open area of the park near the playing fields was spread with stalls and marquees and lined with rows of wooden tables and benches where people were relaxing and enjoying the food they'd purchased. Colourful bunting was strung between the stalls, adding a carnival feel. A band was playing on a tiny stage at one end, and kids were lining up to get their faces painted. The sun was shining, a breeze was blowing, and as Bruce paid the small entrance fee and led them towards the festival tents, Laura was happy she'd decided to tag along.

They wandered the food stalls, enjoying marinated olives one moment, tiny haggis bonbons the next. In one open-sided marquee, a fresh Italian pasta demonstration was in full swing, while in another people were learning cupcake decoration techniques. As Laura and Bruce browsed the stalls, they purchased little cartons of food and were soon heavily laden down.

"This is just greed," Laura said, balancing a bag of bread rolls on top of a stack of food cartons. "We'll never eat all this. I've already scoffed enough free samples to keep me going for a week."

"Most of these tables are taken," Bruce said, looking around. "How about we grab a spot beneath that tree?"

As they headed in the direction he'd pointed, they passed a stall selling picnicware and Bruce stopped and purchased a blanket.

"If I'd known we'd end up here, I could've brought my own," Laura said as he spread the blanket beneath the tree. "I just pulled it from the linen closet this morning."

He laid out the cartons of food and gave her a curious look.

She shrugged and sat down. "I was supposed to be going on a picnic this afternoon with my boyfriend."

"And yet you're here with me. What happened?"

"It's embarrassing."

"Tell me anyway."

She studied a carton of chargrilled vegetables. "He dumped me for Indiana Jones."

Bruce frowned, before clicking his fingers and nodding solemnly. "*Raiders* is showing at the film theatre on Rose Street. I can see the dilemma. It's a tough call."

She gasped and whacked him playfully on the arm.

"I'm kidding! Hey, you hit hard." He rubbed theatrically at his elbow. "Obviously he shouldn't have ditched you for Indiana Jones. It's a no-brainer."

"Apparently not for him."

"So, who is this guy? Want me to beat him up for you?"

She laughed and spread some brie on to a crusty roll. "He's just someone I've been seeing for a couple of months. I don't think it's going anywhere."

Bruce examined the pakora he'd taken from a bag. "So, why are you with him?"

"Good question."

They ate in comfortable silence, watching people walk around the stalls and listening to the band playing on the stage at the other side of the festival.

"This is nice," Laura said, popping an olive in her mouth and stretching out. "And this blanket's much more comfortable than mine. It's got padding and everything. I might have to buy one of these."

"You can have this one."

"Don't be daft."

"Take it. My gift to you, to say thanks for keeping me company today."

"You don't need to bribe me to get me to spend time with you, Bruce."

"I don't? Good to know."

Grinning, she pushed her sunglasses up on to her head and studied him. He was a good-looking guy, although she hadn't exactly registered it until now. She liked his thick dark hair and his grey-blue eyes, which made her think of the way the sky clears after a storm. And he had a great smile, the kind you couldn't help but return when you saw it. He was tall, in good shape, and seemed to look after himself. She found herself wondering what his wife had been thinking, letting him get away.

"When we talked last night on the phone," she said, "you mentioned your ex-wife. I've never heard you talk about her before. We don't really know each other, so tell me if I'm sticking my nose in. But the way you spoke last night, she obviously hurt you. What happened?"

Bruce set aside the food carton he'd been opening. "Let's not put a dampener on a beautiful summer afternoon by talking about it."

"Hey, I told you I'd been dumped for *Raiders of the Lost Ark*. I share, you share."

Although he laughed, she understood it was a sad laugh.

"What happened to me is a little different."

"I can see that. I'm not an idiot. But if you ever want to talk, I'm here. Okay?"

Deciding to let it go, she leaned back once more, looking out at the stalls and the people. And just when she thought the moment had passed, he finally spoke.

"She cheated on me," he said quietly. "My wife cheated on me."

Leaning forward, she squeezed his arm. "I'm sorry."

"People cheat all the time, I know that. I'm not the first person it's ever happened to, and I won't be the last."

"It doesn't matter. It happened to *you*. It hurt."

"It was a guy she knew at work, and they'd been

handling this big corporate account together. One thing led to another. Those are the words she used. I thought people only said things like that in the movies."

She waited, stayed quiet, and let him talk.

"Anyway, it had been going on for months by the time she told me. She said they'd fallen in love." He shook his head at the memory. "That was a punch to the guts. I'd been working non-stop building my business, and had no idea. I blamed myself at first. It was my fault, because I was too busy to notice my wife had fallen in love with some other guy."

"It wasn't your fault."

"So people tell me. And I guess I know it's true. But see, I thought we'd had a plan together. She was my wife and I loved her and I thought we were going to be together forever. It's hard to face up to being dead wrong about something as important as that."

She watched him debate something with himself.

"And then she told me that ..." But he trailed off and looked into the distance and shook his head. "Maybe you won't mind if I finish the story some other time."

"You don't ever have to finish the story, Bruce. You don't owe me an explanation. Listen, we'll change the topic. What's your plan now, for the future? What's next?"

Now he laughed a proper laugh and she felt relief, hating the idea that she'd risked spoiling their lovely afternoon by bringing the conversation around to painful things.

"What's next?" he repeated. "Who knows? When I was living in London with my wife – correction, my ex-wife – I bought and renovated a pub, so—"

"Ah, that's why you're hanging around with your Uncle Keith. You miss your pub."

"That, and don't forget Uncle Keith's sparkling personality is a huge draw too."

She smiled. "I just assumed you were doing some bartending. I didn't realise you were a big businessman."

"I wouldn't describe myself that way."

"Did your Uncle Keith get you into that line of work?"

He nodded. "I worked a couple of summers at The Crooked Thistle while I was at college – this was probably before you started working at Valentino's. It started as a way to make a bit of pocket money. But I loved it. Uncle Keith showed me the ropes, how the place was run. I was doing a business and hospitality course, and when I graduated I decided to go into the pub business. And I've loved every minute of it. It's dominated by the big breweries, but there's space for independents like me, if you know what you're doing. It's challenging, but so is any job.

"I sold my pub in London after my marriage ended and I came home to Glasgow. Uncle Keith let me have his spare room, and I like hanging around The Crooked Thistle, just doing routine jobs, routine work, while I regroup. I'm looking for the right opportunity to present itself to buy something else. I viewed a place this morning, but it wasn't right."

"What are you looking for? In a pub, I mean?"

He considered the question. "I liked what I did in London, taking on a place that was basically a shell but that had a lot of potential. I saw what it could be with care and attention. I say London, but we're talking the outer extremities, because I couldn't have afforded anywhere else. But there was potential. And it worked and it made money. So what I'm looking for is the chance to do the same thing again, here." He plucked at a blade of grass on the edge of the picnic blanket. "I don't know what I'm looking for specifically, but I'll know it when I see it."

"But the place you saw today wasn't it?"

He shook his head. "I didn't think it would be. Wrong location, wrong market, wrong building. Wrong everything, basically. But my brother thinks I'm dragging my heels and keeps harassing me about restarting my business plans, so now I'll be able tell him I've got the ball rolling, which should keep him off my back. I want to move on, and know I *have* to move on, but it's not easy."

"It's hard after a big shock in life." She drank from a bottle of water and picked out another olive from the carton. "After my parents died, it took me a while to get going again."

"How long before you got back on track?"

She returned the olive to the carton and wiped her fingers on a napkin. "I'm not sure I ever did. I mean the life I have now isn't the one I once thought I'd have. But I found Valentino's at a really low point in my life and I liked it there, and so I stayed. Things don't always turn out the way you expect them to, but Valentino's became the one place I could rely on to stay the same. Until now."

"It must have been hard, losing your parents. I can't imagine it."

When she looked at him, she saw his expression was open, an invitation for her to talk, if she wanted to. And she found that she did want to talk, in a way she rarely had before. Something in his eyes made her feel safe and made her want to share what lay in her heart.

"After they died," she found herself saying, "I had to sell our family home, pack up everything and leave. When Natalie told me she was selling Valentino's, my boyfriend, John, asked why I was so surprised. After all, hadn't I sold my family home after my parents were gone to get away from the memories? But he had it all wrong. I didn't sell our home to get away from the memories. I sold because I had no choice.

"At the time, I thought I was being brave, facing up to the fact that I couldn't afford to run the house, that I had to sell it, that I had to relocate to the city to have a chance of getting a job and staying afloat. But there isn't a day that goes by when I don't wish I hadn't had to do it. It was the house I grew up in and I miss it, even now. So I know how much it hurts saying goodbye to a place that means so much to you, knowing that once it's gone, you can't ever get it back."

She looked away and cleared the emotion from her voice before talking again. "Natalie says she wants to get away from the memories in Valentino's, but I worry she might end up feeling the same way I did."

Now it was Bruce's turn to lean forward and squeeze her arm. "I'm sorry about what happened to you. And I'm sorry you're troubled about Natalie."

She waved a hand. "You're sorry for me, and I'm sorry for you."

"We're quite a pair, overflowing with the joys of life like this."

Seeing him grin, she laughed. "The funny thing is I

never talk about this stuff. You're the first person I've shared it with in a long time." She looked at him, and considered. "You're sort of easy to talk to."

"I was thinking the same thing."

They held each other's gaze. Finally, he laughed and gestured towards the park and the festival. "We ought to be enjoying this beautiful afternoon, not sharing these sad stories."

She glanced around and pointed to one the marquees. "I saw a sign earlier for a pancake-making session. How about we go and do it?"

"Make pancakes?"

"Sure, why not?"

"I've never made a pancake before."

"All the more reason to make one now. You said you wanted to see some cookery demonstrations."

"Yeah, see them. Not take part in them."

But he was smiling and already gathering up the empty food cartons. Laura packed everything into a bag, and they walked over to the marquee, arriving just in time to take their places at the preparation counter.

They passed a pleasant thirty minutes, mixing pancake batter, listening to the banter from the cooking demonstrator, and sharing laughs with the other participants when everyone's first attempt at pancake frying ended in disaster. When it was time to toss the pancakes in the air, Bruce managed to throw his halfway across the tent, making Laura double over in helpless giggling.

Eventually, everyone succeeded in sliding at least a couple of pancakes from their pans on to their plates, prompting the demonstrator to break into applause and encourage everyone to join in.

"What do you think?" Laura said, gesturing to her pancakes and the mixed berries she'd artfully arranged around them.

"Not bad." Bruce turned to his own plate, on which sat a tower of charred discs. "I think mine might be inedible."

The grinning cooking demonstrator arrived at their station and issued certificates acknowledging their pancake-making prowess.

"We get a certificate!" Laura said, examining the paperwork with delight. "I can put it on my wall."

"You're really going to put this on your wall?" Bruce said, eyeing his own certificate doubtfully.

"Every small victory counts. Today, we mastered pancake making and I've got this certificate to prove it."

"Maybe you mastered it. I almost burned the tent down."

Laughing, she forked some pancake from her plate and held it out to him. "Eat and learn from a true, and now certified, pancake expert."

Bruce ate the pancake. And then reached out and brushed his hand over her cheek. The surprise stunned her laughter to silence, and the touch of his fingers made her skin tingle.

"You've got flour on your face," he said, seeing her reaction and quickly dropping his hand.

"Oh God, do I?" She rubbed at her cheek and laughed. "Is it gone?"

He reached out once more and gently wiped her face. "All gone."

His gaze held hers, and she found she couldn't look away. His eyes were really something up close, a colour caught somewhere between grey and blue like a storm crossing over a sea. And the way his lips curled just the way they did, when that smile was sneaking in from the side ...

For just the briefest moment, Laura wondered what it would feel like to press her lips against his.

Startled by the thought, she cleared her throat and glanced at her watch. "I should probably think about getting home," she said.

And she quickly walked out of the marquee before she did something really stupid.

THE EVENING TURNED sweet and cool as they drove back to Fairhill, with the windows down and the radio on. Bruce enjoyed the drive with Laura beside him, her honey-blonde hair whipping in the breeze.

He'd almost kissed her. And over a plate of burned pancakes, for God's sake. The way she'd looked with that sprinkling of flour on her cheek, and her hair soft and wispy from the heat inside the marquee, had almost undone him.

But it was impossible to get caught up with a woman again, so soon after the disaster of his marriage break-up. His divorce had only just been finalised, and he was trying to get his life back together. Yet those reasons had been lost as he'd stood beside Laura, letting her feed him pancakes and strawberries and listening to her laugh.

And brushing the flour off her face? That had been a cheesy move. What was wrong with him?

Yet there'd been something in her eyes when he'd done it. Surprise? Annoyance? He wished he knew. Was it possible she might actually be interested in him? It didn't sound like things were exactly rosy between her and this boyfriend. But the last thing he wanted was to start chasing after someone who wasn't interested. He'd been through enough this year already without adding insult to injury. And his Uncle Keith was enough of a cautionary tale in that department to give him fair warning.

Still, something about her intrigued him and drew him in.

When he pulled up outside her tenement block, she was already preparing to jump out before he'd brought the car to a stop.

"Let me help you upstairs with these food boxes," he said.

"I'll be fine."

"You can't carry all those cartons and this picnic blanket too."

"I'm not taking your new picnic blanket."

"That's right, you're not taking it. I'm giving it to you."

Before she could protest any further, he came around and opened her door, helped her out with the boxes and the blanket, and carried the load while she found her keys and made her way upstairs. When Laura stepped in through the wooden storm doors and opened the inside door to her flat, he waited on the landing, and when she turned around he held out the things he'd carried.

Laura looked at his outstretched arms, laden with

boxes, and the picnic blanket dangling off his wrist from its tie cord.

"Come in and I'll put the kettle on," she said, smiling. "The least I can do is offer you coffee after such a lovely afternoon."

"I'd like that," he said, and followed her inside.

He took in the little hallway and saw a living room at the front, kitchen at the back, and a small bathroom. The other two doors off the hallway were closed, and he guessed those were bedrooms. In the kitchen, she began filling the kettle and gestured for him to dump the load he'd carried on the table. It was a bright airy kitchen, the tall windows letting in lots of light from outside. Houseplants crowded the deep windowsill, and a little vase of daisies sat on the waxed pine kitchen table. Pots and pans sat neatly on open shelving in the pantry, with stacks of colourful mismatched plates and cups beside them.

"This is a really nice flat," he said. "Lots of space."

"I don't live here alone," she said, pulling cups from the shelf. "I have a flatmate, Yvonne. She's staying at her boyfriend's for a couple of days."

Shifting her bag on the kitchen table to get at the food cartons, she spied the certificates they'd been given following the pancake-making lesson.

"Oh, I want to pin up my certificate!"

He saw her expression light up as she darted from the kitchen with her certificate in hand. Amused at her enthusiasm, he followed as she disappeared into one of the bedrooms off the hallway. Peeking around the door while she rummaged in a desk by the window, he looked in surprise at her small bedroom. There was barely space for a double bed, and the drawers, wardrobe, and tiny desk were crammed together side by side.

"I guess you drew the short straw when it came to assigning the bedrooms," he said.

She glanced up and looked around the room. "I don't mind, I like it in here. It's nice and cosy." She returned her attention to the desk and finally located a small box of pushpins. "And I had to take this room, anyway. I couldn't get good rent for a bedroom this small, so my flatmate always gets the big bedroom."

"The trials of sub-letting."

"Actually, I'm not sub-letting. I own the flat. I bought it with what was left over once I'd sold my parents' house and cleared their mortgage and bills. I'm lucky to have the place and lucky I didn't end up sofa-surfing after my parents died, but I can't run it without a flatmate paying rent. Waitressing tips in Valentino's are good, but not that good."

She turned to the wall and pinned up the pancake certificate. "There!" she said, grinning. "Now I'm all proud."

Bruce stared at the wall and stepped a little closer into the doorway. He realised that most of the wall between the bed and the wardrobe, up to around head height, was covered with certificates of one kind or another.

"Look at all these!" he said, taking another step forward. "Do you mind if I ...?" He gestured to the wall.

"Sure, if you really want to," she said.

He stepped closer and looked at the array of certificates. There seemed to be one for every imaginable activity. Cocktail mixing. Beginner's Spanish. Kayaking. An archaeological dig. A section completed on the Southern

Upland Way. Argentine tango. And more, far more than he could take in.

"Wow," was all he could say, gazing around the wall.

"Yeah, it's a sickness."

"How can you say that? Look at all the things you've done."

She shrugged. "Not to any degree of proficiency. I just like dabbling. That one there" – she pointed to a certificate acknowledging participation in a watercolour painting class – "was the first one I got." She narrowed her eyes at the date printed on the certificate. "Eight years ago, God. Anyway, it was just a fun thing to do on a rainy Sunday afternoon, and at the end the instructor gave us these certificates. It was a way to get us to sign up for more classes, of course, but I liked having it. Stupid, but there you go. A couple of months later, I walked a part of the Southern Upland Way, and it turned out you could send away and get a certificate for the section you'd completed. So I did. And I liked getting that certificate. It was a tough walk with tough climbs. And since then, I've been collecting these things." She gestured to the wall. "Little triumphs. It helps to remind yourself of them when you've had a tough day."

"And what's this?" he said, pointing to a printed chart pinned to one side.

"Ah, well, that's my training regime. I'm doing a ten-kilometre run next month, and this is my progress record. It's been pretty hard going." She pointed to the numbers on the chart – times logged, distances covered. "When it comes to the actual race, I'll probably finish last, if I don't simply drop dead in the middle of it."

"With this much preparation, you'll be brilliant."

"Hmm, well, we'll see. They give you a great finisher's certificate, all gilt embossed. I already looked at it online. It'll be the nicest certificate I'll have. If I actually get it."

"You'll get it."

"Thanks for the confidence boost, but you haven't seen me wheezing my way around Mungo Park." She tilted her head to the bedroom door. "Kettle's boiled."

He followed her back to the kitchen, his head spinning at all those certificates on her wall. Little triumphs, she'd called them. He liked that.

He leaned against the counter while she made coffee. When she reached to open a cupboard behind him, he moved to let her pull out the coffee jar, only for her to have to ask him to move once again so she could find a new bag of sugar in another cupboard.

"Sorry," he said, shifting.

"It's fine," she said, laughing.

She was close to him as he moved aside for a second time. Close to him as she leaned around to look for the sugar. Her hair brushed against his shoulder as she reached, and he could smell the faint scent of her shampoo, a lingering hint of green apples.

"Sorry. I'm in the wrong cupboard. The sugar must be in this other one."

"Sorry, right."

Moving at the same time, they bumped together and laughed.

Then stopped laughing.

As he looked at her, the kitchen, the flat, everything just seemed to melt away. All he could see was her.

The moment spun on and on. He wondered what it would be like to put his hands around her waist and pull her close. He wondered if she would fit against his body the way he thought she might, and if kissing her would make his heart beat even faster than it already was.

He'd just decided that he absolutely had to find the answers to these questions, when the front doorbell rang.

He jumped back, away from Laura and away from that moment he'd almost seized with both hands.

Laura, her eyes wide, blew out a breath. "I better answer that."

As she ran from the kitchen and unlocked the door, he shook his head and tried to pull himself together.

What *was* that? It had felt like he'd been momentarily transported to a different planet. *Get a grip*, he told himself. *Seriously*.

Once Laura opened the front door, he saw a young woman stomp into the flat with a guy coming in behind her.

"Thank God you were home!" the young woman said, shrugging out of a jacket that looked soaked through. Bruce noticed her hair hung damp too. "What a disaster! Officially, this was the worst romantic day trip ever."

"How can you say that?" said the guy. "We were having a lovely time!"

"We were, until you shoved me into the bloody river!"

Bruce stepped into the hallway, and the new arrivals looked his way.

"Yvonne, Olly, this is Bruce," Laura said, closing the door. "Bruce works in The Crooked Thistle, Yvonne.

Bruce, this is my flatmate, Yvonne, and her boyfriend, Olly." She turned back to Yvonne. "What happened?"

"Casanova here thought it would be nice to go out on a canoe on the river," Yvonne said. "Then, for reasons that cannot be explained, he shoved me in."

"I didn't shove you in!" Olly said, clearly struggling to suppress laughter. "You stood up in the canoe, Yvonne, and destabilised us. I was trying to pull you down on to the seat, and you thrashed out at me and fell in."

"Funny how *you* didn't fall in."

"I was sitting down, which is what you should've been doing."

"Anyway," Yvonne continued, "to cut a long story short, I fell in the river. I had to *swim* to the riverbank to get out. We're in the middle of nowhere and need to return the canoe, so I had to climb back in and sit there, soaking wet, all the way back to the boat hire place. I'm covered in muck and weeds, and this guy's laughing his head off."

Olly said nothing, which Bruce thought was probably a good move.

"Surprisingly enough, I wasn't in the mood for romance after that, so I asked him to bring me home. It was only when we got here I realised my keys must've fallen out when I took a dunk in the river. If you hadn't been here to let me in, I might've flipped out."

Yvonne stopped to draw breath. "So, I need a hot shower and fresh clothes." She turned to Olly and poked a finger in his chest. "I'm not speaking to you, so you can go home."

"Come on, Yvonne, don't be like that."

"You *laughed* at me, Olly. You were in hysterics, while I was splashing around in that filthy river water." She rubbed at her leg and scowled. "I think a fish might've bitten me."

Bruce saw Olly's face creasing dangerously with the effort of suppressing laughter, and he also saw the look that crossed Yvonne's face when she noticed it. He decided it was time to leave.

"Laura, I'm going to head home," he said.

"No, wait!" She spun around. "We were going to have coffee."

"Next time," he said, and turned for the door. "See you soon, and thanks for a nice afternoon. Yvonne, Olly, nice to meet you guys."

He headed out the door, half-jogged down the stairs, and felt relief when he hit the pavement outside.

He'd almost gone and done something stupid, something insanely stupid, and he ought to thank his lucky stars that Laura's flatmate and her boyfriend had come blasting in when they did.

He'd had an amazing afternoon, no doubt about that. He liked being with Laura. And God knows, he'd wanted to kiss her, just grab her and kiss her. The look she'd given him in the kitchen when they'd got in each other's way made him sure she'd wanted to kiss him too. There was no misreading it.

But as he stalked towards Shaw Street and The Crooked Thistle, he made a decision. His heart was still broken after the end of his marriage. His business career was currently non-existent. He was voluntarily living in his uncle's spare room and working for free. All of those things had to be put right before he could even contemplate letting his feelings run wild for a woman.

Having a business, running his own pub, being successful – those things were important and without them he was drifting. He had to feel like himself again and get his hands back into the hard graft of a project. That was what he'd come back to this city for, and he had to focus on actually doing that and only that.

He couldn't think about Laura. He'd only just got divorced.

He had to get back on track. Find a new place, buy it, and turn it into a great pub and a great business. He had to get back into the game.

Only then would he think about grabbing women and kissing them.

Inside The Crooked Thistle, a football match played on the big screen, assorted punters were enjoying their drinks and pub grub, and Keith was behind the bar pulling pints.

"Hey son, we're not too busy yet, but if you've got a minute maybe you could go down into the cellar and—"

"Sorry, Uncle Keith, I can't help out tonight," Bruce said and headed for the back stairs. "I've got some work to do."

Ignoring his uncle's surprised stare, he went to his bedroom, stared at the ugly painting above his bed – his ex-wife's ugly painting, he thought with a groan – before shaking his head and sitting down with his laptop. Pulling up some of the files he'd begun on commercial properties for sale, he noticed with disgust that it had been weeks since he'd actually done any serious work on them. No wonder he'd ended up scouting that dead-end prospect this morning. He had been putting things off and licking his wounds for far too long.

But now that would change. It had to.

And so he would focus on getting his life back on track, and that meant he just wouldn't think about Laura at all. He wouldn't think about how her hair had smelled of sweet green apples. And he definitely wouldn't think about that kiss they'd almost had.

What could be so hard about that?

CHAPTER 8

Laura puffed her way up the hill in Mungo Park. Her calves were screaming at her to stop and it was all she could do not to listen to them. Or to the stitch that had knotted its way into her side.

Every run she'd had this week had felt like this: sore, exhausting, and unpleasant. Last week, she'd thought she'd been on a good roll, feeling stronger, logging better numbers into her spreadsheet. But this week, nothing seemed to be going to plan.

Monday had hurt in her abdomen, but she'd chalked it up to indulging in too many rich treats at the food festival she'd gone to with Bruce. Tuesday had hurt in her thighs, and she'd thought that the poor run the day before was simply having a knock-on effect. But now it was Friday, and not only did every muscle in her body still ache with each step she ran, but she felt utterly exhausted too.

At the top of the hill, she clutched her sides and gasped for air. She didn't think running was supposed to make you feel this wretched.

A woman wearing tight leggings and a designer athletics top ran up the hill and jogged serenely past. She barely had a hair out of place, Laura noticed, barely a single bead of sweat on her forehead. This woman would have no trouble running a competitive race. She probably wouldn't even have to shower afterwards, just touch up her still-perfect lipstick and carry on with the rest of her weekend.

Scowling, Laura wiped her sweaty forehead, shoved her hair back into the ponytail from which it kept escaping, and rubbed at the stitch in her side. She wished she hadn't worn these stupid thick jogging trousers that made her too hot, and wished she'd made time to buy some proper running tops instead of settling for these over-sized T-shirts that made her feel the size of a bus.

But there was no point getting upset. The well-groomed, fat-free woman already rounding towards the park exit had probably been running for years, whereas she'd only taken it up a couple of months ago. She ought to have been prepared for training setbacks. It had been too optimistic to assume that everything would be smooth-sailing.

Laura half-jogged, half-limped her way back to the flat. Writing the morning's running time on her chart on the wall, she felt nothing but dismay to see it was fully four minutes longer than her time a week earlier.

In the kitchen, she found Yvonne at the table hunched over a bowl of Weetabix.

"God, you look awful," Yvonne said when Laura wheezed into the kitchen.

"Thanks."

"Maybe this running lark isn't such a great idea."

"Maybe it's not." Laura filled a glass with water and chugged it down.

"Sorry, I shouldn't have said that," Yvonne said. "What I should say is that you're doing a great thing and you should keep at it, because you're brilliant and you'll definitely succeed."

"Yeah, that's what you should've said." Laura set the glass in the sink and pulled a cereal bowl from the pantry shelf.

"And probably I should apologise again for last Sunday."

"You don't need to keep apologising, there's nothing to apologise for," she said, filling her bowl with bran flakes and adding milk.

"If I'd known you were planning on bringing home a guy who looked as good as he did and snagging him in a lip-lock, I never would've come back."

"Yeah, well, I must've misread things, because not only did he *not* kiss me, but I haven't seen him since." She stabbed unhappily at the bran flakes with her spoon.

"So, *you* go and speak to *him*. *You* go and kiss *him*!"

"It's not as easy as that."

"Why on earth not?"

Laura's phone pinged. She picked it up from the counter and saw a message from John. Ever since he'd dumped her in favour of Indiana Jones, he'd been texting constantly to apologise, and midweek she'd relented and accepted his request to make it up to her by taking her out to dinner. Now she realised she was scarcely in the mood for it, but they'd already arranged it for that evening. Cancelling would look like she was playing tit-for-tat – you cancel on me, and I'll cancel on you.

"I'm going out tonight," Laura said, tapping a reply to John. "The flat's yours if you and Olly want it."

"Going somewhere fun?"

"John's taking me to dinner, some fancy place to make up for last weekend."

Yvonne's eyes practically popped out of her head. "Laura, for God's sake, why are you still seeing that guy? You don't even like him."

"Of course I like him."

"But is liking him really enough?"

"Yvonne—"

"I know, I know, I'm sticking my nose in. But if you and that guy, Bruce, had actually kissed each other last week, would you still be going out with John tonight?"

"Well, no, but—"

"That's your answer, right there. John might be a nice guy, at least as far as you're concerned, although I can't see how, considering he dumped you to go out with his friends. But either way, he's a placeholder. He's not the one. So why are you wasting your time?"

Sighing, Laura dumped her breakfast uneaten into the recycling caddy. "I need to get ready for work," she said, and headed for the shower.

At Valentino's, her shift seemed endless. She was kept busy with Mr Davidson complaining about his eggs, and a noisy lunch group celebrating a birthday, but still the minutes dragged. Potential buyers visited the restaurant in the late afternoon, and she did her best to ignore them as she fidgeted with a late sandwich lunch in an empty booth while Natalie and the commercial estate agents showed them around.

Staring out the window towards The Crooked Thistle, she wondered whether Bruce was in there. Had something happened between the two of them, or hadn't it? The answer to that question should be obvious, and yet she was clueless. One minute, they'd been milliseconds away from kissing, the next he was sprinting out of her flat never to be seen again.

Men said women were complicated. Showed what they knew. They ought to take a good look at themselves.

Idiots. They were all idiots. And if Bruce was over there hiding in The Crooked Thistle, she thought, pushing away her uneaten sandwich, she hoped he damn well knew it.

"You're an idiot," Jack said, as Bruce pulled the car into a parking space.

"Thanks very much."

"I mean it."

"I wish I hadn't told you."

"Well you did tell me. And you told me because you hoped I'd commiserate and say, oh, poor Bruce, still so confused after the collapse of his marriage, and how thoughtless of this lovely woman Lana—"

"Laura."

"Laura, how thoughtless of this Laura, making him want to kiss her and leaving him all muddled about whether he *should* kiss her or just flee like the building's on fire."

Bruce turned off the engine. "That voice you're doing doesn't sound anything like me."

"When you're whining, which you are, it sounds *exactly* like you."

Bruce squinted at the pub they'd pulled up beside. It sat on a corner, towards the end of a line of shops in a leafy residential area on the fringes of Glasgow's west end. There was good footfall, lots of flats and townhouses and shops, and plenty of potential customers within easy walking distance. The place had only been on the market a few weeks. He thought it might be a contender.

"What do you think?" he asked, turning to Jack.

"That you're an idiot."

He sighed. "I mean, what do you think of the pub?"

Jack glanced at the building. "Didn't think you'd be interested in a place with private flats above it."

"I figured it couldn't hurt to take a look."

He saw the agent come through the doors of the pub. The business was no longer trading, and the agent showed them around the empty unit and delivered his sales pitch. Bruce looked at the layout and at the potential for renovation, which he could now see was limited. Still, he decided not to reject the place out of hand. When the agent stepped out, he walked behind the bar and tried to imagine himself there permanently.

He couldn't.

"You're not some confused teenager, unsure about how this is supposed to work," Jack said, poking at the open fireplace that stood on one wall.

"What?" Bruce said, frowning in confusion.

Jack turned around and spread his hands. "Laura. This Laura woman."

Sighing, Bruce looked at the back-bar and down along the counter. “Can we just forget I mentioned it?”

“No, we can’t. Surely you know how to do it.”

“Do what?”

“How to *kiss* her! How to let her know you like her! You’ve been married, for God’s sake.”

“Exactly, I’ve been married. And now I’m divorced.”

“That’s what’s holding you back?”

“Well, kissing one woman when I’ve only just stopped being married to another doesn’t sound like the ideal way to start off a new relationship.”

Jack’s eyes widened. “You think you might want a relationship with this Laura person?”

“Oh, for God’s sake, stop harassing me. You wanted me to start looking for a new pub to buy. And that’s what I’m doing. Now you also want me to throw myself into some romance with a woman I hardly know, when the ink’s barely dry on my divorce papers.”

Jack pointed a finger at his brother. “You think you can line things up in life in order of preferred implementation. First I’ll do this, and *then* I’ll do that. First I’ll stew in my own misery for months following the collapse of my marriage, and *then* I’ll think about putting my life back together again. Life doesn’t work that way, Bruce. When I decided to leave my job at the car dealership and start my own company, we found out that same week that Claire was pregnant with Chloe. Do you know how easy it would’ve been for me to say, well, now that we’ll soon have the responsibility and expense of a kid, I’d be mad to leave this job where I’m making good money and risk it for a business that might fail, so maybe I ought to wait? But I took the risk. And I'm glad I did because it was the right thing."

"Good for you. But I don't know what the right thing for me is, other than finding a new pub. Can't you just be happy I'm taking that step?"

Bruce saw his brother's expression shift.

"Okay, you're right. I'm pressuring you. I'll stop." Jack gestured to the pub. "So, what do you think about this place?"

Bruce came out from behind the bar. "It's not for me."

"Didn't think it would be. Where's next?"

Back in the car, Bruce punched the next destination into his phone and began following the navigation directions. "How are the girls?" he asked as he drove.

"They're good. Oh, I almost forgot." Jack reached into his pocket, pulled out a sheet of paper and unfolded it. "Isla drew this for you."

Slowing for traffic lights, Bruce glanced over and saw a drawing of a stick man with an enormous head. In one hand he held some kind of pole, in the other a squinty rectangle. When the mental adjustment kicked in, and he saw the image through the mind of a small child, finally it clicked. Isla had drawn a picture of him pulling a pint behind the bar.

He laughed. "I love it."

"After we visited you last year in London, Isla talked endlessly about how your job was to pull pints. She got obsessed with this thing about pulling pints, and she's been drawing variations on this picture ever since. When I told her we were looking at a new pub this afternoon, she drew this and asked me to give it to you."

"She's a little sweetheart."

"I'll leave it here." Jack slid the drawing into the glove compartment. "Once you find a new pub, Bruce, the girls are going to love coming to visit you there."

"Me too. Are they enjoying the summer holidays off school?"

"Loving it. Six weeks of me and Claire wrangling child-care chaos."

"Sounds tough."

But Jack waved a hand. "I wouldn't trade it for the world. Those two girls are the lights of my life."

Turning at a set of lights, Bruce felt his brother's eyes on him.

"You deserve those things too, Bruce. Children, a family. I know it's what you want. You'll be an amazing dad one day."

"Can't imagine when that'll happen."

"It'll happen when it's the right time. For all you know, this Laura could be the one you've been waiting your whole life for."

Bruce shot a glance at his brother. "So not only do you want me to kiss her, you want me to have kids with her now, too?"

Jack laughed. "I'm just kidding around." Peering further up the road, he pointed and curled a lip. "Is this the next place?"

Bruce nodded and parked the car, but knew before he'd even turned off the engine that this second pub was all wrong. It was in a bad location next to a scrubby patch of wasteland, and several of the cars parked on the street looked long abandoned. The pub had looked better in the paperwork that had been prepared by the selling agent, and now that he saw it with his own eyes, it seemed cold and hard.

However, as the agent had the desperate look of a man who'd been attempting to flog the property for a long time, Bruce spent ten minutes inspecting the place before thanking him and making good his escape.

"Sorry, that was a waste of time," he said to Jack as they drove off.

"I'm happy to come along for the ride. How many sites did you look at before you bought your pub in London?"

He thought back. "Close to twenty."

"See, there you go. Just keep at it. If we're all done for the day, drop me back at my office. There's some work I want to finish before I go home." Jack turned and studied his brother. "How about we go out tonight, have a few drinks and get some dinner?"

"Isn't Friday night your movie night with Chloe and Isla?"

"Claire won't mind me missing it to be with my brother who needs a pal right now."

"I'm not taking you away from movie night with your girls, and I'm working at the pub anyway. One of the bar staff's got a family member in hospital, and I said I'd cover."

"In that case, come over on Sunday. I'm planning another barbeque. There's a special feature with one of the gas burners I haven't tried out yet."

"Hard to turn down a dinner offer involving a special feature on a gas burner. What time?"

"Six o'clock."

"I'll be there."

"And listen, I'm serious about what I said about this Laura woman. If you like her, don't wait. In life there's no such thing as the perfect moment."

For the rest of the drive home, Bruce found himself wondering if that was true.

And despite not wanting to think about Laura, he found himself thinking about her anyway and whether, that afternoon in her kitchen, he'd somehow stumbled into the perfect moment with her ... and botched it.

KEITH STIRRED sugar into his cappuccino and watched Natalie tapping at her laptop behind the counter in Valentino's. She had a look of concentration on her face he found oddly alluring. "Any interested buyers yet?" he asked.

Glancing up from the keyboard, Natalie shook her head. "These things take time, and—" Her attention shifted to a passing waitress. "Fiona," she called out, signalling the young waitress back. "I asked you fifteen minutes ago to clear tables eight and nine, and they're still a mess."

"Oops sorry, I forgot," the young waitress replied, giggling.

Natalie shook her head as Fiona scurried towards the dirty tables. "Now that's something I won't miss when I leave this place," she said in a low voice to Keith. "Constantly herding staff members who are unable to line up a list of tasks in their heads and get them done."

Keith chuckled and sipped some coffee. "You've got good staff here. Laura's a gem."

"No argument there. Although she has been acting

strangely this week. When I quizzed her, she said she's doing a ten-kilometre race in a few weeks' time and the training is taking a toll. She looked decidedly peaky during her shift earlier. I only hope she isn't coming down with something. The last thing I need right now is to have my best waitress off sick."

Natalie tapped on her keyboard and scowled. "Oh for goodness sake! Sorry, Keith, but I need to go to my office and make a call about an invoicing error. Something else I won't miss when I sell this place – all these constant paperwork mistakes."

"I'll wait until you come back."

"I might be a while," she said, picking up her laptop. "Listen, we can have coffee some other time. I shouldn't have suggested this afternoon – I knew I'd be rushed off my feet."

"Wait, there was something I wanted to ask you."

Natalie, already disappearing through to her office, looked over her shoulder. "Okay, just come through with me while I get this call started."

In her office, she set down her laptop, picked up the desk phone and dialled. Keith made his way to one of the chairs on the other side of her desk. Music was playing in the office. Opera music. Grinning, he felt relief rush through him.

"I just dialled this number and have immediately been put on hold with these clowns at my meat supplier, can you believe that?" Natalie said.

"Disgraceful." Keith set down his coffee cup on the edge of her desk. "Listen, I happen to have a couple of tickets to the opera and I wondered if you'd like to go?" He pulled the tickets from his pocket and waved them in the air before peering at them. "*Rigoletto* at the Theatre Royal."

Across the desk, Natalie looked at the tickets and then at Keith. "You just happened to have opera tickets on your person?"

"Well no, not exactly. Last week at dinner, you said something about liking opera. So I thought I'd find out if there was any opera playing. And there is. The only tickets still available were for tomorrow night. Maybe that's late notice—"

"I'd love to go," she interrupted. "Late notice, yes, but I happen to like *Rigoletto* very much. In fact, I knew some months ago it would be playing but never got around to doing anything about it."

Pleased, he tucked the tickets back into his pocket. "Good. Shall we get some dinner before the show?"

"Can you manage a late supper afterwards? I'll be busy here most of tomorrow."

"That works for me. I'll get Bruce to cover at the pub. I was also wondering—"

She held up a finger, listened into the phone, then sighed and shook her head. "I'm still on hold. Go ahead, what were you going to say?"

"I wondered if you'd take a look at the new whisky menu I've designed for the pub. You've always had a good eye for these things, and I know you helped design Valentino's menus. I'd value your thoughts."

"A whisky menu?"

"For the new single malts I'm introducing, and—"

"Of course, I remember you told me. I'd be glad to take a

look. I'll pop over when—" Leaning forward in her chair, she shifted the phone from her shoulder and spoke into it. "Yes, this is Natalie Fachini at Valentino's. I'm afraid there is a serious problem with the invoice you just sent through."

Keith rose and headed for the door, taking his coffee cup with him. He gave Natalie a small wave, which she returned distractedly while she continued her phone conversation. He was happy not to be the person on the other end of that discussion. Natalie, he could plainly hear, took no prisoners.

In the restaurant, he deposited his coffee cup on the counter and nodded to Paul as he left.

Natalie had agreed to go to the opera with him. He could suffer through opera – for her.

He found himself grinning all the way back to The Crooked Thistle.

THE FANCY RESTAURANT to which John had promised to take Laura turned out to be the Pizza Hut at the nearby retail park.

She had no quibble with pizza, or with Pizza Hut for that matter. But it definitely wasn't fancy, which meant she looked really silly in the sleek midnight blue dress and killer silver stilettos she'd chosen to wear. The waitress, along with just about every diner in the place, had given her long looks as she'd swished through the place. She'd never felt more embarrassed in her life.

John, in contrast, had turned up wearing old jeans and a Darth Vader T-shirt.

"I know I already said it, but you look great," he said, chewing through a slice of spicy meat feast.

Laura jabbed her fork at the ham and pineapple pizza she'd ordered. A family of four sat at the next table, where the kids were currently engaged in a game of who-can-throw-the-pepperoni-slices-furthest-across-the-room. Laura sat clenched in fear that one of those slices would soon be headed towards her and her beautiful dress.

Quite why John had promised fancy if he'd always intended bringing her here was beyond her.

To make things worse, she'd felt a headache brewing just as John had arrived to pick her up – an ill omen, she now decided – and it had only got worse as the evening went on. She wanted to chalk it up to the after-effects of that morning's disastrous training run, and maybe it had actually begun hatching so long ago. But she also knew that the weirdness of the evening – her all dolled up in an evening dress, John slouching across from her in Star Wars gear, the two of them surrounded by the roar of a Saturday night in a fast food place filled with noisy children and screeching packs of teenagers – wasn't exactly helping keep a tension headache at bay.

Plus, John had hardly said a word since they'd arrived. She studied him, munching on his pizza and trying to pretend he wasn't reading a message on his phone.

What am I doing here? Laura wondered. *Why am I with this person?*

Yvonne was right: there was no future in this relationship, if it even *was* a relationship. John wasn't a bad person. He just wasn't right for her. And she just wasn't right for him.

And it was time to do something about it.

"Want to get some dessert?" he asked.

"Um no, I'm fine. Listen, can we get out of here? It's kind of noisy."

He looked in the direction of the ice cream station with an expression of longing, before signalling to the waitress for the bill. Outside, they began walking to where he'd parked his car.

"Want a coffee somewhere?" he asked. "Or a drink?"

"Would you mind just taking me home? The truth is I don't feel too good."

Concern spread across his face. "Was something wrong with your pizza?"

"No, the food was fine. I've been feeling off all day. I probably just need an early night."

"Oh right, okay."

They drove in silence. She decided she had to end this thing – tonight. As soon as they reached her flat, she'd explain that she'd enjoyed their time together but didn't want to see him any more.

Except she couldn't say that, could she? It was too blunt: *I don't want to see you any more*. What an awful thing to hear.

She tested alternative options in her head. *John, we've had a few nice dates together, but we don't really share a lot in common and I think it might be time for us to go our separate ways.*

Go our separate ways? Ugh.

John, you're a lovely guy, but we're not right for each other, and with the way things are at work right now, with the restaurant going on the market, I just think ...

But it didn't have anything to do with the restaurant, so why would she bring Valentino's into this?

There had to be some set of words in the English language that could communicate the essence of a break-up, words that didn't involve half-truths, or leave someone feeling hurt.

John, I think that ...

"Okay, here we are," he said, steering the car into a parking spot outside her flat. She hadn't even realised they were back already. The passing scenery of the city had simply flashed by as she'd been racking her mind for something sensible to say.

And now that they had arrived, she still hadn't thought of a way to say what needed to be said.

"John, um—"

"Laura, listen," he said, switching off the engine and turning towards her. "The two of us seeing each other isn't working out. I think we should call it a day."

Stunned, she could only stare. "What?"

"Don't be upset," he said, making soothing gestures with his hands, like he was trying to calm a skittish horse. "You're a lovely girl. But you're not what I'm looking for. And if I'm being honest, I don't think I'm what you're looking for, either. I'd hoped tonight we might have a final go at things and see if we could find stuff to talk about. But we couldn't."

Literally speechless now, Laura stared at John, then out of the windscreen, where rain had begun falling in hard, thick sheets that had simply blown in from nowhere.

He was breaking up with her. *He* was breaking up with *her*. If it hadn't been so awful, it would've been hilarious.

"Okay," she said, and opened the car door.

"Wait, I've got an umbrella, let me walk you to the door."

But she was too embarrassed to even consider allowing that. *He'd* dumped *her*. And he'd been planning on doing it all the way back, just the same way she had. Except he'd managed to say it first.

Hauling herself out of the car and into the rain, she stumbled, her silver stilettos almost taking her down with their treacherous height. She should never have worn the damn things. And now she'd have to navigate the curb and the uneven pavement and the steps to the tenement door, while her beautiful evening dress – the only one she owned – got soaked and her cheeks burned with the mortification of rejection.

She fished her keys from her bag and fought to unlock the door, her wet hair hanging in rat-tails over her face. Her headache was now firmly lodged behind her left eyeball and blooming into something monumentally catastrophic. As she trudged up the stairwell, she began sneezing too.

It had been a terrible day. Just a terrible day.

The only way to end a day as terrible as this one, she decided, was to get into bed and hope that tomorrow had the decency to be a little less gruesome.

CHAPTER 9

For the second Saturday in a row, Yvonne was packing an overnight bag. This time, Laura was leaving her flatmate to her own devices.

She was too groggy to help locate items of saucy underwear or hear about the spa hotel Olly had booked as part of his continued campaign to convince Yvonne to forgive him for the canoe debacle.

Laura needed some space alone.

After towelling off following the drenching she'd endured while running back to her flat the night before, she'd gone straight to bed. But sleep hadn't come, and her headache had persisted through the painkillers she'd swallowed. She'd tossed and turned, thoughts spinning about her hopeless run in the park, about the potential buyers who'd been swaggering around Valentino's, and about the humiliation of being dumped by a guy she'd been too nice not to dump first.

But sleep must have come at some point, because in the morning she'd woken feeling better. Relieved, she'd decided to make up for her training setback and had gone for a run, hoping to log better numbers.

But that hadn't happened. The first half mile towards the park began well enough, but once she was jogging around the pond, it felt like she was hauling dead weight. By the time she hit the hill around the golf course, she might as well have been running through cement. Since she'd begun her new training regime, she'd never felt so bad.

She hadn't just walked the rest of the way home; she'd all but limped.

After dragging herself to Valentino's for a nine-to-three shift, she'd focused only on getting through each minute, watching the clock hands spin slowly around to when she could go home.

But when Natalie took her aside and told her one of the waitresses had called in with a family emergency and that Natalie herself couldn't work the evening shift because she was going to the opera with Keith, Laura had had no choice but to agree to cover the shortage. After all, she'd been the one who'd set Natalie up with Keith, and if there was any chance the two of them might have something going on, she had to do whatever it took to help it along.

And so she'd agreed to return for a six-through-ten evening shift. But by five o'clock, as Yvonne was finishing packing her bag, Laura was already wondering how she would manage to put in another four hours on her feet on a busy Saturday night.

"You look peaky," Yvonne said, wheeling her little suitcase into the living room. "Do you really think you ought to work tonight?"

"I agreed to do it, so I'll do it," Laura said, unenthusiastically sipping some tea.

Yvonne sat on the edge of the sofa. "Are you feeling any better after what happened last night?"

"Not really."

"You should've dumped him ages ago."

"Tell me something I don't know."

"Sorry."

Outside, a car horn blasted. Yvonne looked out the window and picked up her suitcase.

"Does Olly know we have a doorbell he can ring?" Laura asked. "That he doesn't have to honk his horn and make our neighbours hate us?"

"He knows." Yvonne leaned over and kissed her on the forehead. "You feel too warm. Are you sure someone else can't cover this shift?"

"I'm sure."

"Come home early if you feel any worse. And if you need me back here to look after you, just phone. I mean it."

"I'm fine. Stop worrying about me."

Outside, the car horn blasted a second time.

"See you soon," Yvonne said and darted for the door.

"Bring me something nice from the spa if—"

But the door had already slammed before she could finish the sentence.

She glanced at the clock on the bookcase. It was five fifteen. All she wanted to do was curl up on the sofa and close her eyes. But that, she knew, would be a bad move.

After carrying her teacup to the kitchen, she got ready for her second shift at Valentino's. Four hours, that was all she had to get through. It was probably just one of those twenty-four-hour bugs that disappeared as quickly as they came.

And Saturdays were always hectic at the restaurant, so the time would fly. She'd be home before she knew it. And tomorrow morning she wasn't scheduled to work until ten o'clock, so she'd sleep late. No running. The running would have to wait until she felt like herself again.

Once she'd changed into her uniform, she stood at the door checking her pockets for her phone, her purse, her keys. And found herself swaying on her feet, as the hallway tilted and fuzziness clouded her brain.

This was a bad idea, surely? If she was on the cusp of illness, she shouldn't go back to work.

But then she thought of Natalie, who was probably already hoping to take herself off into her office so she could get ready for the opera with Keith. If she didn't show up, Natalie would cancel the date.

Four hours, she reminded herself, shaking off the funny spell and heading out towards Valentino's. Four hours and then her lovely warm bed would be hers.

NATALIE LET the soaring music of the finale of *Rigoletto* wash over her, felt her skin prickle as each crescendo was reached and the tale unfolded to its tragic conclusion. The story itself was ridiculous: a young woman who allowed herself to be stabbed to death in order to save the life of her unfaithful lover. Absurd, as indeed so many of the stories that comprised operas tended to be. Women always seemed to be dying and sacrificing themselves, and the operatic tragedies were never complete until female blood had been spilled.

Yet she loved these operas just the same. They reminded her of being a new bride on her honeymoon with Angelo and going to the open-air Arena di Verona to see *Tosca*. The two of them had sat in the gauzy heat of a summer's evening, high up in the amphitheatre seating terrace, sipping the wine they'd brought along. As Natalie watched the final scenes of *Rigoletto* on the stage below, she realised this was the first time since Angelo had died that she could recall such memories without tears immediately brimming in her eyes.

Not that she would have cried here anyway. She was having too much fun, and even if she hadn't been, she wouldn't embarrass Keith by crying in front of him. He had taken a risk in making the opera booking and it had paid off. Natalie was glad she had agreed to come. It had been a long time since she'd gone to the opera.

And she couldn't have imagined enjoying this man's company so much, she thought, stealing a look in his direction as the curtain fell and the audience applauded the performance. In all the time they'd run their respective businesses on either side of Shaw Street, he had simply been Keith, the landlord of The Crooked Thistle, a man who continually found himself entangled with an endless parade of women seemingly intent only on hurting him.

She and Angelo had given small presents to Keith on each of his three weddings. But while Angelo had shaken his head in bafflement as each marriage disintegrated, Natalie had felt tremendous sympathy for this perpetually unlucky-in-love man, who epitomised the triumph of hope over experience. Keith was a good man and had surely deserved more than he'd got from those women on to whose fingers he'd slipped those wedding rings.

Yes, he was a good man and a gentleman too, she decided, as he retrieved their jackets from the cloakroom and helped her into hers. And not a bad-looking one either, when he took the time, as he had again tonight, to tame those mad tufts of hair that sprouted from his head.

Or maybe that was just the wine talking. He'd insisted on treating her to pre-theatre drinks and had also ordered champagne for the intermission, waving away her protest that she would be well and truly sozzled by the time they sat down for their late supper. As they exited the theatre, Keith held out his arm, and she smiled as she slid her hand into the crook of his elbow.

"You're old style, Keith," she said as they walked companionably along the pavement.

"Old is the only style I know." Looking up, he gestured to the summer sky that was deepening to twilight above the city. "It's a fine night."

Liking the way he turned and smiled at her, his eyes twinkling beneath the streetlights, she moved a little closer as they walked and thought how amazing it was that life could manage to pleasantly surprise you, just when you needed it most.

"How are those travel plans of yours coming along?" he asked.

"They're not, and they won't, not until I have my buyer in place. I'm not prepared to jump the gun and make assumptions about how this sale process might play out."

"Smart thinking. You'll make a grand old go of things,

Natalie, whatever you decide to do in the future. I've no doubt about that."

"What's in the future for you? What are your plans?"

He half-shrugged, half-laughed. "I'm thinking I ought to take a leaf out of your book and organise a trip somewhere. Ever since you told me about these travel plans, I've been thinking I should get myself out there, see more of the world."

"Good for you."

"Since I started thinking about stocking more single malt whiskies in the bar, I've been doing research into some of the distilleries, and I might take a trip to visit one or two of them."

"That sounds wonderful. I didn't know you could do that."

"What, visit the distilleries? Oh aye, that's a big tourist industry. And it'll help with this whisky menu I'm planning if I can say something about visiting the distillery myself. To begin with, I'm going to keep the menu simple, but later, once I've got a few trips under my belt, I'd like to tweak them."

"I love that idea."

"And I've probably spent far too much time behind the bar at my pub over the years. I'll be nice to get out and about."

"In our business, work isn't something we can just set aside because we feel like taking a trip. You committed yourself to your pub and that's not a decision to regret. You have a good, solid business there, Keith."

"Luck has been kind to me."

"We make our own luck."

He glanced in her direction and gave her a smile that struck her as filled with mystery and mischief. "Maybe we do."

He stopped walking, stepped closer, and when he looked in her eyes, Natalie understood he was searching for hesitation or discomfort. Knowing he'd find none, she savoured the moment as he moved closer still and kissed her. The tingles that rippled across her skin felt exquisite as his lips gently brushed hers.

She laid a hand on his arm and kissed him back and thought that it felt wonderful. Surprising and lovely and wonderful.

BRUCE, still asleep long after the sun began sliding between the curtains, was caught in a dream where he stood beneath the shade of a tall oak tree beside a riverbank, looking towards an old tumbledown red sandstone building that glowed in late afternoon sunshine. Some of the windows were broken, many of the roof slates had slipped, and the guttering was hanging off at one end. But Bruce – dream Bruce – liked standing there looking at it just the same. It felt peaceful beneath the boughs of the tree, listening to the gentle rippling of the river.

He felt somehow that he knew this place, knew this spot beneath the oak tree, and knew that red building. It all felt familiar, in that eerily tantalising way that happens inside dreams.

He opened his eyes and the dream slipped away. Sitting up in bed, he glanced around the room. For the last few mornings, every time he awoke it seemed smaller than when he'd gone to sleep the night before.

Just a trick of the imagination. Still, if he didn't find someplace else to live – and soon – he worried he might wake up one morning and find the room had grown so small that his arms and legs were poking through the walls. What had started as a comfortably compact space where he could lick his wounds was fast turning into a self-imposed prison cell.

He showered, hauled some clothes from a drawer, and made a mental note to get some laundry done. As he buttoned his shirt, his gaze wandered to the painting that hung above his bed, the one he'd bought for Heather and then taken to spite her.

It truly was an ugly painting, he thought, wincing at the harsh brushstrokes, the cold greys and acid yellows. He felt prickly just looking at it. He didn't understand how anyone could *enjoy* looking at it. No doubt that was just one of the many reasons his marriage had collapsed. He simply had not understood why Heather had found the painting so alluring, because he had never really understood Heather.

And why exactly was he already torturing himself with these gloomy thoughts, less than ten minutes after waking up?

No mystery there. He was living in a room the size of a shoebox and keeping in plain sight a memento from his marriage that would always make him unhappy.

Downstairs, he began cleaning up the public bar. They'd had a good busy night, and he'd been pleased to hold the fort for the second Saturday night in a row while Keith went out with Natalie. He'd always loved the buzz of a Saturday night in his old pub in London and loved seeing people having a good time, laughing and talking, dancing to the music, drinking a little more – sometimes a lot more – than was good for them. Mostly, the drunkenness had never resulted in anything more sinister than too-loud laughter and some ill-advised gyrating on the little dance floor near the DJ booth.

God, he missed that place. He missed the pub that he'd made his own.

Yet just as he'd loved the noise and energy of a good Saturday night, he'd also loved the quiet that followed on the Sunday morning, when he was alone amongst the detritus of empty glasses and soggy beer coasters and getting ready to do it all again. If you knew what you were doing – and Bruce did – there was as much money to be made from the Sunday lunch and dinner crowd as there was from the Saturday night hordes. In fact, it hadn't been unusual in his old pub for the Sunday takings to be highest of the week. He'd always booked a band for Sunday evenings, which drew in punters looking for some live entertainment before the start of the regular working week, and his pub had quickly earned a reputation as a Sunday hot spot.

One day, he hoped, he'd have that again.

With this thought now at the forefront of his mind, he finished clearing up in the bar and sat down with his laptop to look at some pub market opportunities he might have too readily dismissed.

When Keith appeared downstairs a short time later, smartly dressed and wearing a grin that stretched from ear to ear, Bruce could hardly keep his own smile off his face.

"Looks like you had a good night, Uncle Keith."

Keith slid his hands into his pockets and rocked on his heels. "Natalie is quite a woman, Bruce. She takes my breath away."

Bruce stared, thinking this through. "Um, is she ..."

"Is she what?"

"Well, is Natalie still ..." He sighed. "Should I put the kettle on and take her a cuppa?"

Keith looked at him in confusion and then towards Valentino's across the road. As understanding dawned, his eyes bugged. "We didn't spend the night together! What's the matter with you?"

"When people like one another, spending the night together seems like a natural step to me. I just assumed you had, judging by the look on your face."

"For God's sake, we've only been out together twice." Keith looked thoughtful. "But I do like her, Bruce."

"You haven't forgotten she's selling up and leaving, have you?"

"Of course not, I'm not addled."

"I'd hate to be responsible for pairing you up with the next woman who's destined to break your heart."

"I'm a grown man, and my heart's my own business."

"Hmm."

Keith smiled and waved a hand. "Don't worry yourself son, I can look after myself. Come on, I'll buy you breakfast over at the restaurant, there's plenty time before we open."

Immediately, Bruce thought of Laura. He'd successfully avoided her all week. But appearing as a customer in her place of work would almost certainly bring that policy of cowardice to an end.

"Actually, I've got a few things I need to do before—"

"Nonsense, you've got time to sit down and eat some breakfast," Keith said, already heading for the door. "Let's go, my treat."

There was no easy way out that wouldn't look strange and require explanation, so Bruce found himself reluctantly tagging along. When they arrived at Valentino's and settled into a booth, the place was far busier than he'd expected.

And with relief, he saw no sign of Laura.

In fact, he noticed that there were only a couple of servers working – Paul and a young woman he didn't recognise, and both were struggling to keep up with the pace.

"It's hectic in here today," Keith said, gesturing to the messy tables and the plates of food piling up at the kitchen order station and the obviously annoyed customers still waiting to be served.

Just then, Natalie rushed from her office, stabbing furiously at her phone before hustling to the order station and carrying a backlog of breakfasts to waiting customers. Only once the plates of food had been delivered did she notice Keith and Bruce.

Briskly walking over, she brought their coffee order with her. "Good morning, Keith. Good morning, Bruce. How are you both today?"

"We're good," Keith said. "And you?"

"Oh, I'm just fine," she said, absently waving a hand. "I'd

still be basking in my enjoyment of *Rigoletto* last night, but for the fact we're short-staffed this morning."

"Can we help?" Keith said.

"I wouldn't hear of it." She looked down at her phone when it pinged and sighed. "I hoped that might be Laura. I've been trying to reach her all morning. She was supposed to start her shift at ten but hasn't turned up. It's not like her to be late and even less like her to be late and not call ahead to let us know."

A tremendous crash erupted by the counter. Bruce turned to see the lone waitress staring in dismay at the tray of coffees she'd upended, while Paul gaped at the mess and then let out a yelp as the milk steamer on the coffee machine went into overdrive and sprayed hot foam all over his shirt.

"Oh, for God's sake," Natalie said. "We're officially in meltdown. I better go and restore order."

Keith rose. "We'll help you, Natalie."

"No, please—"

"Don't be daft, we're not going to sit here watching you sink." He rolled up his sleeves. "Bruce, you start clearing the dirty dishes off these tables. I'll see to these new customers waiting to be seated."

"You're very kind," Natalie said, making her way to the spilled coffee and retrieving the mop from the store cupboard.

Within fifteen minutes, the extra hands had helped smooth over the chaos. Food was leaving the kitchen promptly, drinks orders were being filled, tables cleared, new customers seated, and no more accidents had taken place. All in all, not a bad result, Bruce thought as he stood by the counter, lifting a forkful of the omelette he'd ordered and watching Keith dig into his bacon and eggs.

"You two saved my life," Natalie said, preparing pots of tea and glasses of orange juice for an order. "You're a fast worker, Bruce. Your uncle says you're looking for a pub to buy, but maybe you ought to think about putting an offer in for this place instead."

Bruce laughed. "If I were in the restaurant business, I'd be mad not to buy this place, Natalie. But I've got my heart set on finding a pub."

"Fair enough." She pulled out her phone and jabbed at the screen, then sighed and disconnected. "I still can't get hold of Laura. This is very unusual." Glancing up, she looked beyond the restaurant windows in the general direction of Laura's flat. "Maybe I should go over and knock on her door and see if everything is alright."

Another ear-splitting crash reverberated around the restaurant as the waitress knocked a stack of dirty glasses from a table. Bruce saw tears swim in the young woman's eyes as every customer in the place turned to look at her.

"Dear God," Natalie said. "Clearly there is no way I can leave this place for even a second, given the mess we're in."

She strode off to help clear up the broken glass, and Bruce felt his uncle's gaze upon him.

"You should do it," Keith said, biting into a slice of toast.

"Do what?"

"Go and knock on Laura's door."

"Me?"

"You two know each other, don't you?"

"Not really."

"The two of you were thick as thieves, setting me and Natalie up together."

"You've known her longer than I have."

"And wouldn't that look strange, some old man knocking on her door at eleven o'clock in the morning?"

"It would look just as strange if it was me knocking."

"No, it wouldn't. Look, Natalie's worried about her. All you have to do is go over there and see if she's in. What's so hard about that?"

There was nothing hard about it, Bruce knew. And he couldn't deny he was concerned about why Laura wasn't at work and wasn't answering her phone. What if she'd gone out last night and something had happened to her, and no one knew about it yet? He couldn't go about the rest of his day with an idea like that stuck in his head when the solution was right in front of him.

"Okay, I'll go."

"Good lad. I'll help Natalie hold the fort."

As Bruce headed for the restaurant door, his heart knocked wildly in his chest, and he desperately wished he hadn't behaved like a fool all week by avoiding Laura – and that he hadn't run out of her flat in the first place.

Because if he hadn't done those things, going into her building and knocking on her door wouldn't feel as horribly awkward as it did.

CHAPTER 10

Laura rarely had the nightmares any more, but she was having one now, in which she stood on the side of the road and watched her parents' car crash head-on into the van that had veered suddenly and treacherously on to the wrong side of the road.

She hadn't been there when the accident happened, but she was always there during the nightmare that re-enacted it, watching the look of horror cross her father's face, then her mother's, as they realised what was now inevitable. In slow motion, Laura saw her father turn the steering wheel with all his might. But it was always too late. And so she stood helpless on the dark verge, the rain falling in sheets from a thick night sky, watching the collision and hearing the terrible sounds of the impact.

She cried, screamed, and tried to run, but found herself rooted to the spot as always, as the crash ended and an awful silence filled the quiet country road.

A banging sound began. That was new. There had never

been banging in the nightmare before. After the crash, there was only ever deadly silence. Why was there banging now? Were her parents still alive somehow in that car? Could she reach them? Save them?

Laura forced her feet to move from the roadside verge and tried to run through the thick treacle of the dream-world.

Suddenly, the banging sound was gone, replaced with a ringing noise. Then the banging resumed once more.

She ran, ran and ran, but got no closer to the car wreck. With a frustrated sob in her throat, she realised that the banging and the ringing was getting louder and closer.

Bang, bang, bang. Ring, ring, ring.

BANG, BANG, BANG.

She opened her eyes. The nightmare clung to her, tearing fresh grief from her heart. She couldn't remember the last time she'd dreamt the nightmare that had plagued her for long months after her parents' deaths. Lying in bed as sleep departed, she realised that the nightmare had left her clammy all over.

No, not just clammy. She was absolutely drenched in sweat. Her palms were slick and a hot sweat coated her forehead. The nightmare had made up for its years of absence.

BANG, BANG, BANG.

"What the ...?" She sat up and immediately regretted it. Every muscle ached and groaned and she was sore to the marrow of her bones.

BANG, BANG, BANG. RING, RING, RING.

What was that noise? Where was it coming from? It seemed so close, but also so far away.

And now the room was spinning.

BANG, BANG, BANG.

"Laura? Are you in there?"

Someone was at the door, banging on it and ringing the doorbell. Why had it taken her so long to figure it out?

She would have to get to the door, would somehow have to move herself from her bed to the hallway to the door. Surely that was impossible.

What on earth was wrong with her?

Whimpering with each tiny movement, she pushed up on to her feet. The room spun harder, like she was on board an out-of-control fairground ride.

There were probably only eight steps from her bed to the front door, but climbing Mount Everest could scarcely have been more difficult. Clutching at the door knob, more for balance than anything else, she peered through the etched glass panel to see who was there.

But there was only darkness. With a sinking feeling, she realised that the outer storm doors of the flat were closed too. Of course they were closed. She always closed them at night.

When she opened the inside door, the chill that snaked in from the tiny porch was enough to leave her gasping.

"Who's there?" she said, the words like rough sandpaper against her throat.

"It's Bruce."

She frowned. She didn't know anyone called Bruce, did she? Although the name did sound familiar. "Who?"

"It's Bruce. From The Crooked Thistle."

Cogs whirred and laboured inside her head. Finally she

remembered – yes, of course, Bruce from the pub – and she shook her head against the fuzziness.

As she unbolted the storm door, she realised the nightmare must've really sunk its claws in to leave her so confused. And as for the terrible achiness, well, she must've fallen into a strange position while sleeping, no doubt thanks to the nightmare, and was now paying the price with numbed limbs.

She hauled open the storm door and saw Bruce. "Hi Bruce, what do you want?" she said, hugging herself against the chill of the tenement stairwell.

"I came to see if you're okay." He looked her up and down with an expression that seemed half-surprised, half-alarmed. "Natalie's worried about you."

She frowned. "Why?"

His gaze moved to her face. "Because you're supposed to be at work, but clearly—"

Realisation seized her. "Oh my God! What time is it?"

"Nearly eleven thirty. But it looks to me like—"

But she was no longer listening as she rushed into the stairwell.

"Hey, for goodness sake!" he said, hooking an arm around her when her legs buckled and she almost fell. "Don't go tearing off, you're not even dressed."

Glancing down, she saw her pyjamas. Of course she was still in her pyjamas. She'd known that.

"I need to get changed." Disentangling herself, she stepped unsteadily into the flat. "I must've overslept. Wait, hang on, why exactly are *you* here looking for me?"

"I was having breakfast at Valentino's with Uncle Keith.

Natalie's short-staffed and it's pandemonium. She's been phoning and when you didn't answer, I came over."

"Oh God!"

She never overslept. Most mornings she woke before the alarm even began bleeping. Pulling a fresh uniform from the wardrobe, she felt the room begin to spin again and felt the fogginess creep into her head. Fiddling with the buttons on the shirt, she told herself to get her act together. She'd let Natalie down, and now she had to get to the restaurant and put things right.

She was about to haul her pyjama top over her head when she realised that Bruce was standing out in the hallway, staring.

"Do you mind?"

"What?"

When she gestured with the fresh shirt in her hand, his cheeks coloured.

"Oh. Um, I'll, um ..." He cleared his throat, and turned his back. "Listen, do you really think this is such a good idea?"

"Do I really think *what* is such a good idea?" Struggling with her pyjama top, she tried not to wince as she awkwardly raised her arms to get it over her head.

"Do you really think going into work is such a good idea?"

"I'm supposed to be working right now. Why wouldn't I think it's a good idea to get over there, before I'm any later than I already am?"

"Laura, you don't look well." He turned his head slightly in the direction of her bedroom. "In fact, you look awful."

"Thanks very much."

"I mean you look ill, really ill, like you might have the flu or something."

Having finally managed to yank her pyjama top over her head, she now contemplated the shirt she'd have to get into. "I'm fine. I had a bad dream last night and must've slept funny. Once I'm up and moving, I'll be fine."

With her arms in the fresh shirt, she looked at the buttons and decided they'd have to wait until her fingers were up to the challenge of such a dexterous task. Instead, she focused on getting into her trousers, and began sliding her pyjama bottoms down. Realising that the vertical movement would leave her dangerously off-balance, she shifted to sit on the edge of her bed.

And let out a shriek as she missed the bed altogether and landed in a heap on the floor.

"Jesus! Are you okay?" Bruce said, racing into the bedroom.

She might have been woolly-headed, but she couldn't let Bruce see her sprawled on the floor with her shirt unbuttoned, her pyjama bottoms pulled down to her knees and her underwear in plain sight. As he rushed towards her, she imagined how she must look, and the sheer embarrassment was enough to propel her up on to her feet like a jack jumping out of his box.

"I'm okay! Don't look at me!" she shouted, yanking her pyjama bottoms up with one hand and hauling her shirt closed around her with the other.

"Laura, did you hurt yourself—"

"I said, don't look at me!"

"Fine, fine." Hands out in surrender, Bruce turned his

back once more. "But just tell me one thing. Do you really feel up to going into Valentino's?"

"I'll be okay once I get there."

"That's not what I asked. Do you really feel up to going into Valentino's?"

"Well, maybe not, but I don't have a choice, and—"

"Do you really feel like running around after customers, and serving their food, and clearing their dirty plates, and wiping up the messy tables they leave behind?"

She pulled the shirt tighter to ward off the shivering. "Well when you put it like that, not really, but—"

"And do you feel achy and sore and hot?"

Now she sagged. "Yes."

"And do you want the customers at Valentino's to end up feeling that way too, because you insisted on going into work and infecting them?"

She sat down on the bed, this time successfully. "No."

"That settles it." He risked a glance over his shoulder. "Can I turn around?"

"Okay."

Turning, he smiled kindly. "How does this sound? I'll call Natalie and explain that you're ill and can't come in to work."

She paused before nodding. "Tell her I'm sorry, and I didn't hear my phone ringing, and—"

Bruce held up a hand. "She'll understand. We'll get you into some fresh pyjamas. We'll get you settled on the sofa while I change your sheets, because I can see that these ones are in a bit of a muddle."

She closed her eyes. "This is too embarrassing."

"No, it's not. I'll make you a hot drink, get you loaded

up with paracetamol. Make you something to eat, if you want?"

She curled a lip, shook her head.

"Nothing to eat, understood. We'll get you back into a nice clean bed and get you some rest. How does that sound?"

"It sounds good. But you don't have to stay and change my sheets or make me hot drinks. I can do those things myself."

"Sometimes it's nice to be looked after, don't you think?"

She stared at the floor. "Yes."

"Okay, where do you keep your clean PJs?"

"I can get them."

Once more, he held up a hand. "Where do you keep them, Laura?"

His smile dissolved her, and she pointed to a drawer by the window. "Get me the ones with the giraffes on them. I like those."

Opening the drawer, he rummaged around and located the pyjamas. They were pale yellow and covered with images of giraffes eating leaves from a tree, drinking water from a pond, and galloping across a savannah. They never failed to cheer her up. She noticed Bruce trying to hide a smile and blushed at his obvious amusement.

"And where do you keep your clean bed linen?"

"The cupboard in the living room. My stuff's on the second shelf. Don't take anything from the third shelf, those are Yvonne's things."

"Where is Yvonne?"

"She's with Olly for the weekend."

"Should I call her? Maybe you ought to have someone with you …"

"No, don't call her, I'll be fine."

He studied her. "What about your boyfriend, what's-his-name? Want me to see if he can come over and keep you company?"

She paused for just a beat before answering. "We broke up."

A look seemed to cross his face, but she was too muddled to be sure what the look might have been, or what it might have meant, or whether it had even been there at all. He gave a nod and began moving towards the door.

"I'll get some clean sheets, and you can get changed while I'm gone." He looked at her uncertainly. "Unless you think you'll need a hand ..."

She managed a smile. "Slick move, cowboy, but I'll manage."

He grinned, and then once more looked serious. "What about a shower? Do you feel like having a shower to freshen up?"

But already she was shaking her head. "I can't even bear to imagine it."

With a final nod he left the room, pulling the door behind him. Laura remained on the edge of the bed and began unfolding the clean pyjamas and removing the assemblage of mismatched garments.

She felt horrible, just horrible, and wondered how long she might have continued sleeping had it not been for Bruce coming to the door. She figured that she'd slept close to thirteen hours straight, and that she could sleep thirteen more, easily.

She was ill, no doubt about it.

Once changed into her fresh PJs, she heard a soft knock at the door and found Bruce with a stack of clean bed linen in his arms.

"Let's get you settled on the sofa while I change your bed," he said, laying the new sheets down and ushering her out. "I found a blanket in the cupboard to keep you warm."

In the living room, she slumped on the sofa and let Bruce wrap the soft blanket around her. It felt good as the warmth returned to her body. He brought her tea, along with a glass of water and paracetamol, which he instructed her to swallow. She smiled in resignation when he loitered to make sure she took the pills.

"You'll be okay for a minute while I sort your bed?"

"Of course I will."

But still he stood there, and she couldn't mistake the concern in his face.

"Sorry you're so sick."

"Me too."

"We'll get you better in no time."

"Promise?"

"Promise," he said, and once more headed to her bedroom.

As she sipped her tea and settled back into the blanket, exhaustion swept through her from the physical efforts of the last ten minutes. She was aware of Bruce, wrestling with the bedding, but the sounds grew distant, as if she was floating into the sky.

She set down her mug of tea, laid her head against a

sofa cushion, and tucked up her legs. She'd just close her eyes for a minute while Bruce finished dealing with the new bed sheets. Just close her eyes and wait.

Just for a minute.

THE FRESH BED linen that Bruce took from the cupboard wasn't a matching set, he realised – only after putting the duvet and pillows inside their covers. He considered finding the correct matches, but thought better of it. Laura was in the grip of a seriously nasty bug and needed to get back into bed and sleep. Matching pillowcases were the least of her concerns.

He stepped into the living room to tell her the bed was ready, but stopped short when he saw her stretched out on the sofa fast asleep. He thought of waking her, but couldn't bring himself to do it. Her bed might be more comfortable, but the sofa would do just fine for now.

He certainly wasn't going to leave her alone, though, to wake up confused on the sofa. When she woke, maybe she'd want to eat, so if he stayed he could make himself useful and fix something.

He'd wait. It was the decent thing to do.

In the kitchen, he dialled the number Natalie had given him and summarised the situation.

"I should've realised something was wrong," Natalie said. "That girl is never off-colour. If I hadn't gone out with your uncle last night, I wouldn't have asked her to cover the shift, and maybe she wouldn't have ended up so ill."

"I doubt working has changed the course of events," Bruce said. "She's picked up a virus, and the virus will do what it does. I'll stay for a while in case she needs anything."

"You're a good boy, Bruce. One of my other waitresses is starting her shift early, and when she arrives I'll pop over with a carton of Tanya's chicken and lentil soup. We can put it in the fridge for Laura – she'll need something good in her stomach."

"Would you tell my Uncle Keith what's going on?"

"He's standing right next to me and says you should stay with Laura as long as she needs you."

They ended the call, and when he checked again on Laura he found her still asleep. Back in the kitchen, he quietly washed up the dishes that sat in the sink, and as he dried them and found where they belonged in the cupboards, he took the place in more fully than he had during his previous visit.

He liked this kitchen and the way Laura had it laid out and organised. It felt good in the space, warm and comfortable. He could imagine her standing at the hob stirring something in one of those pans that lined the pantry shelf. He could imagine her chopping vegetables on the scarred wooden board propped up against the turquoise wall tiles, could imagine her watering her herb pots or fiddling with her ancient coffee machine. This kitchen was a place where a person could be content, where a person could be happy.

Which, he thought grimly, was in stark contrast to the clinical kitchen installation Heather had insisted upon for their home, six months before they'd split. While he'd been glad to see the back of the tired units and vinyl flooring they'd inherited from the previous owner, he hadn't anticipated that their new luxury kitchen would consist of a palette of greys and cold whites that made him feel depressed every time he walked into it. But he'd figured it was all just part of the compromise of marriage. Heather's heart had been set on the vision she'd created, and so he'd consoled himself that he had his lovely pub to retreat to with its warm woods and clever colours on the walls. It never occurred to him that it should've been his home that he thought of as his sanctuary, not his place of business.

Thinking of that hard, cold kitchen of Heather's while he stood in this warm, lovely kitchen of Laura's, with its mismatched tableware and pretty plant pots and bright tea towels, made him realise just how his own vision of what a home should look like had never really matched up with that of his ex-wife's. These days, it seemed he only ever found himself baffled that they'd ever had enough in common to get together in the first place.

After making coffee he headed to the living room, where Laura still slept. He picked up a magazine and flicked through it, before scanning the rows of well-thumbed paperbacks in the bookshelf alcove and selecting a thriller to pass some time.

Lowering himself into the armchair by the window, wincing in case of any noisy creaks, he realised that this was the chair he'd made gentle fun of that night he and Laura had chatted on the phone while Keith and Natalie had gone out on their date. She'd explained that the chair had belonged to her father, and he found himself imagining the man, sitting in this chair watching golf on television, just as she'd described him.

It was a nice memory for her to hold on to. He

wondered what it must have been like for her to lose her parents so young. She'd been only nineteen, he calculated. He couldn't imagine his parents not being around when he'd been nineteen. Even now, he spoke to them most weeks at their cottage on the coast. When his marriage to Heather had been collapsing, it had been his parents, and Jack, who'd got him through it during countless phone conversations while the end had spun out.

Who'd been there for Laura since her parents' deaths? Who'd watched out for her?

In that moment, he understood a little better Laura's devotion to Natalie and her devotion to Valentino's – and the anxiety she felt at what lay ahead.

Watching her, tucked up inside her blanket, she looked beautiful. Even in the grip of illness, her face left him mesmerised.

He thought about what she'd said about her boyfriend no longer being on the scene. It made sense that she must've ditched him after he'd stood her up that day for an Indiana Jones movie. She would've been crazy not to.

No boyfriend. No entanglements.

If he wasn't still licking his divorce wounds, he wondered if he might have allowed his heart to open instead of keeping it snapped closed.

LAURA WOKE, although it was more like surfacing after being trapped below ground. Groaning, she screwed her eyes against the light. Although every muscle still ached, they didn't ache quite as badly as before, and for that she could only be grateful.

Opening her eyes, she shifted and heard heavy rain lashing against the windows. As she looked to the dark, gloomy skies outside, she saw a figure sitting in her father's old armchair, and once her vision adjusted she realised it was Bruce.

"What are you still doing here?"

He closed the book he'd been reading. "I didn't want to leave you alone, in case you needed something."

Swinging her legs off the sofa, she grimaced at the sharp spears of stiffness in her calves and thighs.

Bruce studied her for a few seconds. "How do you feel?"

"Like I've been run over by a twenty-tonne truck." Rising, she waited until the room stopped whirling around her before testing one foot in front of the other. "I need some water."

"I'll get it. How about tea, too?"

"Yeah, I'd like that."

Heading for the door, he paused. "Natalie brought you some soup from the restaurant. Chicken and lentil, Tanya's speciality, apparently. Want some?"

"What a lovely thing to do. But I didn't hear anyone at the door."

"You were out for the count. You have been for the last three hours."

"Three hours?" Her gaze darted towards the clock, and she saw it was the middle of the afternoon. "God, I've slept most of the day."

"You needed to sleep. And now that you're awake, just take it easy while you get your bearings."

In the bathroom, she looked at her reflection in the mirror and groaned. After splashing cold water on her face and brushing her teeth, she felt a little better although her reflection looked just as awful.

As she walked into the kitchen, drawn by the smell of warm soup, she heard Bruce talking on the phone cradled at his ear while he stirred the pot on the hob.

"Tell the girls I'm sorry, and I'll see them during the week," he said, pouring soup into bowls. "Yeah ... yeah, I know ... yes, I do understand about fluid intake requirements for sick people, I'm not a moron. In fact, I'm heating soup right now ... Okay, have fun, and don't set your hair on fire with that barbeque." He hung up and shifted his attention to the soup-pouring.

"You had plans today," Laura said.

He turned and smiled when he saw her in the doorway. "Just a visit to my brother and his family, no big deal."

"I feel terrible."

He set the pot in the sink and hurried over. "I'll help you back to the sofa—"

"No, I don't mean that. I mean I feel terrible you've stayed with me instead of visiting your family."

He looked at her, his gaze level. "There's nothing for you to feel terrible about. You didn't ask me to stay, I chose to. Anyway, Jack just wants to show off his new shiny barbeque."

She turned to the rain-spattered kitchen window and the leaden skies beyond. "Your brother's having a barbeque in this weather?"

He laughed. "He bought one of these all-weather, all-purpose barbeques of the gods. Rain just gives him another opportunity to test its capabilities."

"He makes his family sit in the rain so he can have a barbeque?"

"God, no. Jack will be out in the rain, Claire and the girls will be warm and dry inside. You've saved me from hovering at his kitchen door, passing the meat tongs while he lectures me about marinade techniques. This virus of yours has really helped me out."

She laughed, and then groaned as the muscle movement sent fresh aches darting through her. Bruce ushered her back on to the sofa and set her up with a lap tray.

"Thank you," she said, taking in the soup bowl, the linen napkin he'd dug out of the drawer and placed inside a napkin ring – how had he even known what those were for? – and the glass of iced water that sat tantalisingly alongside.

"Eat as much or as little as you can," he said. "Natalie wants an update once you're finished."

She drank down half her water in one long, thirsty gulp, and began eating the soup. Although it was delicious, she felt herself begin to fade away after six or seven spoonfuls.

"That was good," she said, setting her lap tray on to the table. "But I can't eat any more."

"Want anything else?" Bruce asked.

She shook her head. He continued eating for a few moments longer before also setting down his spoon and giving her a look she couldn't decipher.

"What?" she finally asked.

"I'm glad you broke up with your boyfriend," Bruce said. "Ditching you like he did last weekend, well, he deserved to get dumped."

She cut her eyes towards him before looking away. “Actually, he dumped me.”

Bruce gaped. “How did he …? What, you gave him another chance after last week?”

Laura blushed. “I know, I’m an idiot. He said he was sorry and asked to take me to dinner to make it up. Then after he brought me home, he broke up with me. I’d been going to end things with him, and he ended up dumping me. That’s what happens, I suppose, when you try to dodge making a difficult decision.”

“I can testify from personal experience, it’s always better to be the dumper than the dumpee.”

She gave him an unhappy look. “I put on my beautiful dress and my killer heels because he said he’d take me somewhere fancy. And we ended up at Pizza Hut. Hey, don’t laugh!”

“I’m not,” he said, attempting to clear his expression.

“Yes, you are.”

“Only because of how you described it.”

“Great, have a good chuckle.”

“Sorry, I’m not chuckling,” he said, serious now. “This guy sounds like an idiot.”

But she shook her head. “That’s the thing, though. He’s not an idiot. He’s not mean or horrible. He just wasn’t right for me, and I wasn’t right for him. He liked going to the movies, and we’d just sit there in the cinema, no work required. I don’t know why I thought that’s what I wanted. Stupid, right?”

Bruce looked at her for a moment, and when he answered his voice was soft. “Not stupid, no.”

She sighed and shifted her blanket. "I'd like to close my eyes again for just a little while. Do you mind?"

"Of course I don't."

"You don't have to stay."

"Do you want me to go?"

She thought about it and shook her head. "Is it okay if you stay?"

"It is."

WHEN LAURA WOKE AGAIN, it was eight in the evening. She'd only meant to nap for a few minutes. Cursing the virus, she propped herself up and found herself alone in the living room.

Bruce must have left. Of course he'd left. Why would he hang around for another boring four hours while she snored?

But when she opened the living room door, she heard noises from the kitchen. She wandered through, her legs still stiff and achy, and found him working at the counter with a wooden spoon and a mixing bowl.

"Hey," she said, rubbing sleep from her eyes.

Bruce turned and smiled. "Hey, sleepyhead. Hope I didn't wake you."

"You didn't. What are you doing?"

Glancing at the bowls and ingredients and general mess on the counter, he laughed. "I was planning to surprise you. I'm making muffins."

"You don't have to make muffins, you've done enough already."

"Ah, but these aren't just any muffins. These are magic muffins."

At her sceptical look, he laughed and gestured to the mixture in the bowl. "My sister-in-law, Claire, makes these for my nieces when they get sick. I happened to be there once when she was making a batch. They're amazing, so I called her and she talked me through the recipe. I thought you might like them."

She sat at the kitchen table and watched him spooning the mixture into cases.

"I didn't know I even had muffin cases."

"You didn't. I asked my Uncle Keith to bring round a few things." He finished filling the cases and slid the tray into the oven. "How are you feeling?"

"Not any better, but not any worse, either. Think I might like a shower, though."

"I'll warm up some more of the soup Natalie brought, and it'll be ready when you are."

A hot shower, warm soup to eat afterwards, the smell of muffins baking in the oven, and someone running around to help her – it was exactly what she needed. As the water cascaded over her sore body – bliss, pure bliss – she wondered what had possessed Bruce to give up his Sunday for her. There was no obligation, no expectation. As she towelled off, she thought of the afternoon they'd spent at the food festival, just a week ago, although it felt far longer, and wondered at that moment they'd shared in the kitchen before he'd suddenly darted off.

Was there something there or not? Was he interested in her, her current state notwithstanding? Or was he just a nice guy doing a nice thing for someone who could use some help?

Drying her hair, she pushed the thoughts aside. She was in no fit state to start speculating about such things. The man was here and being sweet while she was ill. That was enough.

Back in the kitchen, feeling fresher and more like herself, she found him washing dishes, the previously messy countertops now cleared, while a saucepan of soup once more warmed on the hob.

"A man who bakes, cleans up after himself, and makes nourishing meals for the sick. Do you have your own superhero cape, too?"

Laughing, he set a bowl of soup before her. She tasted it and her hunger pangs instantly cried out for more. When the oven timer pinged, Bruce removed the muffins, laid them out to cool, and the sweet aroma of apple and cinnamon had Laura's stomach growling. That had to be a good sign, she decided.

When you wanted to eat, the virus was in retreat.

Her mother's little saying.

She was about to smile at the recollection, but in a flash so sudden it almost took her breath away, the memory of the nightmare that had gripped her so violently came thundering back. She shivered as its edges raked over her, and found herself once more standing at the edge of that dark, wet road, watching her parents' car being obliterated by the speeding van, hearing the deafening roar of the collision, feeling the cold rain on her skin as the silent aftermath enveloped her.

As she jolted on her chair, her soup spoon clattered to the floor. Bruce leapt to his feet.

"What's wrong? Are you alright?"

Not for a long time had she experienced one of these waking nightmares. First, there had been the nightmare while she slept. Now, she was having one while awake. And the sensation of it hurt so badly inside her heart that tears spilled uncontrollably down her cheeks.

"What's the matter?" Bruce, now beside her, grabbed her hand. "Are you in pain?"

She managed to shake her head. "I'm fine, I'm okay." She sipped from the glass of water he'd set on the table. "I just remembered a nightmare. I'm fine, really."

"You're not fine, you're shaking. And you're freezing cold."

He left the kitchen, and when he returned he'd brought the blanket she'd slept beneath on the sofa. Wrapping it around her, he pulled his chair closer and took her hands and began rubbing them between his own.

She watched his hands move over hers, felt his skin against hers.

"Tell me about this nightmare," he said, his voice soft.

"It's nothing."

"Tell me. Please."

His eyes were on her, and she found she couldn't look away, couldn't do anything other than what he was asking, as his hands rubbed warmth back into hers.

Rain ticked against the darkening kitchen windows, and she found herself beginning to talk, talking like she'd never done before, not with anyone.

"I used to have nightmares about the car crash that

killed my parents. I haven't had them in a long time, but I had one last night, or this morning, I'm not sure. I wasn't there when they died. But for a long time, I dreamt about what the police told me had happened. I used to daydream about it too, although daydream's the wrong word. My brain would just start playing this film in my head of the final seconds before the crash. I haven't had those nightmares, awake or sleeping, for years. But now I've had two, one while I slept, right before you came to my door, and one just now. I know that sounds crazy, a waking nightmare, but it's the only way to describe it. I don't know why it's happening now."

"Illness messes with the mind as much as with the body."

She watched his hands moving more slowly now, almost caressing her.

"You don't have to keep doing that."

"Shh. You need to be comforted. Let me comfort you."

She blinked back tears. "This bug's turned me into a wreck. I'm a disgrace."

"No, you're not."

More tears come to her eyes. She told herself not to start sobbing, because if she started, she thought she might not be able to stop.

"It's just been a strange few days," she said, clearing her throat against the emotions. "Natalie putting the restaurant up for sale. John dumping me. And I had an awful training run the other day and it made me feel completely useless. And now I've got this virus. God, listen to me moaning."

"Things mount up. It happens."

"Yeah, and now I'm ..."

Now she was sitting in her kitchen, almost sobbing, while this perfectly lovely man who'd been looking after her all day patiently listened and rubbed her hands.

Hands which were now lovely and warm. But still he rubbed them. And it felt good. Very good.

Clearing her throat, she pulled away. "I think I ought to get to bed."

He sat back in the chair and nodded. "You don't want to finish your soup?"

"I've had enough."

"Okay, we'll get you settled and I'll clear up in here."

"No, you've been running around after me, baking for me, and ... God, I didn't even ask to taste the muffins you went to the trouble of making."

"You want one now?"

She shook her head. "Tomorrow, though, I'll probably eat the lot. But you've been here long enough already, you don't have to stay and—"

"I'm not letting you wake up to a messy kitchen in the morning, end of discussion."

Resigned, she nodded. "You're a good guy, Bruce." She began heading towards her bedroom. "Before you go, could I ask one more favour?"

"Just one, then I'll have to charge my standard hourly rate."

Seeing him grin, she relaxed. "There's an extra pillow on top of my wardrobe, but I'm too stiff and sore to reach up. Would you mind getting it?"

"Consider it done."

In her bedroom, she pointed to the pillow and Bruce

tugged it down from the wardrobe, but it caught the edge of a cardboard folder and sent it tumbling to the ground.

"Sorry," he said, picking up the pile of documents and paperwork that had fallen out.

Realising what the folder contained, Laura darted over and began stuffing the papers back inside. But Bruce was already staring at the paperwork he'd scooped up.

"I didn't know you'd gone to university," he said, inspecting the degree brochure that had slid across the floor.

She sighed. "I didn't. Or at least, I didn't finish."

Frowning, he picked up a couple of handbooks – *Introduction to American History, Europe Since Napoleon* – and flicked through them. "You decided you didn't want to study history after all?"

She sat on the edge of the bed. "No, that wasn't it, but …"

When she said nothing further, he looked up. It only took a moment for his confused expression to disappear as realisation dawned.

"Your parents died."

She nodded. "A few weeks before the start of my second year. I suspended my degree while I dealt with the funeral and sold the house. I always intended to go back eventually, once I'd sorted everything out."

She ran her hand over one of the university brochures, remembering that time and the pain that had come with it.

"I bought my flat and got the job at Valentino's to pay the bills, and thought that once I'd got over what had happened, I'd start my degree again. The first anniversary of the accident came and went, and I told myself that things would be better the next year, and I'd re-enrol. But then that next year came and went too. And time just got away from me, I guess."

She looked at Bruce and he nodded.

"And then I ended up falling in love with Valentino's. It was easy being there and I liked the work. And so long as I worked there, I didn't have to put myself on the line, all alone, and go after something I might never accomplish."

His gaze travelled to the wall and to her collection of certificates. She turned, looked at them as he did, and uttered a sad little laugh.

"You don't have to be a psychoanalyst to work out what's going on there. I never got my degree, so now I compensate with these useless things instead."

"They're not useless. Don't say that."

But she shook her head. Her little triumphs, she called those certificates. And maybe that's what they'd been to begin with, a reminder that she could still achieve things, no matter how small. But didn't those certificates just remind her of the degree she'd once longed for and had never completed? Didn't they just remind her that she'd never been brave enough to start again?

"I had these dreams, once," she said. "And then one day those dreams were gone, and I knew I'd never get them back again."

Bruce turned, and his smile was so tender it almost brought back her tears. "That's the virus talking. You're ill, exhausted, and your mind's being cruel. What you need is to get well."

He gathered the rest of the spilled documents back into

the folder and returned it to the wardrobe top. "You have to promise you won't lie in bed thinking about this stuff."

"I promise."

"I mean it."

"I know. And I do too. I promise. Or, at least, I'll promise to try."

Once he'd cleared up in the kitchen, she walked him to the door.

"Thanks for today, Bruce. It really means a lot."

"You'll go straight to bed?"

"If I don't fall asleep here in the hallway."

He paused, his hand on the door knob, as if considering something.

Then he moved closer and kissed her cheek, and the kiss was so soft and gentle that her skin hummed beneath his lips.

"Goodnight, Laura."

When he leaned back and held her gaze, those storm-grey eyes were all she could see.

"Goodnight, Bruce."

He stepped into the stairwell, pulled the storm door behind him, and was gone.

She stood for a moment, the kiss still tingling on her cheek, and only thought to move when the chill of the stairwell began sneaking around her aching body.

When she fell into bed, sinking into the pillows and pulling the duvet around her, she groaned with the comfort of it. But although all she wanted to do was sleep, she found her mind racing with the freshly disturbed thoughts about her parents and painful memories of her long-lost dreams.

So she tried to block the unhappy thoughts by thinking about Bruce instead. She thought about how kind he'd been. She thought of how his hands had warmed hers. She thought of his eyes and how they made her want to fall into their grey storm.

And she thought of the way his lips had brushed her cheek, and how her heart had begun beating faster because of it.

With these thoughts in her head, sleep finally came and claimed her, and it was a sleep so deep and peaceful that no nightmare could break through.

CHAPTER 11

The man could bake a muffin.

Standing at the kitchen counter in her pyjamas and bathrobe, Laura broke off a piece and savoured it. The apples were soft, the cinnamon warm and comforting, and the texture was melt-in-the-mouth perfection. By the time the kettle had boiled for tea, she'd already eaten an entire muffin and begun another.

It was partly hunger after more than thirty-six hours of near starvation. Mostly, though, it was because they tasted awesome.

Like a dark veil being lifted, she'd woken to find the virus had loosened its grip. Sunshine slanted through the curtains and the previous day's summer rainstorm had passed. She felt better, lighter. And although far from recovered, she felt once more like herself.

Despite making these arguments to Natalie, her boss wouldn't hear of her going into work and assured her that if she appeared at the restaurant, she would simply be sent back home again.

Laura sent a message to Bruce, thanking him for all he'd done and for the muffins, which she invited him to come over and enjoy before she ate the lot. When he replied that he was glad she felt better but would be gone for most of the day viewing pubs for sale, she was disappointed. She wanted to see him and thank him properly for his company and help. But also because ... well, just because.

The days that Natalie compelled her to take off work to recover passed quickly. Yvonne arrived home from her trip with Olly, bursting with stories she eagerly shared and commiserating with Laura over her illness.

"You should've called, and I would've come back," Yvonne told her. "At least Mr Hottie was here to sponge your fevered brow."

"Don't call him that."

"You're blushing."

"No, I'm not. I'm still getting hot flushes from the last of this bug."

Yvonne rolled her eyes. "So what are you going to do about this?"

"About what?"

"About Mr Hottie? You ought to go round there and ask him out to dinner."

"For God's sake, I'm not going to ask him out to dinner."

"Why not?"

"Because."

"You're so old-fashioned, Laura."

It was a relief when Yvonne finally left again for work.

Yet Laura found herself sitting at the living room

window in her father's old armchair, peering down the street and towards The Crooked Thistle. Before going back to work, she'd go in there, she decided, and thank Bruce. That was all, just thank him. Make sure he knew how much she appreciated the time and care he'd taken with her.

Remembering how she must've appeared to him – the near hysterics over the awful nightmare, not to mention blubbering about that folder of old university paperwork – made her cringe.

He'd probably run a mile if he saw her again.

There wasn't much she could do about the nightmare she'd suffered. But that folder of old university stuff? Why was she still clinging on to it?

Marching into her bedroom, she pulled the folder from the top of the wardrobe and strode through to the recycling bin in the kitchen.

And almost – *almost* – dropped it in.

Sighing, she returned to the bedroom and all but threw it back where she'd found it. She didn't know why she couldn't part with it, and supposed there were just some things in life that were hard to let go of.

She pulled on a jacket and left the flat. She needed fresh air. The sun was out, summer temperatures had returned, and a walk would do her good.

She wasn't yet up to running, even if the ten-kilometre race was now perilously close. But walking, that would be good.

And it was.

. . .

After two days of searching, Bruce had found only disappointment.

Eight pubs. And not a single one ignited even the slightest interest.

Too small. Too big. Wrong price. Wrong location.

Keith, tagging along on a couple of the viewings, remonstrated with him about being too picky. Jack remonstrated with him for the same reasons.

Bruce tried to explain. He now had a vision in his head of what he wanted, but nothing he saw came close to matching it. He wanted a bright space with lots of potential, and maybe enough room for a beer garden, and a nice place upstairs where he could live, and some beautiful trees around the place, maybe even a little stream or river nearby, and ...

It was the place he'd dreamt of. That place with the tumbledown red sandstone building, where he'd stood beneath the tree, with the stream bubbling nearby. The image was caught in his head, and he couldn't get rid of it. It wasn't what he'd been looking for when he'd returned to Glasgow. But ever since he'd had that dream, it had become all he wanted.

And there was nowhere that looked even remotely like it. He wondered if he was chasing a mirage.

Returning to The Crooked Thistle late one evening after yet another frustrating viewing, he installed himself behind the bar and began pulling pints for Jimmy Pearson and Big Kev, who were on their usual stools at the counter.

"No joy?" Keith asked, as he ferried a tray of dirty glasses to the kitchen.

Bruce shook his head.

"Must be hard," Jimmy Pearson said, winking and elbowing Big Kev, "wondering what to do with your millions."

"It's a tough life for the wealthy," Big Kev agreed.

"Give it a rest, boys," Bruce said, serving them their pints. "I'm not wealthy."

"So you didn't make millions when you sold that last place of yours?"

He opened his mouth to reply, but realised there was no sense getting dragged into a conversation with them. He wasn't in the mood.

"I'm taking Natalie out again this Friday," Keith said, returning from the kitchen. "You'll be okay to cover me?"

"No problem. You haven't forgotten she's—"

"Leaving? How could I, when you keep reminding me?"

Bruce pointed to a box on the floor. "You want these fresh bottles opened?"

Keith hurried over. "Not yet. These are the new whiskies I've brought in. They just arrived this morning. I want to clear some of these shelves and make a nice display." He frowned at the bottles crowding the bar shelves, before picking one up and inspecting it. "I mean, when did we last sell advocaat in here? Or that disgusting banana liqueur? We need a clear out to make space for my lovely new Scotches. Bruce, have you looked at the new whisky menu I'm working on yet? Bruce? Earth to Bruce?"

"Hmm?" He turned and saw Keith looking at him in puzzlement.

"Just staring out the window at her won't make anything happen," Keith said.

"What are you ...? I wasn't staring at her."

"Yes, you were," Jimmy Pearson chimed in. "I'm surprised Wee Blondie can't feel the force of your laser gaze from across the street."

"If it was any more intense, you'd burn a hole in the wall," Big Kev said, chortling.

"Ignore these two." Keith waved a hand dismissively. "But if you like that lovely wee Laura, you need to tell her."

"I'm just wondering how she's feeling after being ill."

"So, go over and ask her."

"She's busy, look." Bruce gestured to the window. "It's packed over there this evening."

"Then wait until closing time."

"She'll be exhausted after her shift."

"She came in here earlier looking for you," Keith said, picking up one of his new bottles of whisky and admiring it.

"She did?" Bruce turned from the window.

"Seemed a bit disappointed when I said you were out for the day."

"Disappointed?"

"Disappointed."

"Definitely disappointed," Jimmy Pearson said.

"Aye, that's the word," said Big Kev. "Dis-app-ointed."

"Shut up, you two." Keith walked over, and clapped his hand on Bruce's shoulder. "Son, if you're waiting for the perfect moment to go and talk to her, let me save you some trouble and tell you there's no such thing."

But Bruce only sighed as he watched Laura over in Valentino's, delivering a tray of drinks. When she disappeared from sight, he turned back to serve a punter at the bar.

And as the evening wore on, he realised that Keith was right. He probably should go over there and speak to her. They'd exchanged messages since she'd been ill, but that wasn't enough and he knew it.

Although they'd spent that long rainy Sunday together while Laura had been ill, the fact remained that the last time he'd seen her before that, he'd been doing the hundred-metre sprint down her tenement stairs.

And then he'd ignored her for a week.

That had to be dealt with. He couldn't act like he hadn't done those things, couldn't act like he expected her to forget he'd stood there in her kitchen, almost kissing her before legging it out the door.

He ought to go over once Valentino's closed, as his uncle had advised. Tell her how happy he was to see her up and about again. Tell her he was sorry he'd acted like an idiot before. Tell her he was sorry he hadn't kissed her that day in her kitchen.

But he couldn't say that. If he said he was sorry he hadn't kissed her, didn't it imply that he wanted to kiss her now?

Did he want to kiss her now?

Of course he wanted to kiss her! He wanted to kiss her so badly it almost hurt to think about it.

So why was he tying himself up in knots with these stupid debates inside his head? Why was he over-thinking everything? Looking for every possible way in which doing anything – anything at all – might cause him to make a wrong move? Why was he letting his head rule his heart?

The answer was obvious. The last time he'd listened to

his heart instead of his head, he'd ended up married to Heather.

No, that wasn't fair. He'd been happy with Heather for a long time, and she'd been happy with him, as far as he could tell. There'd been no way of knowing how things would end, no way of knowing that things even *would* end. Sure, they'd had their differences, but those hadn't been differences that would automatically condemn a marriage to failure. What Heather had done – the affair, and the terrible revelation that had come with it – could never have been anticipated.

Could it?

And now, he realised, he was still playing pointless mind games with himself.

A flicker of movement across the street caught his eye as he cleared empty glasses from a table. Looking up, he saw the window blinds being pulled down in Valentino's.

They were getting ready to close.

Bruce stood, staring. He should go over there. He should catch Laura while it was quiet, before she went home. He should tell her ... what?

But he already knew. Had known from the first moment he'd set eyes on her.

Yet the idea was absurd, ridiculous, terrifying ...

He felt a hand on his shoulder, and turned as Keith removed the empty glasses from his hand.

"Go," Keith told him.

And he did.

CHAPTER 12

Laura cleared the last table in Valentino's, set it with fresh silverware and napkins, and made sure everything looked smart and neat. Pleased, she looked around the empty restaurant.

She loved these times, just before or after service, when the place was quiet and lovely and she was alone. Tanya and her kitchen crew and the rest of the waiting staff had already gone home. Laura had volunteered to lock up once the last of the customers had departed, and she'd taken her time about it. Once Valentino's was sold, there might not be any more moments like these, after new owners arrived and began doing things their own way.

So she savoured the space while she still could. Music played quietly, tonight's choice a playlist of the old easy-listening love songs that Angelo had always enjoyed. The lights were low and candles still burned on the tables. The restaurant looked pretty and romantic in candlelight. So pretty and romantic, in fact, that Laura could hardly bring herself to blow them out.

A knock came at the door. With the blinds pulled down, she couldn't see who was out there. Not that it mattered. The restaurant was done for the night.

"We're closed," she called out.

"It's Bruce. Can I come in for a minute?"

She felt a tiny flutter in her stomach as she walked over, turned the heavy lock, and opened the door to find him standing there, smiling.

"I wanted to see you before you went home," he said. "How are you feeling?"

"Much better. Natalie made me take a few days off, but I'm glad to be back."

"You're not too tired after your shift?"

"I'm fine, I feel fine."

"Good, that's good." He thrust his hands in his pockets and shifted his feet. "Listen, could I maybe come in, just for a minute?"

"Oh, sure." She opened the door wider to let him step through and locked it again. "I want to thank you for being so sweet on Sunday. You stayed when you didn't have to, and that meant a lot."

"I wouldn't have left you, given the state you were in."

She felt her cheeks flush. "Yes, I was in a state. I'm sorry."

"There's nothing to be sorry for. You were sick."

"No, I mean ... I'm sorry for getting upset about the nightmare, and about—"

But he held up his hands. "You don't have anything to be sorry for Laura."

She fidgeted for a second. "Well, anyway ..."

A long beat passed. The candles flickered on the tables.

Frank Sinatra sang something softly into the quiet of the night.

And Bruce held her gaze, kept her pinned with those eyes that made her quiver inside. Quite how many seconds passed before she finally looked away she didn't know.

"It's late, and I need to lock up and—"

"I'm sorry I ran off that day, after the food festival," he said quickly, before taking a deep breath. "I shouldn't have disappeared like that. We had a perfect afternoon together, and running off at the end of it wasn't what I'd been planning."

She studied him. "What *had* you been planning?"

"This."

He moved in, pulled her close and laid his lips on hers. The sudden sensation of it sent shivers across her skin as his hands glided around her waist and over her hips.

Then the kiss was all she knew.

His lips moved over hers, wild and tender at the same time. The kiss turned her inside out and made every nerve ending sing. She ran her hands over his arms, over his shoulders, feeling the strength that lay there, the strength he used to hold her close.

When he finally stopped kissing her, she thought she saw fireworks detonating above their heads.

"Wow," was all she managed to say.

Everything shimmered, as if the softly lit restaurant had been draped in delicate silver gossamer. The candles still flickered. The love song still played. But all she could think about was Bruce, standing before her, and the way he looked at her.

Now she was the one who moved forward, grabbing his

shirt and pulling him close until his kiss was once more wrapped around her. He pushed her back against the bar counter, and when his mouth hit the sweet spot behind her ear, she thought she might've become a puddle on the floor but for him holding her up.

It was like no kiss she'd ever had in her life. It was like no kiss she thought could exist in this world.

Then the kiss moved from blind passion to gentle caress, which was a new kind of wonderful. He kissed her forehead and tilted her face towards his.

"You have no idea how long I've wanted to do that," he said.

"How long?"

"Since the first moment I saw you. It just took me a while to realise it." He kissed her lips and the tip of her nose. "I want you."

Her surprised gasp escaped before she could stop it, and he laughed softly.

"What I mean is I want to take you to dinner."

She threw him a glance. "You *don't* want me?"

"Oh, I want you. But I think I ought to buy you dinner first."

Laughing, she let him pull her even closer.

"So, can I take you out?"

"Sure, if you promise me something."

"What?"

"That afterwards you'll kiss me again the way you just did."

"It's a deal."

As he once more found that sweet spot on her neck, she

sighed. If there were still brains inside her head, they'd turned to mush.

"How about Friday?"

"I'm working Friday night while Natalie goes out with your Uncle Keith."

"Damn, I knew we should never have set up those two."

She laughed. "Saturday?"

"Saturday it is." He stepped back and studied her. "You said that on the last date you had with what's-his-face, he told you to get dressed up for a big night out, and he ended up buying you pizza. Get dressed up for our date. You won't regret it. I'll treat you right."

"I don't expect anything fancy."

"Get dressed up anyway. It's our first date, and it's going to be special." He laid his hands gently on either side of her head and kissed her once more. "Want me to walk you home once you're finished here?"

"I think I can manage."

They said goodbye at the door with another kiss that left her breathless. When he was gone, she collapsed against the bar counter, her lips bruised and tingling and her heart thundering in her chest. At some point the music had stopped playing, but she couldn't have said exactly when.

She blew out the last of the candles still burning on the tables, locked up Valentino's, and all but floated home.

CHAPTER 13

The whisky distillery sat on the north shore of the River Clyde, and Keith had bagged the best spot from which he and Natalie could enjoy the view. There were two trios of whisky samplers set out on the table, the evening had turned the sky outside the huge bank of windows a pretty shade of blue, and Keith was as happy and content as he could ever imagine being.

"Here, try this one," he told Natalie, pushing a whisky glass in her direction. "This might be more to your liking."

Her expression was unconvinced. She'd already sampled two whiskies and hadn't enjoyed them. But he was pleased she appeared to be giving this third measure a fair chance.

As soon as it hit her tongue, she shook her head. "It tastes exactly the same as the last one."

He laughed. "That's impossible. The last one was an Islay malt, heavily peated, very distinctive flavour. This is a Speyside, aged in sherry casks, quite different."

"If you say so."

"There's some work to do yet to develop your palette."

"I think I'll keep my palette as it is and stick to wine. Do they have wine here?"

"I'm sure they do. Hang on, I'll be right back."

He headed to the little tasting station, inquired about wine, and a glass of red was soon produced. He'd hoped Natalie would enjoy this trip to the whisky tasting at the distillery. She'd been so helpful when she'd come to take a glance at the whisky menu he'd drafted for The Crooked Thistle, and had given him so many good ideas about how to describe the new whiskies he'd be selling, that he couldn't help but think she would love actually sampling them too.

Clearly, though, Scotch was not her thing.

She had told him as much, in fairness, when he'd suggested this little jaunt. All she'd done, she explained, was take the whisky descriptions Keith had already written and spiced them up. That didn't mean she liked whisky.

But, convinced of his own wisdom, he'd set out to convert her. And had failed.

Still, as he carried her wine to the table, she was smiling and looked happy enough enjoying the river view while picking at the little plate of Scottish antipasti they'd ordered.

The evening was not a total bust.

"Here," he said, setting the wine before her. "Get a good glug of that down you. I've got six whiskies to drink by myself now, so you'll have to keep up with me."

"I can assure you, my days of keeping up with anyone in the drinking department are long behind me."

Spearing a thin slice of venison, he laughed. "I do enjoy

myself when I'm with you, Natalie. I haven't had as much fun with a woman in very a long time."

"Keith, you deserve nothing but happiness, in love and in life generally. You simply have to stop searching for it in all the wrong places."

"Maybe that's something I've realised, since we started seeing one another."

Natalie said nothing and looked away as she topped an oatcake with smoked salmon. Watching her carefully, he swirled his Scotch, the amber liquid catching the light. He didn't want to scare her off. This was just supposed to be a couple of old friends enjoying one another, no more, no less. If he pushed it too hard, he'd blow it.

A change in conversational direction was required.

"I suppose you've heard the good news about Laura and Bruce? They're off out to dinner together tomorrow night."

Natalie smiled. "Yes, it's wonderful. I don't think she was keen on that other boy she was seeing, although she may have been trying to convince herself otherwise. My gut tells me that Bruce might be a far better match for her."

"He's had his cap set in her direction since he came to live with me. The first time she came into the pub, he was as good as struck deaf and dumb. Not that he realised it at the time."

"I'm glad they've decided to give things a go. Laura needs a push in life, and I'm sure it wouldn't hurt for your Bruce to be reminded that he is an attractive young man who deserves another chance at love."

"You think it might be love?"

She grinned over the edge of her wine glass. "I've seen with my own eyes how lit up Laura's been these past few days. And I like to be an optimist, where important matters such as love are concerned."

"I hope things take a turn for the better for the boy. They'd make a nice pair, Bruce and Laura. And, had it not been for them meddling in *our* lives, maybe they wouldn't have got together at all. So, cheers to them, and cheers to us, too."

They clinked glasses. Outside, a pleasure cruiser passed on the river, its deck lights lit up. He watched Natalie as she sipped her wine. She looked wonderful tonight, with the coppery glint of the whisky still exhibit that dominated the space highlighting the burnished tones in her hair and the deep amber of her eyes.

"How's the restaurant sale going? Any interested parties yet?"

She wiped her fingers on a napkin and shrugged. "We had several people come around this week, but I don't think they're likely buyers. One of them wasn't even in the restaurant business. I gave the agent a telling off about that, believe me. I only plan to sell to someone who knows what they're doing."

"There's a lot of history in Valentino's. I can understand why you want to make sure the right people buy it. You know, I wondered if you might be upset that your kids won't be taking over."

She waved a hand. "Angelo and I raised them to make their own choices in life. They both have wonderful careers and were never even slightly interested in running the restaurant. Angelo was different – he loved working there with his father and, when he was younger, his grand-father. Three generations running a family business is quite something, but we realised when the kids were teenagers that it would end with us. We gave them jobs in the restaurant so they could earn a little money for themselves and see how things were run, but although they worked hard, their interest ended when their shifts did. I'm glad they've made their own lives, on their own terms."

She sipped her wine and gazed out at the river, where dusk was falling fast, before turning back to Keith and grinning. "And now it's my turn to live my life on my own terms too. I don't regret a moment I spent at Valentino's with Angelo. But now that the decision to sell is made and is in motion, I'm excited about what will come next. I want to see if there's still something new for me, out there in the world."

Keith smiled. "You have a wonderful spirit, Natalie."

"No matter how amazing the past has been, we have to believe that the future will be even better. Or else what's the point in living?"

"That's a nice way of thinking."

"It's the *only* way of thinking."

"Hey, you're speaking to a man with three failed marriages behind him and a string of broken hearts long enough to loop around the moon and back. It's hard to see how my future can be better when I keep making the same mistake over and over again."

"So stop making the same mistake. Stop giving your heart away so easily. Only give it to someone who deserves it."

"When you say things like that, it makes it very hard for me not to just give my stupid old heart to you."

She laughed. "Well, Keith—"

"Natalie, I like you. I like you a lot. It would be nice if this – me and you – turned into something, don't you think?"

"Keith, listen." She held up a hand, and when she spoke again her voice was soft. "We're having a lot of fun together. But I'm not the right woman for you, and you're not the right man for me. And I think you know that."

Keith didn't know that. In fact, the more time he spent with Natalie the more convinced he became that she was *exactly* the right woman for him. And he, with time, could learn to be the right man for her.

"I hoped we could just be friends who enjoyed one another's company," she said. "I don't want anything more than what we have already. I should never have let you kiss me after the opera. And I should never have kissed you back."

"I hope that's not true. I enjoyed that kiss."

Her lips curved, ever so slightly. "I enjoyed it too. And, if I'm being honest, I'd have to say I'd hoped we'd have the opportunity to kiss again, if it could be strictly no strings attached. Kissing you was very cathartic."

"Cathartic?"

"I haven't kissed anyone since Angelo. But I enjoyed kissing you. It's nice to know I still have it in me to kiss a man and to have a little fun. But it's not fair for me to have a little fun if it's going to end up with you nursing another broken heart."

Keith was torn. He was falling for her. He couldn't help himself. Almost forty years he'd known her, and not once had he thought of her the way he was thinking of her now.

She'd been a married woman, and then a devastated widow. But now something had changed.

Yet she was being clear about how she felt. She wasn't leading him on. He had a chance to step back, because she was giving him one.

He didn't want that chance.

There were no buyers yet for her restaurant. Wasn't it possible that she could still be here months from now, waiting to sell? And if they enjoyed each other's company in the meantime, who knew where things might lead?

"I'd just like to have some fun," Natalie said. "No strings, no relationship, no nothing. Just fun. Can you do fun and only fun, Keith?"

Keith crossed his fingers beneath the table. "I can."

"Good. In that case, you'd better get me another glass of wine."

CHAPTER 14

The menswear section in the department store was Saturday-afternoon busy, filled with confused-looking men pawing at clothes racks. Bruce was being supervised in his choices by his nieces, who, he'd discovered, were drawn to the most garish colour combinations possible.

"What about this?" Chloe held up a shirt in neon pink that almost had him shielding his eyes.

"No, sweetheart."

"How about this?" said Isla, waving a shirt covered in a bizarre design of purple whales.

"Um, no."

Jack reappeared from his own foraging and held up a shirt in steel grey. "This?"

Bruce shook his head. "Too boring."

"Or this?" In his other hand, Jack held a designer shirt in smart petrol blue.

"Yeah, maybe."

"Are you wearing a suit or blazer and smart trousers?"

"A suit." Bruce held up the suit he'd chosen while Jack had been wading through the luxury shirts.

"You don't think a suit's maybe a little overboard?"

"The last guy she was with promised her somewhere fancy and then took her to Pizza Hut. I want to wow her. I want to sweep her off her feet. I want her to take one look at me and know I made as much effort as I possibly could to impress her."

"Sounds like this last guy set the bar pretty low. The suit might scare her off."

"I'd rather risk scaring her off than disappointing her."

Jack grinned. "You really like this girl."

Bruce rummaged through a stack of shirts – and rejected them. "I really do."

"I can't tell you how much I like hearing that. But if you're trying to sweep her off her feet, this shirt won't do it." Jack set aside the blue shirt, picked up another in white and held it up against the dark suit. "Yeah, this is what you want. Great suit, white shirt open at the neck, no tie."

Bruce considered it. "I like it. It's simple."

"Just like you, buddy."

Bruce gave him a look, and Jack snorted. Chloe and Isla bounced over and frowned at the shirt in Bruce's hands.

"You're not going to wear that, are you Uncle Bruce?" Chloe said, appalled. "It's boring."

"So boring," Isla agreed.

"This is the shirt, girls."

"I suppose it's sort of okay," Isla said, running her little hand over the sleeve. "Will we choose a tie to go with it?"

"Get this tie, Uncle Bruce." Chloe grabbed a tie covered

in a vivid design of yellow and orange circles from a nearby display.

"No tie, girls."

"Do you need any of these things?" she asked, pointing to a display of cufflinks.

Bruce considered the question and inspected the range.

"You must have at least a couple of dozen sets of cufflinks," Jack said, frowning. "Come to think of it, you must own a suit and white shirt that would do the job too. Do you really need all this new stuff?"

Bruce raised an eyebrow, and a look of understanding finally crossed his brother's face.

"You don't want to wear anything that might make you think about Heather, so you're buying everything new."

"Can you blame me?"

"Not really."

Bruce chose a set of pewter cufflinks that would look good with the suit shade. "Okay, let's go and pay."

Once everything was bagged and paid for, they headed down the escalators to the ground floor and navigated the alluring displays of home accessories fanned out around the exits. The girls skipped along, inspecting items for sale and chattering.

"What's the lady's name you're going out with tonight, Uncle Bruce?" Chloe asked.

"Laura."

"You should buy Laura a present. You should buy her this!" She grabbed a little vase of artificial flowers from a display shelf.

He paused. "I should buy her flowers."

"Buy her these ones!"

"I don't think fake flowers would set the right tone, Chloe. But I should buy her actual flowers. Is there a florist nearby, Jack?"

"Sure, we can go there once —"

"No, wait, not flowers." He shook his head. "It's too predictable."

Walking beside him, Jack looked at his brother and grinned. "You've got it bad."

"Yeah, I do. And I'm terrified."

Jack frowned. "Why?"

"I just got divorced, Jack. And we hardly know each other. It shouldn't feel like this already."

"You still think there's a set length of time you have to be miserable and alone before good things are allowed to happen to you?"

"No. But I'm scared I'll push things too fast."

"Bruce, for God's sake, you haven't even been out with her yet. How can you possibly be worried about things going too fast?"

But when Bruce thought of the kiss they'd had in Valentino's, he knew only too well that things could definitely move too fast between them. All he'd wanted to do was kiss her to see what it would be like. But something had happened in that moment that had been beyond anything he could've imagined.

"I think there might be more between us than I expected."

Jack laughed and checked his girls were out of earshot. "Look, it's been a while Bruce. You've got an itch, that's all."

"I'm not just looking to hop into bed with some random woman, Jack. I'm *nuts* about this girl."

"Okay, cool your jets. Being nuts about her, that's good."

"But I'm terrified too."

Jack spread his hands. "You're nuts about her, but you're terrified?"

Bruce shook his head, exasperated. "Jack, what if I'm turning into Uncle Keith, barely out of one disastrous relationship before getting embroiled in another? I love Keith, but I'd hate to make the same mistakes he's made."

Jack blinked at him. "That's what's worrying you? Look, you need to switch your brain off, Bruce. One minute you want to wow this girl, the next you're worried it's going too fast. One minute you're nuts about her, the next you're imagining it ending in disaster. Want some advice? Stop thinking, and ..." Jack glanced up and saw the girls over by a display of delicate ornaments. "Hey girls, don't touch those. You break them, you buy them."

But Bruce's attention had been caught by the display his little nieces had crowded around. It was animal-themed and comprised animal-print cushions, gilded bird cages, animal-themed stationary, and a collection of pretty animal ornaments. Chloe was examining a painted glass elephant, while Isla studied a brightly coloured parrot.

Walking over, he honed in on the item that had caught his eye – a lovely, long-necked porcelain giraffe, around six inches in height. Picking it up, he thought of those amusing pyjamas Laura had asked him to find when she'd been sick.

"I'll get her this."

While Chloe and Isla clapped their hands, delighted at his choice, Jack only gaped at him. "Why on earth would you give her that?"

Bruce smiled, mostly to himself. "Because her favourite pyjamas have giraffes on them."

Jack stared at his brother. "What happened to worrying it was all moving too fast? What happened to being terrified?"

Bruce looked up from the giraffe and frowned. "You're the one who told me to get on with my life."

"Are you sure you don't just want to give her a bunch of flowers?"

He shook his head. "I want to give her this."

Jack considered the little ornament. "You're sending a message if you give her that on your first date."

"I know."

Jack laughed and shook his head. "I hoped you'd start seeing some women now and again and get back into the swing of things. But maybe you've fallen head over heels straight out the gate."

"I think I might have, yeah."

Jack met his brother's goofy grin with one of his own. "You really want to sweep this girl off her feet?"

"More than you could believe."

"In that case, I've got an idea."

LAURA ANGLED herself in front of the mirror in the hallway. "You don't think this dress is too much?"

Yvonne, perched on the edge of the living room sofa, shook her head. "It's perfect."

Deciding the dress she'd worn on her final doomed date with John was now tainted by bad luck (not to mention the downpour of rain), Laura had forced herself to go shopping to buy something new. When she'd spied the pale blue dress with gauzy sleeves and embellished cuffs, she'd instantly raided her savings to buy it. Now, though, she was having second thoughts.

"After the last time I got dressed up for a night out with a guy, I'm anxious."

But Yvonne waved that off. "The dress is perfect, stop agonising over it. Any idea where Bruce is taking you?"

"None, which doesn't exactly help." She sighed at her reflection again and poked at the silver circles cascading at her ears. "These earrings are too big. I need something simpler."

Heading into her room and rummaging through her little jewellery box, she switched the dangly circles for studs. Not diamond – she owned nothing like that – but they were still sparkly enough to catch the light the same way as the embellishment on the cuff of the dress.

She slipped into the heeled sandals she'd chosen and returned once more to the mirror. She didn't often dress up – she didn't often have a reason to – and it felt strange being head-to-toe in a whole new outfit. She'd never gone to so much trouble before for a night out with a guy.

Although it didn't really feel like trouble, not when she thought of the guy the night out would be with.

"Those shoes make your legs look amazing," Yvonne said. "If I didn't love you, I'd hate you right now. All that running has given you calves to die for."

"God, don't talk to me about running. The race is in two weeks, and it's the last thing I want to think about. I'm nervous enough about tonight."

"It's good that you're nervous."

Laura narrowed her eyes. "It's good that I feel like I might faint?"

Yvonne's eyes only grew wider. "Yes! It means you really like this guy. God, please tell me you've had tummy flutters over guys in the past."

"Well, maybe a little, but nothing like this."

Yvonne clapped her hands together. "This just gets better and better! He's the one, Laura, he's the one."

"Oh for God's sake, we haven't even gone out together yet."

"And I'll be staying at Olly's tonight, so you've got the place to yourself if you decide to bring Mr Hottie back to see him naked."

Laura blushed and shook her head. "That won't happen."

"Never say never." Yvonne gave her a side-long glance. "Listen, there's something I want to tell you. I've been spending a lot of time with Olly, and we've been talking about things, and ... and I've decided to move in with him."

Laura glanced up from the clutch bag she'd been organising. "Really? I mean, that's amazing, but don't you think it's a little fast?"

"I really like him. And I really like being with him. I think he feels the same way about me. Why wait?"

Laura smiled. "I wish I had your courage, Yvonne."

"You have your own courage, which is exactly the right sort of courage for you." Yvonne walked over and laid a hand on her arm. "I'll miss you when I leave."

"I'll miss you too."

They hugged, and Laura felt a lump come to her throat.

When she leaned back and looked in Yvonne's eyes, she saw tears there.

"Okay, that's enough, or I'll start crying and have to redo my make-up, and there's no time for that. He'll be here any minute."

"I'll watch at the window." Yvonne darted to the other side of the room to peer outside. "Okay, I see a taxi turning on to our street ... no, it's driving past ... Oh, here's a car stopping outside our door, but that can't be it ... wait a minute ... Oh my God! Laura, you have to come and see this, quick!"

"If it's the neighbour across the street parading around naked again, I'm not interested, and—"

"It's not the naked neighbour! Just get over here, hurry!"

Laura rushed to the window. "Oh my God."

A Jaguar luxury saloon car sat outside, its sleek curves waxed to perfection, its signature front grill gleaming. A uniformed chauffeur was opening the rear passenger door. She watched in disbelief as Bruce got out, looked up, and smiled when he saw her at the window.

"Holy crap!" Yvonne said. "He looks good enough to eat! I'm actually salivating! And he came to pick you up in a chauffeur-driven Jag! This is absolutely amazing!"

Laura stepped back, stepped forward again, and checked she was seeing what she thought she was seeing. As the chauffeur closed the door, Bruce waved up.

"I can't believe this," Laura said.

"Believe it."

"I better go down."

"What? Are you crazy? He's come for you in a *chauffeur-driven Jag*, Laura. You wait until he rings the doorbell."

"I'm not making him wait when I can see perfectly well he's already here."

"Too late." Yvonne glanced down. "He's on his way up the front path."

When the flat doorbell rang, Yvonne raced to answer it. Laura remained rooted to the spot, and Yvonne turned back and led her by the arm to the hallway.

"You are going to have such a wonderful night," Yvonne said. "Just take deep breaths."

"He looks pretty good, doesn't he?"

"He looks fantastic. Okay, go on, open the door."

Laura took a breath. Her head was spinning. He'd come for her in a chauffeur-driven car. Nothing like that had ever happened to her before.

And he looked good. So good, in fact, it made her knees almost knock together.

When she opened the door, she discovered Bruce looked even better close up. If he'd told her he'd just flown in from a red-carpet premiere at Cannes, she wouldn't have been even the least surprised. She caught the drift of his aftershave, and it actually made her mind go fuzzy.

"Wow," Bruce said. "You look gorgeous."

"You look pretty good yourself."

He stepped forward and kissed her cheek, reminding her of that first kiss they'd shared in Valentino's. She pushed the memory from her head, knowing that if she didn't, they wouldn't make it out of the flat at all.

"Oh, hi, Yvonne," Bruce said, when he finally noticed her hovering by the living room door.

"Hi, Bruce."

But he'd already turned back to Laura. "Shall we?" he said, and offered his arm.

Smiling, she slipped her hand into his elbow, gave Yvonne a wave goodbye, and let Bruce lead her down the hallway stairs and out to the waiting car.

"I can't believe you hired a chauffeur and a car," she said when they got outside.

"Actually, I have a little confession to make. That's my brother, Jack. He has his own limousine company, so he came in pretty handy tonight. Jack, this is Laura."

Jack held out a hand. "Pleasure to meet you."

"And he also likes to dress up like this," Bruce said, as she shook Jack's hand. "Any excuse, really, to wear that cap. And, of course, drive around in his new toy."

"My pride and joy awaits you," Jack said, opening the door, "Ma'am, sir."

"He just calls me that so I'll have to tip him," Bruce whispered as they got into the car.

She laughed and looked around the beautiful interior. "This is a really amazing surprise, Bruce."

"There's more to come."

"You didn't say where we're going."

"You'll find out when we get there."

Jack got in behind the wheel, and soon they were moving. She looked out the window as they turned on to Shaw Street and saw Valentino's rush past, the tables filled with Saturday night diners, the place buzzing, and she saw Natalie, too, framed in the windows and waving at the passing car. Delighted, and realising that Natalie must have known the details of this part of the evening, she waved back.

She decided the start of her first date with Bruce couldn't have gone any better.

She was wrong.

"I thought of bringing you flowers," he said as they sped along Shaw Street. "But I brought you this instead."

He handed her a gift box, pale pink wrapped in a lavender ribbon.

"You didn't have to do that."

"Open it."

She untied the ribbon, and let out a cry at the sweet little porcelain giraffe inside. "This is so lovely," she said, admiring its impossibly slim legs and long, elegant neck.

"When I saw it, it made me think of your—"

"Pyjamas!" they both said at the same time, and laughed.

"I don't know whether to be embarrassed about the pyjamas or pleased about the gift."

"You like it?"

"I do."

"Then that's all that matters." He reached over and laid a hand on hers. "I hope you have a wonderful time tonight, Laura."

As the car glided along the road, the summer's evening stretching before them like a promise, she glanced at Bruce as he looked out the window. She'd felt something shift inside her heart when he'd stepped out of the car and looked up and smiled.

Now, as she ran her fingers over the silly, sweet little giraffe gift he'd bought her, and marvelled at the man he must be to know how much she'd like it, she thought she could feel herself beginning to slip, beginning to slide.

Beginning to fall.

CHAPTER 15

They drove west out of the city, headed south towards the Ayrshire coast, and when the Jaguar finally pulled up at the luxury beachfront hotel, Laura could only stare.

The grand building stood elegantly elevated above the stretch of sand dunes that swept down to the shoreline, set in grounds that had been landscaped to perfection. Jack rolled the Jaguar to the entrance, lit along its length by concealed illuminations that glowed softly in the deepening summer evening.

A doorman opened the car door on Laura's side, while Jack exited the driver's seat and opened the door for Bruce. Taking it all in as she stood beneath the entrance canopy, she felt light-headed. It was like something out of a fairy tale.

"Have a good evening, sir, ma'am," Jack said with a wide grin, before tipping his cap and getting back into the car.

Bruce took her hand, and they walked through the brass-trimmed door held open by the doorman and into a marble floored reception space, and on again until they reached the restaurant in the south wing. As they were greeted by the maître d', Laura gazed around the beautiful room. Banks of windows looked out towards the sea, tables draped in pristine white table covers were spread across the room, and glittering crystal chandeliers hung from one end of the ceiling to the other.

She was happy she'd splurged for the new dress. Nothing else in her wardrobe would have looked even remotely appropriate.

A waiter led them to their table by the windows – and the stunning sea views beyond. Her breath caught when Bruce rested his hand on the small of her back as he stepped around to pull out her chair.

"You really know how to treat a woman. I'm officially seduced."

"Terrific. In that case, we can leave."

She laughed and tried to focus on the menu, but found her attention being drawn to those beautiful sunset views across the sea.

And to Bruce. It was almost indecent how good he looked in that suit.

What on earth had his wife – ex-wife, she once more reminded herself – been thinking when she'd left him for another man?

Laura found the seduction continued when he ordered champagne, but she began fidgeting when he suggested oysters to start.

"You don't like them?" he asked.

"Actually ... well, the truth is, I've never had one. But I can't imagine eating anything more disgusting."

"Thank God. I can't stand them either. The one time I ate them, I had to make my excuses and sprint for the bathroom. That's a true story."

She laughed, enjoying the way his eyes danced. "So why'd you suggest we order them?"

"I want this to be a romantic evening. People say oysters are romantic." He paused and grinned. "I don't know who these people are, exactly, but it's what they say. Anyway, I just want tonight to be perfect."

"It already is."

The waiter arrived with their champagne, filled their glasses, and Bruce touched his against hers.

"Thanks for letting me take you out to dinner."

"After you kissed me the other night, I would've agreed to anything."

"Damn, I wish I'd known."

She laughed again – already, she'd probably laughed more in the time she'd spent with Bruce than during the entirety of any previous relationship she'd had – and sipped the champagne, enjoying its sparkling fun.

"I like you, Bruce."

Gazing over his glass, he smiled. "I like you too. More than like you, actually. The way you look in that dress is ... well, you look beautiful."

"Thank you."

"And I like what you've done to your hair."

She raised a hand and patted the soft curls she'd spent almost forty-five minutes working into the style – and cursing every time she burned herself with the edge of the curling tongs.

"If we're trading compliments, you should know I think

you look amazing in that suit. And the chauffeur-driven Jag was really something special."

"The Jag was Jack's idea, although I should've thought of it myself. If I'd driven, I couldn't have enjoyed this champagne with you."

"I'm glad you *are* enjoying it with me. It wouldn't have been as much fun otherwise. And this place is wonderful. I've never been anywhere like it."

He frowned. "I find that hard to believe."

She shrugged and looked out of the window to where the sea sparkled golden beneath the setting sun.

"What kind of men have you been going out with that they didn't see sense and take you to the places you deserved to go?"

She shifted in her seat. "Not everyone has money to afford chauffeur-driven cars and luxury restaurants. That doesn't make them bad people."

"No, it doesn't. And the truth is that it's got nothing to do with money or how much is spent. But first dates are important, and they ought to be special. Especially when the woman is as wonderful as you are."

The compliment tripped her up. "My first dates haven't been much to write home about."

"Tell me."

"It's too embarrassing, especially as you seem to know so much about these things."

He set down his champagne glass and laid his hand on hers. "I'm sorry. I sounded like an arrogant twat just then, and I didn't mean to. My plan tonight was to sweep you off your feet, but I'm not flash, that's not me."

She met his gaze and thought she saw agitation in his

eyes. Maybe he was just as nervous about this date as she was.

"I don't think you're flash," she said. "And I don't think tonight is flash, either. It's beautiful and romantic. I'm not used to that. The guy I was seeing, John? He was a big movie fan, and we went to the cinema on our first date, which was fine. That's a nice first date. Or it would have been, if he hadn't tripped getting into his seat and spilled his bucket of popcorn all over me."

Bruce attempted, and failed, to hide his grin. "Sorry."

She felt her own smile widen. "It's funny now, looking back. It wasn't at the time, which is a shame. It could've been funny, you know? One of those cute stories you look back at and laugh about. But John was just upset he wouldn't have a full metric tonne of popcorn to chew during the movie. Maybe I should've recognised that for the sign it was. Although John was an improvement on the last guy I'd gone out with, Lee. For our first date, he took me for a Sunday afternoon walk in the park, which sounds lovely, until the part where he asked to borrow money so he could buy us both an ice cream cone."

More suppressed laughter from Bruce. Laura shook her head, finding herself amused to recall these hideous incidents from her extremely limited and vanilla love life. "And before Lee, there was Steve, who arranged for us to have our first date at this late-night jazz club. Again, it sounded promising, and the perfect opportunity for budding romance. Except he spent the entire night doing this jazz rhythm thing with his hand on his thigh and shushing me any time I tried to start up a conversation."

Now Bruce was shaking with laughter. "Laura, where did you find these guys?"

"I don't know. It's like I have some kind of moron magnet. Although, that's not really fair, at least not on John. Movie Boy," she added when Bruce looked confused. "He wasn't a moron. He just liked spending his time at the movies, and I didn't. I'm glad we're not together any more, but I really only wish him well. I hope he finds someone he can be happy with."

"You're incredibly sweet."

"Gullible, you mean."

"No, I mean sweet."

"Anyway, enough about me." She gestured to the restaurant and the sea views. "Is this your routine for first dates? Full shock and awe?"

Bruce sat back in his chair and blew out a breath. "Actually, I don't have a routine. The last woman I took on a first date was my wife. My ex-wife. I don't know why it still feels strange to call her that."

"How long were you married?"

"Two years, but we were together a while before that."

Seeing the sadness creeping into his expression, Laura regretted the turn the conversation had taken. "We don't have to talk about it."

"Good. In that case, we won't."

The waiter arrived to take their orders, and by the time the starters arrived the conversation had shifted.

"How's your pub search going?" she asked.

"It's not. I haven't seen anywhere that comes even close to what I want. My Uncle Keith and Jack both think I'm looking for somewhere that doesn't exist. They may be right."

"Don't give up, and don't compromise."

"To be honest, compromise is inevitable, I know that. We can't have everything just the way we imagine it. But …"

"But what?"

He waved a hand and glanced towards the sea. "This will sound insane. But I had this dream. Actually, I've had it a few times. And in it, there's a tumbledown old building and a beautiful tree next to a stream. And I feel like I know the place, except when I wake up I don't recognise it. I can't get it out of my head, and now whenever I view a commercial property for sale, I measure it against this place I've dreamt about. That's madness from a business perspective. But somehow I can't help myself."

She watched him and thought about what he'd said. "You want the perfect place. There's nothing wrong with that. And maybe your perfect place is out there waiting for you to come along and find it."

"That's a nice thought. I hope it's true."

"It is. You just have to believe."

Bruce looked at her, a smile at the edge of his lips. He laid down his fork. "What perfect place is waiting out there for you, Laura?"

Glancing up, she thought about it. "For a long time, I thought I'd found it in Valentino's. I love it there. I know that will change when Natalie moves on. *If* she moves on. She's had a lot of potential buyers visit, but nothing has come of it yet. And I can't help but hope that maybe, just maybe, something will happen with your uncle, and

Natalie will fall in love with him and change her mind about selling. That would be my perfect happily ever after."

Bruce sipped some wine. "Once upon a time, though, you had a different happily ever after in mind."

She picked up her napkin and fussed with it. "Yeah, that's true. Listen, Bruce, there's something I wanted to say. When you came to my flat and looked after me while I was ill, and I got all weepy when those university forms fell on the floor, and I made a fool of myself—"

"You didn't make a fool of yourself, Laura."

"Well, anyway, I'm sorry."

"I don't know why you think you have to keep saying sorry to me, because you don't."

She shrugged. "That night, I garbled something about once having a dream for my life, and how it disappeared after my parents died."

He nodded, and when she looked up and into his eyes, she wondered at how it could be so easy to talk to him about these things when she'd never been able to talk to anyone about them before.

"My plan had been to go to university and study history," she continued. "I loved history and wanted to become a teacher. Just like my parents. They were both teachers. My mum taught high school chemistry, and my dad was a primary school teacher. They were always around during the school holidays, and I didn't realise how unusual that was until I was older. We had amazing summers, the three of us, with day trips and picnics and silly little adventures. And when I decided to go to university, that's what I wanted. To have the same life they'd had. A job I loved, teaching something I loved, and being able to spend all those long school breaks off with my kids, whenever I got around to having them."

She glanced towards the sea. "That was the perfect life I'd been working for. I think it would've been nice."

"It still could be. You could still finish your degree."

But she shook her head. "I'm twenty-nine years old. I can't imagine going back to university now, alongside all those kids in their teens. I'd be in my mid-thirties before I was even qualified to teach."

"So?"

"Don't you think it'd be a bit sad?"

"Not sad. Brave. Starting again and taking a chance on a dream you thought you'd lost? That's brave. That takes courage."

"More courage than I've got."

"You doubt yourself too much. Look at all the amazing things you do, Laura. You're running a ten-kilometre race, for God's sake. That takes guts."

"Yeah, it'll take guts and also a team of paramedics to resuscitate me. I haven't gone for a training run since I got sick."

"You've been recovering. You'll get back to it soon."

"I think I might just cut my losses and forget about the race."

"That's a shame. I was planning to come along and cheer you on."

"You were?"

"I'm kind of interested to see how you look in tight running shorts and a skimpy T-shirt."

She laughed, but stopped when she saw his serious expression return.

"Seriously, Laura. Believe in yourself. And don't think the future you hoped for is lost. You just told me a minute ago that I had to believe my perfect place was out there, waiting for me. You should believe the same thing."

Smiling, she picked up her fork and began eating again. "I don't know how you do it, but you make me feel better about myself, Bruce."

"I could say the same thing about you. Maybe that makes us a perfect fit."

Before she knew it, they'd finished their main courses and the champagne and the waiter was delivering dessert menus.

"I can't believe how fast tonight has gone," Laura said, looking out to where night had fallen across the sea, leaving raspberry twists of summer sunset along the horizon.

"Shall we order dessert?"

"I couldn't eat another thing."

"How about we split something and have brandy?"

"After the champagne, I'm already tipsy."

"I like you tipsy. And I think I'd like you even tipsier."

"Believe me, Bruce, if you want to take me to bed, you don't have to get me drunk."

Her eyes popped wide, and she clapped her hands to her mouth and stared in shock across the table to where Bruce sat grinning.

"Oh my God, I can't believe I just said that." She lowered her head to her hands. "I *never* say things like that. See, this is what happens when I'm tipsy."

"Good to know. Okay, no brandy, we'll order coffee

instead. If we're going to bed together in a while, I want to be at my best, too."

"Oh God, I'm mortified."

But he just laughed. By the time the chocolate torte arrived, with two spoons, she thought her cheeks might no longer be burning hot enough to risk setting the table cloth on fire.

"Laura, I've had a wonderful time," Bruce said a little while later as he paid the bill and dealt with the tip.

"Me too."

"You should know I'm planning on kissing you very soon."

"Thank God."

Laughing, he pulled out his phone when it pinged and checked the screen. "Jack's nearly here. How about we go outside and get some fresh sea air?"

After the candlelight and wine, the night air was refreshing and cooling. Bruce took her hand, and they walked along the front of the hotel, admiring the lights of the building against the dark sky, and found a little illuminated waterfall set in the middle of a pretty garden terrace.

Bruce turned towards her, and her skin tingled as he moved his hands around her waist and pulled her close. When he kissed her, her head spun deliciously.

The moment was interrupted when Bruce's phone began ringing. Giving her a wry smile, he pulled out the phone and answered.

"Jack's here, we better get back," he said when he hung up.

When they returned to the entrance, there was no sign of the Jaguar in which they'd arrived. Instead, Laura saw

Jack stepping from an SUV, and his earlier chauffeur uniform had been replaced by jeans and a sweater.

Jack spread his hands as he came around to meet them, an anxious look on his face. "Bruce, I'm sorry! Claire got called into the hospital on an emergency, and there was no one who could watch the girls this late at night, so I had to bring them and come in our own car. All my drivers are booked tonight or I would've sent someone else."

"We could've got a taxi back, Jack," Bruce said. "It's too late for the girls to be up."

"Are you kidding? A night-time adventure in their pyjamas? They're loving every minute of this. But look, I'm sorry. I know this ruins the end of your evening."

"Don't be silly." Laura stepped forward and waved into the car, where she saw a little girl in a booster seat up front and a smaller girl strapped into a child seat in the back. "I'd love to meet Bruce's nieces."

"Jack," Bruce said, taking his brother by the shoulders. "It's fine. You haven't ruined the evening, that's just stupid talk. Now, let's get home so you can get those girls to bed."

Laura climbed into the back of the car, while Bruce got in the other side, with the child seat between them.

"Hi, Uncle Bruce," the two girls said in unison.

"Hi, girls. Chloe and Isla, this is my friend, Laura."

Two little heads swung in her direction. "Are you Uncle Bruce's girlfriend?" Chloe asked.

"Well …"

"Yes, she is," Bruce said, as Jack, laughing behind the wheel, got the car moving.

"Did you kiss her?" Chloe wanted to know.

"Chloe, I did kiss her, as it happens."

Both girls, finding this hilarious, giggled and gawped at one another.

"We're in our pyjamas," Isla said. "Mine have My Little Pony on them."

"I see that," Laura said. "They look nice and cosy."

"My pyjamas have got Wonder Woman, Laura, see?"

"I do see. Wonder Woman rocks."

"Do you have Wonder Woman pyjamas, Laura?"

"Actually, I don't."

"She does have giraffe pyjamas, though," Bruce said, grinning. "They're kind of cool."

"Giraffes are nice, I like giraffes," Isla said, before turning once more to Laura and laying a pudgy little finger on the embellishments on the cuff of her sleeve. "I like your pretty dress."

"Thank you."

"Are these real diamonds on the dress?"

"No, sweetheart. These are just pretend."

"Why aren't they real diamonds?"

"Because I think it would cost too much to put this many diamonds on it."

"How much would it cost?"

"Probably a gazillion pounds."

Chloe and Isla looked at one another and giggled.

"Dad says you and Uncle Bruce were having a fancy dinner," Chloe said.

"That's right."

"What did you have for dessert? Ice cream?"

"Chocolate cake."

"We love chocolate cake. Dad, can we have chocolate cake when we get home?"

"No."

"Why not?"

"Because I fear your mother too much to be foolish enough to feed you chocolate cake at this hour."

"But Dad—"

"Hey, girls," Bruce said, reaching into his pocket. "Would you like the little chocolates that came with our coffee? We were too full to eat them."

"Yes!" the girls shouted, as their father shook his head at Bruce in the rear-view mirror and made time-out gestures with his free hand.

"They're tiny chocolates, Jack, don't worry," he said, unwrapping them and handing one each to the girls.

Silence descended as the chocolate was consumed.

"Well, what did you think?" he asked his nieces.

"Yummy."

"Are there any more?"

"That's all I've got."

Spying Isla's sticky fingers, Bruce grabbed a packet of tissues from the door bucket and began wiping them. Watching, Laura found herself charmed to see Isla keep hold of Bruce's hand after he'd finished wiping her fingers and fall asleep with her hand still tucked inside his palm.

And when Bruce leaned over and kissed Isla's sweet little head as she dropped into dreams, Laura knew she was falling in love.

BOTH LITTLE GIRLS were fast asleep by the time Jack stopped the car outside Laura's flat. With whispered thanks, they got out and Jack drove off to take his daughters home.

Laura pulled her keys from her bag and walked up the path to the door. When Bruce remained on the pavement, she looked back over her shoulder.

"Are you coming up?"

"Am I invited?"

"What do you think?"

She smiled when he followed her into the tenement, catching the scent of his aftershave as he walked close behind her. As she slid her key into the lock, he laid a hand on her arm.

"Wait Laura, um, your flatmate, is she at home, because …"

"She's at Olly's."

Smiling, he moved his hand down the curve of her back and let it rest at her waist. "Good."

Inside the hallway, a lamp burned softly. The rest of the flat stood in darkness and silence. Her pulse raced at his closeness and the expectation of what would come next.

"Do you want coffee, maybe more wine, or—"

He caught her hand, pulled her close, and kissed her. Her breath hitched as he moved his lips from her mouth and down her neck.

"All I want is you," he said.

The joy of his kiss and those whispered words made her heart soar. "You make me nervous, in a good way," she said.

He gazed at her and once more took her hand in his. "And you terrify me."

"I …"

But he put a finger gently to her lips. “Maybe we don’t talk any more. Maybe we just see what happens.”

It was so simple and so obvious. In his eyes, she saw only the promise of something wonderful, right now, if she would open herself to it.

She led him to her bedroom, her heart thundering, and there, with moonlight slanting through the window, there was no more talk, no more thought.

There was only the heat and the dark and the moment they made together.

Laura’s head lay on his chest as his fingers moved slowly through her hair. She was shimmering, floating. The warm smell of his skin felt like home.

“Can I stay tonight?” he asked.

“If you try to leave, I’ll tie you to the bed.”

“On second thoughts, maybe I really ought to go.”

Laughing, she grazed her teeth against his neck and smiled when a soft sigh escaped him.

“I liked taking you out tonight, Laura. And this – us together – it means something.”

“It ought to.”

“No, what I mean is ... since my marriage ended, I couldn’t imagine taking this step. But since we’ve got to know each other, I’ve been able to imagine it. In fact, it’s all I could think about. You’ve possessed me, Laura. I’m bewitched.”

Rising on her elbow, she studied him. She knew she was falling and falling fast, and the urge to tell him so, as those silvery grey eyes held her, was almost irresistible.

Almost.

But it would be too much. The man was only just coming out of the darkness of divorce. If she was the first woman he'd taken to bed, the last thing he'd want to hear were teary declarations of love.

He said he was bewitched. Bewitched was something, wasn't it? She'd take it, and be satisfied with it. There would be time enough for whatever else might come, if anything else ever did.

"I had fun tonight, Bruce."

His gaze pinned her, and she thought he was about to say something. But he only smiled, laid his head back against the pillow, and began stroking her head. A flicker in his expression – doubt? disappointment? – made her regret her too-casual tone.

"The sunset over the sea tonight was beautiful," she said.

"It was."

"And so is this."

She kissed his neck, slowly, softly. Being with him was like being wrapped up inside a dream she hoped would never end.

As he caressed her and kissed her, she felt sure she heard him murmur something against her heart where his lips touched her skin.

I love you.

She stared in amazement, caught in shock and wonder. But his head remained buried against her, his face hidden, and as his kisses continued she wondered if she'd only imagined it.

Later, as she drifted off with his arms around her, she decided it had only been wishing thinking after all.

BRUCE WOKE to sunbeams floating through the bedroom window and the distant murmur of the radio in the kitchen. Turning, he saw Laura already gone from the bed. He could still smell the perfume she'd worn, caught on the pillow.

He'd been in love only once before. He'd loved his wife, of course he had, and he'd never imagined loving anyone else, at least not until the catastrophic end of the life that he and Heather had built. Since the divorce, he'd tried to think about what love might feel like in the future, although mostly it had been a purely theoretical exercise. Love had seemed like an impossible dream.

Until Laura.

He didn't understand how it had happened, or how it could have happened so quickly. But it had. He'd fallen in love with her, unexpectedly and completely.

And he'd gone and blurted it out last night, in that blinding moment when she'd been wrapped around him. He hadn't even known the words were coming until they'd been said. Lucky for him, she hadn't appeared to hear his cack-handed declaration.

He pulled on his clothes and wandered through to the kitchen where he found Laura at the counter in her bathrobe, making toast and scrambling eggs.

"I was going to surprise you with breakfast in bed," she said.

Wrapping his arms around her from behind, he kissed her neck. "I can hop back in there."

She laughed and turned off the heat beneath the pan of eggs. "My shift starts at ten. If I go back to bed with you, I won't make it in."

"I *am* irresistible."

Another laugh as she plated their breakfast, before she turned and slipped her arms around him. "I had an amazing time last night."

"I can't tell you how happy I am to hear that." He kissed her and had to resist the urge to keep kissing her. "When do you finish work?"

"Four." She stepped out of his arms and set a teapot on the table next to the mugs.

"Can we get together after? Maybe I could take you a drive somewhere."

"Actually, after your little pep talk last night, I was thinking I ought to do a training run, get back into it while I still have a chance to get ready for this race."

"Want me to come and carry your water bottle?"

She laughed as she sat down and forked up some eggs. "My own personal water carrier. That's tempting. But I like to run on my own."

"Let's get together after."

She studied him over the rim of her tea mug. "You haven't seen enough of me after last night?"

"Not nearly enough."

Smiling, she nodded. "Okay, I'd like that. So, what have you got on today?"

He poured their tea and told her about his plans for the

day. Sitting across the table from her in her pretty little kitchen, eating breakfast, talking – it felt good.

Like how it always ought to be.

When they'd finished breakfast and he was kissing her goodbye, he found himself marvelling at how quickly things could change in life.

And about how love could come when you least expected it.

He thought about this as he walked towards Shaw Street and the pub. And, because he couldn't help it, he thought about Laura. Just yesterday, he'd told Jack about what he felt for her and how it terrified him. Now, there was no terror, no fear. There was only the certainty that something wonderful was happening in his life, and it was all because of her.

As he crossed Shaw Street, his phone pinged. Grinning, he pulled it from his pocket, hoping it was a message from Laura.

It wasn't.

It was a message from Heather.

The shock of seeing his ex-wife's name on the screen caused him to come to a dead halt in the middle of the road. A van driver honked his horn. Bruce glanced up from the phone, saw the traffic coming at him, and quickly jogged to the safety of the pavement, raising a hand in apology to the drivers who'd had to slow to avoid him.

He looked in stunned disbelief at his phone. He'd deleted Heather's details from his contacts long ago. But she must have anticipated this, because she'd begun the message by identifying herself.

Bruce, this is Heather. I need to talk to you. Could you call me?

The last time he'd spoken to her, he'd been hauling the last of his things from their home. And it hadn't been speaking so much as a sort of seething grunting. He hadn't even been able to bring himself to look at her. Ever since, they'd communicated through solicitors. Once the divorce was finalised he'd never expected, or wanted, to hear from her again.

But still he stared at the message. Why did she need to talk to him? And why now, when he was finally getting his life back together?

He had a choice. He could reply to her message. Or he could ignore it.

The months of hurt and anger he'd endured because of what Heather had done crowded his mind. Behind him lay darkness and a pain so deep he'd thought he'd never recover.

But he had recovered. And he'd found Laura. Thinking of her now, those months of heartbreak blew away like dust.

Bruce tapped the phone and his finger lingered only for a second before he deleted the message Heather had sent. What he wanted was the hope that lay in the future, not the torment that skulked in the past.

But still he found himself unable to stop wondering why Heather had sent that message and what possible reason she could have for wanting to talk to him. It was just basic human curiosity.

And for the rest of the day, those questions gnawed at his mind and wouldn't let go.

CHAPTER 16

Not even old Mr Davidson, complaining furiously that his omelette was tasteless, could spoil Laura's mood during her shift that morning at Valentino's.

"It's disgusting!" Mr Davidson wailed. "What kind of chefs do you have here?"

"We'll make you another omelette."

"Another? Don't torture me by making me eat another. Just bring me a bacon roll. Surely the chef can manage that."

"Okay, Mr Davidson."

"And why are you smiling like that, young lady?"

"I suppose I'm just happy today."

"Happy? What's there to be happy about?"

Natalie appeared at the table. "If she told you, she'd only blush, and you wouldn't like the answer anyway."

Steering Laura away, Natalie drew her to the counter and pushed forward a tray of coffees that were ready to be served. "Don't let that grumpy old fool spoil your mood."

"Nothing could spoil my mood."

A sly smile crept across Natalie's face. "I take it you and Bruce had rather a lot of fun last night?"

Laura blushed and Natalie laughed. "Good for you. You have every right to look smug this morning."

"I look smug?"

"It's not a criticism, Laura. Enjoy it."

Still blushing, Laura delivered the coffees, returned to the counter, and checked the order slip on the next tray waiting to be prepared.

"You two looked good together last night when I saw you drive past," Natalie said, working the milk frother on the coffee machine. "I looked out the window, saw you both in the back of that car, and thought – now, there goes a fine-looking couple. I'm assuming you two will go out together again."

"We're seeing each other tonight."

Natalie grinned over the fresh tray of drinks she was preparing. "That's wonderful. You think there might be something serious between you?"

"Maybe, but …"

"But?"

Laura twisted her apron tie between her fingers and shrugged. "His ex-wife messed him up really badly. Sometimes I get the impression he might not be over that."

"I imagine it will take him some time yet to recover. I know from Keith that Bruce's wife had an affair and that it completely floored him."

Laura ducked behind the counter and helped Natalie finish an order by adding some glasses of orange juice to the tray. "I'd hate to find out I was just his rebound fling."

Natalie dusted chocolate over a cappuccino. "I doubt I'm speaking out of turn here, but Keith says Bruce has had a serious soft spot for you ever since he got here."

"He has?"

"Apparently. And I happened to see how Bruce was looking at you last night as you drove past. That was not the look a man gives a woman when he's interested only in a rebound fling. At any rate, don't over think it. Things will be as they will be."

"You're right, I shouldn't over think it. I should just enjoy it."

"A good strategy."

And Laura discovered that it was simply too easy to enjoy how she felt. Her lingering concerns about Bruce's feelings following his divorce couldn't puncture the glorious bliss bubble she bounced along inside all day.

Even during her after-work training run, she felt as if she was cocooned inside something wonderful.

She'd been dreading the run. It'd been more than a week since she'd last pulled on her trainers and hit the pavement. And while there was no ignoring the stiffness she felt to begin with, the muscle memory soon kicked in, and by the time she reached the gates at Mungo Park, she was in full flow.

There was work to be done to get back to where she'd been in terms of speed and stamina before the virus had struck. But, as she stood at her usual spot at the top of the hill, catching her breath and looking out over the city, she decided the run was going far better than she could have expected.

She felt strong and ready for anything. The ten-kilometre race was less than two weeks away, and as she jogged back to her flat, she knew she would be there to compete. And not just because she wanted that participant's certificate on her wall, but because she owed it to herself to see what she was made of. She'd cross that finish line, no matter how much it hurt.

This race would be one of the biggest challenges she'd faced in a long time. Training for it had cost her. It had forced her to work hard, forced her to question what she was capable of, and forced her to silence the voice inside her head that told her she just wasn't good enough.

She'd be at the start line for that race. And she'd be at the finish line too, one way or another.

Maybe she'd ask Bruce if he was serious about coming along to cheer her on. If he didn't run a mile in the opposite direction when he saw her sweating and puffing her way around the course, then it might just say something about him.

Later that evening, she was still imagining him at the finish line of the race, encouraging her as she pounded out those final steps, when he rang her doorbell to pick her up. When she opened the door and saw his smile, the feelings that had swept through her as she'd watched him so tenderly kissing his little niece in the back of his brother's car swept through her once again.

"Ready?" he asked.

She was ready, she realised. Ready for whatever was about to begin.

BRUCE DROVE them north out of Glasgow and into the

Campsie Hills, along twisting roads that rose high above the city. He pulled into a parking area and turned the car around towards the view of the town spread out below. The summer evening was glorious, the blue sky softening into dusk, and Laura settled back in the seat to enjoy it.

"Have you ever been up here before?" he asked.

She shook her head. "Never. It's really a beautiful view."

"Once I'd learned to drive, this was the first place I came by myself. It was a taste of freedom. I could go anywhere I wanted. Well, so long as my dad let me borrow his car."

He laughed and then turned serious as he looked out at the view. "And, in case you're wondering, I never brought Heather up here."

Laura turned, surprised. "I wasn't wondering that at all."

"Really?"

She frowned. "No."

"I'd hate for you to be thinking about that, wherever I take you. I'd hate for you to be wondering if I went here or there with Heather when I brought her up to visit family."

She studied him, confused about the sudden turn in the conversation. "Will you be wondering the same thing if I suggest we go somewhere together? Will you wonder if I suggested the same place to an old boyfriend?"

"Well, no, not really. But Heather and I were together a long time, we were married. It's different."

Still watching him as he looked out across the city spread below, she laid a hand on his arm. "Bruce, is everything okay?"

He glanced quickly in her direction. "Of course, why wouldn't it be?"

"You seem edgy."

He squeezed her hand in his. "I'm fine."

"Listen, if you want to talk about your ex-wife, we can, and—"

"I don't want to talk about her. Sorry, I don't know why I mentioned her."

"It's okay if you're not over her yet."

The pain that flooded his expression made Laura ache. He whipped his head around. "I'm over her. Of course I'm over her."

"You don't have to say things that aren't true because you think that's what I want to hear."

"But it is true! I'm over her."

Laura couldn't understand how the perfectly lovely evening had turned so wrong, so quickly. Bruce was upset about something, she could see that plainly. And if he didn't want to share whatever was on his mind, well, that was fine. They'd only just started getting to know one another, and he didn't owe her a full account of any aspect of his life.

But if he was still hurt and angry about his ex-wife – and why wouldn't he be? – she wished he would just say so. He'd mentioned her completely out of the blue, and Laura felt sure he'd done so for a reason only he understood.

"Listen, I'm sorry," he said. "I wanted us to come up here and be alone together and enjoy these beautiful views. I shouldn't have mentioned Heather."

"You can mention her whenever you want to, Bruce, I mean—"

Just then, his phone pinged. When he pulled it from his pocket and checked the screen, Laura saw his face turn pale and his jaw set hard.

"What's the matter?"

He stared at the phone before jamming it back in his pocket. "Nothing."

"Are you sure?"

The smile he gave her couldn't have looked more plastic. "I'm sure."

He must have registered her expression, because the plastic grin quickly disappeared.

"Laura, truly, everything is fine."

She wanted to believe him, but found she couldn't. Something was troubling him. But she should have expected that. He hadn't been involved with a woman since his divorce, and he'd been with his wife for a long time before that. Maybe it stood to reason that it wouldn't all be plain sailing.

But Laura found herself wishing it could be. She hadn't planned to fall for Bruce, but it was happening, and now there was nothing she could do about it. Still, the last thing she wanted was to get hurt because she'd made the mistake of loving someone who might never recover from the past enough to love her back. Loving someone meant taking risks, and she'd never allowed herself to be involved with anyone who might make her want to take that risk.

Until now.

"You practically turned green when you got that phone message, Bruce. Are you sure everything's okay?"

He nodded. "I promise you."

She cleared her throat. "I'm here for you, Bruce, if you

want to talk. You're taking a big step, spending time with me. I understand that."

"Laura, if only you did understand how big this step really is."

"Then explain it to me."

"If I did, you'd ..."

"I'd what?"

But Bruce waved a hand before starting the car engine again. "Look, let's just have a nice evening together. That's all I want. I don't want to start yapping on about my troubles. It's time I put those troubles in the past. Right now, I just want to be with you and have fun. Okay?"

She watched him for a moment before answering. "Okay."

"There's an ice cream shop not far from here. Interested?"

She smiled and pushed away the strangeness of the last few minutes. "Definitely."

He drove them back down the steep hillside, and the conversation soon turned to easier topics. And, a few hours later, after ice cream cones and a walk in the twilit, and a long, lingering kiss from Bruce that had her almost lifting up off the ground, Laura just wanted to forget all about his earlier strange behaviour.

But found that she couldn't.

CHAPTER 17

They spent a couple of great weeks together. Laura couldn't remember the last time she'd been so happy.

They walked around the city hand in hand, ate out, visited museums, and drank endless cups of coffee in cafes, which turned into long, lazy glasses of wine once evening came. They shared their stories, their hopes, their dreams. And with every day that passed, Laura found her feelings for Bruce only grew deeper.

It was delicious. Terrifying. Exhilarating.

She loved learning about him. His likes and dislikes. His habits and routines. She loved their conversations, which sometimes went on for hours. And if he closed down when those conversations stumbled into the terrain of his ex-wife, she chalked it up to him no longer wanting to dwell on the past. He hadn't talked about Heather at all since that strange half hour when they'd been parked up in the hills, and Laura felt sometimes like a shutter now came down across his features whenever his ex-wife came up. She couldn't help but wonder about it.

For now, though, Laura was happy to know she was in love and that maybe one day, Bruce might be in love with her too.

In the meantime, life continued around her.

"I can't believe I'm leaving when you've finally fallen in love and I won't be here to see you enjoy it," Yvonne said, as she ran tape across the top of the box she'd just finished packing.

Laura had been surprised to discover that while she'd been spending all her free time with Bruce, her flatmate had been pressing on with her plans to move out. Space had been cleared at Olly's place for all her things, a van had been hired to transport her stuff to the other side of the city, and now Yvonne was ready to go.

"I didn't say I'd fallen in love," Laura said, folding a stack of Yvonne's towels.

"Please. You are in love. Have you told him yet?"

"We've only been seeing each other a couple of weeks."

"Don't wait too long. Someone else might nab him, otherwise. If it wasn't for Olly, I might've nabbed him myself. Other women will be watching him. Don't let them steal him away."

Laura set the bag of bed linen on the floor. "I got you a leaving present."

Yvonne's eyes widened. "You did?"

"Of course."

Laura headed to her bedroom, picked up the gift she'd already wrapped, and returned to Yvonne's room with it. "It's just a little thing."

Yvonne pulled off the ribbon and the gift wrap, and Laura saw her friend's expression soften at the framed photograph inside.

"I remember this. That was my first Christmas here, wasn't it?"

"We stayed in our pyjamas all day, drank too much wine, and burned the turkey. I think we took this picture just after we'd opened the bottle of Baileys."

They were grinning out of the photograph, both of them three years younger and looking a little worse for wear on account of the booze. They wore Christmas garlands draped around their necks and tree baubles on their ears.

"We had a lot of fun," Laura said. "You're the best flat-mate I've ever had."

"Obviously." Yvonne's lip began to tremble. "Damn it, you've gone and made me cry. And I promised I wouldn't cry."

They fell into a hug as the tears came.

"I hate goodbyes," Yvonne said.

"It's not goodbye. You're only moving to the other side of town. We'll still be friends. We'll still see each other."

"But it won't be the same."

"Yeah, I know."

Finally they let go of one another, wiped their eyes and laughed.

"I got you something, too," Yvonne said, rummaging through the piles of clothes and books and boxes scattered all around the flat.

Laura took the little box Yvonne held out. When she opened it and looked inside, she found a silver necklace with a heart-shaped pendant. Engraved on the pendant were the words *Follow Your Heart*.

"This is just lovely," Laura said, taking the necklace from the box and fastening it around her neck.

"It's what you should do, Laura. It's what I hope you'll do. Follow your heart. You know where it will take you if you do, and you shouldn't be scared to go there."

Caught by her friend's words, by their unexpected depth and wisdom, Laura ran a hand over the heart-shaped pendant and felt her eyes begin to fill once more. "What will I do without you?"

"You'll pine for a while, wrench at your clothes, wail at the world. But you'll get over me." Grinning, Yvonne hauled the last of her bags to the door. "So, got anyone lined up yet to take my room?"

"Not yet."

"Is that code for 'I want this place to myself so I can sleep with my amazing new boyfriend whenever and wherever I feel like it'?"

Shaking her head, Laura laughed. "I hope you'll be happy with Olly. You deserve it."

"And I hope you'll be happy with whatever comes next for you, Laura. You deserve it too."

Laura opened the door, and then stood and smiled at her friend. "We won't say goodbye."

"Because it's not goodbye."

"Maybe I can just tell you I love you."

"And I love you too."

"Okay, go, quickly, before we start blubbering again."

Laura pulled Yvonne to her, and they hugged one last time before she set off to start her new life.

At the window, Laura waved and blew a kiss as Yvonne got into the van next to Olly. Then they drove down the street and were gone.

Laura looked into the bedroom that now lay empty. She would repaint it before advertising for a flatmate. In the meantime, it would be nice to have the place to herself for a few weeks, and not just because Bruce was now in her life.

She'd never lived alone. Since buying the flat, she'd always been fortunate enough to have someone renting the big bedroom and helping to pay the bills. She figured a few weeks of luxurious alone time wasn't too much to ask and wouldn't make too much of a dent in her finances.

Enjoying the silence, Laura headed to the living room, lay back on the sofa, and revelled in it. As she stared at the ceiling, she ran her fingers once more over the pretty pendant Yvonne had given her and thought about what she'd said.

Follow your heart. You know where it will take you if you do, and you shouldn't be scared to go there.

In the quiet of her empty flat, Laura thought about those words for a long time.

"You've already met my brother and my nieces," Bruce said. "I don't see how meeting my sister-in-law too is such a big deal."

Laura stared. He truly didn't seem to understand. "This is a proper get-together with your closest family. When I met Jack, I didn't even know he was Jack until you told me. I just thought he was the chauffeur. And I can't believe how weird that sounds. Plus, I obviously didn't expect to see your little nieces that night. But this is a special lunch."

"It's not special. Jack's throwing a few burgers on the barbeque."

"But I've been *invited*. That makes it special. This is a come-and-meet-my-family thing."

He gave her a look. "Are you nervous?"

Again, she stared. "Bruce, of course I'm nervous. We've only been seeing each other a few weeks. Now you want me to meet your family."

She looked at the flower bouquets on display. She'd insisted on a trip to the supermarket so she could pick out something to take to this lunch that Bruce had sprung on her with barely any notice. But while the bouquets were eye-catching, they were probably too showy. If she showed up at his brother's house hauling one of these huge bouquets, she'd look like she was trying too hard, which could look worse than not trying at all.

A display of houseplants in pretty ceramic pots stood next to the buckets of flowers. She inspected the glossy leaves of a peace lily and saw there were new fronds already growing at the base, as well as flower buds waiting to open. She picked up the pot and turned it around.

"Does your sister-in-law like plants?"

Bruce glanced at the plant. "She'll love it. Okay, let's go."

"I'm not finished yet. I need to take a bottle of wine, and I want to pick up some little gifts for the girls too."

Bruce scratched his head. "They'll think it's Christmas morning."

"I've been invited to lunch. I want them to know it's appreciated."

"Okay, I'll buy the wine and you pick out something for the girls. Don't spend too much. Claire and Jack won't want you spoiling them."

In the toy aisle Laura scanned the shelves, overwhelmed with choice. She spied several My Little Pony and Wonder Woman items, and, remembering the pyjamas the girls had worn that night in the car, she figured they might work. But she hesitated, wondering if they already had those particular toys. She didn't want to risk arriving with gifts the girls already owned.

In despair, she wandered around and ignored Bruce, who was waving at her from the top of the wine aisle and pointing at his watch.

Finally, she stumbled into the kids' clothing section where she found a display of girls' accessories. She spied a pretty necklace with a Wonder Woman decal on the pendant which she chose for Chloe, before noticing a set of sweet little bracelets with My Little Pony charms attached which she chose for Isla.

Relieved, she rushed to the checkout where she found Bruce paying for the wine he'd picked out. Laura showed him her loot.

"Will the girls like these?"

"Absolutely. You don't have anything to worry about. But it's sweet that you're taking it so seriously."

"Of course I'm taking it seriously." She swiped her items at the self-service checkout and paid. "Okay. I'm ready. I think. No, I'm ready, I am."

She fidgeted all the way there in the car. She saw Bruce slide her occasional glances and smiles and wondered if he really understood how big a deal this was.

The last woman he'd been with had been his *wife*. No matter how things had ended between them, there was still a big yardstick against which she would be measured.

On the one hand, Laura knew Bruce's family would be comparing her to the Heather they'd once loved – because surely they must have loved her, or at the very least liked her. The two of them might have lived in London, but surely there would have been special family occasions, Christmases and so on, when they spent time together. Claire in particular must have had some kind of relationship with her former sister-in-law, and the new female on Bruce's arm might have a lot to live up to.

On the other hand, Heather had broken Bruce's heart, and so his family would be understandably protective. They'd want to make sure he wasn't about to hook up with a woman who was likely to do to him what the last one had done. And Bruce's separation was only a few months in the past, so it stood to reason that his brother and sister-in-law would be wondering if he was moving too fast with another woman when the wounds inflicted by the last one were still raw, and whether ...

"Are you okay?"

Laura's head snapped around. "What? I'm fine. Why?"

"Because you've totally shredded that paper tissue you're holding."

Looking down, she saw tufts of tissue all over her legs. "Oh for God's sake, now I'm covered in fluff." She began sweeping it off her jeans.

Bruce laughed. "That's right, get it all off you and on to the floor of my car."

"Oh God, I'm sorry, I—"

"Laura, I'm kidding. You're getting yourself all worked up about this visit, and there's no need to."

"I can't help it."

"Just relax. And just be you."

When Bruce pulled the car into the driveway, she felt the weight of the moment bearing down. If she didn't feel the way she already felt about him, this wouldn't be a big deal.

But she did, and so it was.

The front door of the house was thrown open, and Chloe and Isla came barrelling out towards the car, chattering and holding aloft the action figures they clutched in their little hands. And then Jack and Claire appeared in the doorway, waving and smiling, and Laura somehow understood that the afternoon was going to be okay.

Her anxieties began to relinquish their grip.

"I've got Captain America!" Isla shouted as she raced around to where Bruce was getting out of the car.

"And I've got Iron Man!" Chloe waved her action figure in Bruce's face. "Do you like Iron Man, Uncle Bruce?"

"I do like Iron Man. In fact, don't you think I look a lot like Tony Stark?"

As the girls dissolved into shrieking giggles, Claire came down the front steps. "Laura, we're so glad you could make it," she said, embracing her. "And that plant you've brought is beautiful. I hope it's for us."

"It is," she said and instantly relaxed. "I thought it'd look nice in a kitchen window."

"Laura's kitchen window is like something from the Botanic Gardens," Bruce said, taking her hand and squeezing it.

"In that case you can give me some advice about a house plant Jack's been trying to kill for the past two months."

"I haven't been trying to kill it."

"You're saying it's committing suicide?"

Bruce handed over the wine he'd brought. "Sounds like we're going to need this."

"I'm already a beer ahead of you." Jack herded his daughters into the house. "I'm trying a new marinade on the chicken. And Bruce, my back might be turned, but I know you just rolled your eyes."

Bruce – who had in fact done just that – grinned. "Laura, whatever you do, don't ask Jack about the marinade or we'll be here for the rest of the afternoon while he describes it."

"So, Jack, what's in this marinade?" Laura asked, and when everyone laughed, she felt little tingles of happy relief.

"Well, there's olive oil, obviously," Jack said. "Then there's my special herb mix, which includes basil, thyme, a touch of oregano, with just the tiniest hint of lemon juice to—"

"Go to your barbeque, we don't want to hear any more," Claire said, kissing her husband and pushing him gently towards the open doors out to the garden.

"My wife, the queen of subtlety," Jack said, and disappeared outside.

"Hey girls, I brought you both a little treat." Laura reached into the carrier bag and pulled out their gifts. Both girls began jumping up and down and shouting in delight as they removed the gift wrapping.

"It's so pretty!" Chloe said, putting on the necklace and tilting the pendant so she could admire it. "I love Wonder Woman."

"I know you do."

"And I like My Little Pony," Isla said, holding the clutch of pastel-coloured bracelets in her hands. "I've got My Little Pony pyjamas."

"That's why I thought you'd like these."

"Can you help me put them on, Mum?"

"I'll help you," Laura said, and carefully pulled off the tag before sliding the row of bracelets over Isla's little wrist. "There you go, what do you think?"

"I think they're pretty. Thank you, Laura."

"You're welcome, sweetheart."

"Thank you, Laura," Chloe said, and gave Laura a kiss on the cheek before turning to her sister. "Let's go and show Dad."

The two girls dashed outside at high speed. Bruce, who'd watched the scene from where he stood against the kitchen counter, gave Laura a wink.

"That was sweet of you," Claire said, positioning the peace lily by the window. "Chloe's been taking an interest in jewellery and accessories lately, and naturally Isla is copying her, so you hit the jackpot with those gifts."

"That's good to hear. They're sweet kids."

"Bruce, Jack is signalling to you from the prow of his grill," Claire said, peering out the window. "Well, I suppose he could just as easily be signalling to me, but as I'm about to pour two big glasses of wine for Laura and myself, I think you ought to get out there and see what he wants."

Bruce kissed Laura's cheek. "Wish me luck."

Once he was gone, Claire turned to the fridge. "I'll pop this wine Bruce brought in here. I've already got one chilled. White okay for you?"

"Perfect. And I want to thank you for inviting me over."

Claire opened the wine and poured. "My girls have been yapping on about you ever since that night they went with Jack to drive you home from your date. Although their yapping is nothing compared to Bruce's. You're all he's talked about these past few weeks. I wanted to see for myself this person who'd finally put the spark back into his eye."

"He's a great guy."

"He is."

Seeing Claire's expression, Laura began fidgeting. "And you want to know if I'm planning on messing him around."

But Claire simply laughed. "Is that what you think I'm wondering?"

"I'd be surprised if you weren't."

Claire laughed again. "Jack and I would make for pretty terrible relatives if we weren't worried about Bruce after all he's been through. But just to be clear, we didn't invite you here to grill you. Believe me, since my husband got that barbeque of his, there's plenty grilling going on in this house without adding any more."

Laura laughed and took the wine glass Claire passed over.

"We want you to relax and have fun," Claire said, and held out her own glass. "Cheers."

Smiling, Laura clinked glasses. "That's what Bruce said."

"And he was right." Claire sipped some wine before turning to the salad she was preparing on the counter.

"Bruce says you're running in a ten-kilometre race next weekend."

Laura groaned. "The closer it gets, the more terrified I feel."

"You'll do fine. Are you running for charity? We'd be glad to sponsor you."

"No, I'm not fundraising. I just thought I'd enjoy the challenge."

"And have you?"

"Let's just say I've bitten off more than I can chew, and if I get to that finish line without collapsing it'll be a miracle. But at the same time, I've sort of enjoyed running too. Well, at least when it doesn't feel like my chest is about to explode."

Claire laughed. "I used to run before I had the girls. I promised myself I'd get back into it, but I never did. Now the two of them come in very handy whenever I feel guilty. All I have to do is try to imagine fitting a running regime into a schedule that already includes their afterschool activities and all the endless social commitments with their little friends, and any guilt I have just disappears."

Laura sipped the wine and smiled. "This is a beautiful house, Claire."

"Thanks. We love it here. The moment I saw the place, I knew it was ours. Jack says you live in town, in one of those beautiful old tenement blocks."

"I do, and you're right, they are beautiful. I'm lucky to live there, so close to work. My flatmate just moved out, so I've got the place to myself while I think about finding a new renter. I miss my flatmate, but I'm also getting used to the peace and quiet."

"When I was doing my medical training, I lived in a rented house with six other student doctors. It was chaos. The mess, the irregular hours everyone kept. When Jack and I got together and eventually got our own place, it was like heaven." Claire stopped chopping and sipped her wine, then laid a red pepper on the board and picked up her knife again. "There's nothing like having your own place. Sometimes I think of Bruce, living in that spare room at his Uncle Keith's pub after having his own house, and I truly wonder how he manages it."

"I hope he finds a new pub soon. It would be good for him to feel he's settling down."

"Believe me, he deserves exactly that after what happened. His ex-wife really put him through the wringer."

Laura said nothing, just sipped her wine. Claire glanced up from her salad-chopping.

"Sorry, that's uncomfortable territory. New girlfriends don't want to hear about their new boyfriend's ex-wives."

"Bruce has talked about it a little. It's obvious he's still getting over what happened."

Claire laughed, but it was devoid of humour. "You can say that again. Heather's affair was bad enough. But when she told him the rest of it? I can't imagine how Bruce must've felt."

Laura, raising her wine glass, frowned. "The rest of it?"

Claire turned from the chopping board. "Well, sure, I mean—"

But as soon as she registered Laura's confusion, her expression changed, and Laura understood she'd been about to say something more and had caught herself, just in time.

"What I mean is ... well, Heather just blurted out to Bruce that she was madly in love with this other man and that she was leaving him," Claire said. "That must've been hard to hear."

But Laura was no fool. Claire was covering and back-pedalling from whatever it was she'd been about to say. She'd assumed Laura knew more than she did.

What more could there be to know? Had Heather squeezed him in the divorce settlement? Somehow managed to get more than her fair share of the pub business Bruce had worked so hard to build? Or had Heather betrayed him with someone he was close to?

Laura realised she could speculate all she liked because she had no idea. As Claire finished preparing the salad and moved the conversation on to safer terrain, she pushed the matter from her mind. She knew there was more to Bruce's divorce than he'd told her already, but knew also that it was his business and his choice to share or not share.

But they'd already shared so much with one another. She couldn't help but wonder what it was that he still wanted to hold back.

"The hamburgers are ready," Bruce said, appearing in the doorway. "Coming out to eat?"

"We're coming," Claire said. "Laura, if you bring that bread basket, I'll bring this salad."

When Claire disappeared into the garden, Bruce wandered over and put his arms around Laura's waist. "Everything going okay?"

"Everything's fine."

Bruce returned her smile and kissed her head. "Good. Come on, let's eat."

"I'll be right there."

The afternoon lay ahead, and she was looking forward to it. But still, as she watched Bruce join his family in the garden, she couldn't help but wonder what it was he'd not yet told her, and what it was he'd decided not to share.

It was an hour before opening time at The Crooked Thistle, and Bruce was stocking beer bottles into the under-counter fridges when his phone pinged.

His stomach clenched when he glanced at the screen and saw it was a message from Heather.

He'd ignored all the others she'd sent. Since that first out-of-the-blue message, he'd lost count of how many more had come. He'd blocked her, but she must have begun using other numbers to contact him, because the messages continued. He knew it was stupid, and cowardly, but the idea of responding to her request for contact, and possibly ending up in some convoluted discussion with her, was unbearable.

Grabbing the phone from the bar top, he stabbed at it to delete the message.

"Punch that thing any harder and you'll crack the screen."

Bruce looked up and saw Keith coming through from the back, hauling the vacuum cleaner.

"What's the matter with you?" Keith said. "It's not like you to have a scowl on your face."

"It's nothing."

"Suit yourself."

Keith plugged in the vacuum and moved it to the carpeted area by the television. Bruce watched him and sighed.

"Heather's been in touch."

Keith laid down the vacuum nozzle and turned around. "Heather? What does she want?"

Bruce shrugged. "I don't know. She's sent messages asking me to contact her. She doesn't say why."

"And have you contacted her?"

"No."

"Because?"

"Because she clicked her fingers and ended our marriage. She doesn't get to click them again and have me at her beck-and-call."

Keith laughed and shook his head. "Son, you will never move on if that's your attitude."

"I've been trying to move on. I was doing a pretty good job of it too, until Heather started contacting me. Now she's …"

"Now she's what?"

"Now she's going to ruin whatever it is that's happening with Laura. Things were going fine. Things were going great, actually. But now I can't get Heather out of my head. And Laura knows something's off, I'm sure of it. How could she not know when I'm acting like an idiot?"

"If you're acting like an idiot, it's because you're choosing to."

"Thanks, Uncle Keith. This is really helpful support and advice."

Keith laughed again. "Look, I know what you've gone

through because I've gone through it myself. And I understand why you don't want to be in contact with your ex after what she did. Not just the affair, but ... well, the other thing too. Calm down, I'm not about to start talking about any of that, I know you can't stand it. But here's a question to consider. Why do you think she's contacted you?"

"Like I said, I have no idea."

"Okay, I'll ask another way. What's your worst fear about why she's contacted you?"

The question caught Bruce short. Beneath Keith's blunt facade, he often forgot there lay a surprisingly emotional and tuned-in man.

"I guess my fear is that things have gone wrong with Dan and Heather's looking for us to get back together."

Keith nodded. "And is that your fear because it's what you want or don't want?"

"I don't want it! I don't want Heather back, not after what she—"

Keith waved his hands in a calming gesture. "Okay, so why do you fear it?"

He sighed and closed his eyes. "Because I'm scared I'd want to throw it in her face, just to see how much it would hurt her. I'd want to hurt her the way she hurt me. And I hate knowing that's the sort of man I might be."

"So, if Heather walked into this bar, right now, and said exactly that – Bruce, I'm not with my fancy man any more, will you take me back? – you would use that to hurt her and get payback?"

He thought of the scenario Keith had just painted and tried to imagine his ex-wife coming to him in distress and asking for another chance. He tried to imagine laughing in her face and asking her how it felt to be rejected and telling her to get out.

It wasn't possible to imagine it. He couldn't conjure the scene in his mind and couldn't imagine causing her that sort of hurt deliberately. He didn't want her back. But he didn't want to hurt her, either.

"No, I couldn't do that."

"So, you're not the man you fear you are. And quite why you'd think you might be is a mystery. For God's sake, Bruce, you're a good man, a decent man. Why would you think you could be spiteful and vengeful? It's not who you are, you must know that."

Rubbing the bridge of his nose, Bruce shook his head. "Heather hurt me so much, Uncle Keith. I was scared that amount of hurt might've, you know, changed me. When I left her, I …"

"What?"

He sighed, realising how dumb it would sound. "I took a painting that Heather loved. She'd asked me to buy it for her because she loved it, and I gave it to her as an anniversary gift. And then I took it to spite her. That's not who I was before she did this to me."

Keith stared. And then began laughing. "That ugly monstrosity you have hanging on your bedroom wall upstairs? You took that to get back at her, and now you're worried you're turning into some monster?"

"Look, I know how it sounds, but …"

But Keith was laughing too hard. Bruce frowned. "Great, laugh it up at my expense."

Keith wiped his eyes. "Sorry son, but you really need to get things into perspective. We both know the only person getting hurt by that painting being upstairs is *you*. You hate that painting, for good reason, and if you have reasons for forcing yourself to look at it every day, I can't understand them. Here's my advice, for what it's worth. Take that painting off your wall and move on with your life. And if you don't want to have contact with Heather, then just tell her that. It's time to get out of your own way, Bruce."

With another shake of his head, Keith turned on the vacuum cleaner. Bruce stood behind the bar, thinking about what his uncle had said. He glanced out the window towards Valentino's across the road, and saw a flash of blonde hair as Laura dashed around inside, working her morning shift. His heart swelled up just to see her.

It didn't make sense, fixating on Heather and her reasons for contacting him when he had within his grasp the chance at a future with a woman he'd fallen head over heels in love with.

He picked up his phone. Heather's message was still there, not yet deleted.

Bruce, please just call me, or answer when I call you. I need to talk. Please.

Instead of deleting it, he replied: *I don't want to talk to you, Heather. Just leave me alone.*

He pressed send. And immediately that black feeling inside him began to disappear.

Leaving his uncle to finish cleaning the bar, he went upstairs to his bedroom and looked at the soul-sapping grey and yellow painting that hung on the wall. Taking it from Heather made no sense. He knew that and had known it all along.

Reaching up, he lifted it from the wall hooks and laid it

on the floor, with the painting facing the wall. Now, he didn't have to look at it any more. That was a relief.

And it was time to return it to its rightful owner anyway. He'd get it wrapped up, book a specialist courier service, and contact his solicitor to arrange for the painting to be sent to Heather's solicitor's office in London.

It was time to make a choice. And so he made it. He'd leave the past behind once and for all and move towards the future, a future that he hoped would have Laura in it.

If he hadn't already jeopardised what they'd begun together.

CHAPTER 18

The ten-kilometre race had seemed entirely feasible when she'd first signed up. But once she was in the middle of it, Laura could only wonder what on earth she'd been thinking.

She'd begun strongly enough, just like the other enthusiastic participants. Ignoring the athletic specimens who'd raced past, she'd focused only on keeping moving. A few kilometres in, she'd begun to slow down and worry seriously about her pace. And at the halfway mark, with tears in her eyes and a lump in her throat, it seemed impossible that there were still five kilometres to complete.

Rain started to fall. And then it got heavier. She wondered if anyone would notice if she ducked under the race cordon and caught a bus home.

But at least one person would notice, because Bruce was waiting for her at the finish line.

She couldn't give up. Everything ached, but she had to get to that finish line and prove to herself that the impossible could be made possible.

So instead of thinking about how she hurt every time her feet hit the road, she thought instead of Bruce and of what he now meant to her.

She loved him. There was no question about it.

But she wondered, too, about what it was that he was holding back about the collapse of his marriage. Her mind, tired from the race, offered up sneaky thoughts about whether the thing he was holding back might be big enough to tear apart what they had together.

It had to be. Or why else hide it?

She pushed the ideas away. Every moment they spent together told her only that they were happy.

So, instead of dark thoughts about the secret she feared Bruce harboured, she thought instead about good things. She thought about the grace of unexpected love and how lucky she was to have it come into her life.

And then, as if a miracle had taken place, she saw the finish line in front of her.

She almost laughed as she crossed it and her mind filled with a whirlwind of amazement and sheer exhaustion. Someone in a steward's vest handed her a bottle of water, while someone else put a medal around her neck and gave her a bag of goodies.

When she glimpsed inside the bag she saw the finisher's certificate she'd thought of so many times as she'd worked towards this moment.

She pulled out the certificate and smiled as she studied it. A space was already cleared on her bedroom wall to hang it up.

Just then, another runner bumped into her and knocked the certificate from her hand. She grabbed for it, but too late to stop it from landing in a puddle, where it was immediately soaked through.

"Oh no!" She reached down and pulled the sodden piece of paper from the puddle as the clumsy runner who'd knocked into her apologised.

"We can get you another certificate," said one of the stewards.

Staring at the wet certificate, the ink already running, Laura felt a smile come to her face and shook her head. "I got soaked most of the way around the course. Maybe it's okay that this got soaked too."

When she looked up she saw Bruce. As he walked towards her, all the aches in her body begin to lift.

"You're amazing," he said, opening his arms.

"Don't hug me. I'm drenched in sweat, rain, mud, some other stuff I can't identify."

"Doesn't matter." He hugged her and kissed her. "Well done. You did it."

"I'm still breathing, and that's more than I was hoping for at the halfway point."

He pulled a towel from the backpack slung over his shoulder and began dabbing at her face. "You've got mucky spots, let me ..."

Something changed in his expression as he looked at her. And despite all that was happening around them – runners crossing the finish line, crowds cheering from the sidelines, noisy stewards directing people here and there – Laura felt like everything had gone still and quiet.

That look in Bruce's deep grey eyes held her spellbound.

"I love you, Laura."

She was stunned into silence for a long moment. “What?”

He took her hands and pulled her closer. “I’m in love with you. I’ve been in love with you since that day we spent at your flat when you were sick. I’ve tried to hide it because I didn’t want to scare you off. But I can’t do it any more. I love you.”

She felt the smile curve at her lips. “Why’d you have to go and say something like that when I’m standing here covered in sweat and muck?”

“The sweat and muck don’t matter. You always look beautiful to me.”

They stood in the rain, the bustle of runners around them forgotten.

“I know we’ve only been together a few weeks,” he said. “And I know love’s a big word. I don’t expect you to feel the same way, and I don’t want you to feel obligated to—”

“Bruce, I love you too.”

A look of utter joy and surprise crossed Bruce’s face, and Laura’s heart did a little somersault in her chest.

“I never expected to love you but I do,” she said.

He stepped forward and pulled her close. “I probably should’ve waited for a more romantic moment to tell you how I feel.”

“Oh, I don’t know. Rain can be romantic.”

And she laid her lips against his as the rain turned into a downpour.

THE BLINDS around the banks of windows in Valentino’s were down and the doors were locked, but inside the lights burned brightly as Natalie showed her visitor around. This was the third tour she'd given Ruby Leighton in as many days, and she knew that the woman was more than just an interested viewer.

She was about as in love with the place as Natalie thought it was possible to get.

"I used to come here with my parents for ice cream sundaes," Ruby said, looking around with unconcealed excitement in her eyes. "When I heard it was on the market, I only wanted to take a look before it changed hands. I almost can't believe I'm about to buy it." She glanced at Natalie and shook her head. "I probably shouldn't be telling you any of this. No doubt I'm blurting away my bargaining position with every word."

"Don't think for a minute your enthusiasm for this restaurant will compromise whatever bargaining position you might have. I'm only interested in selling Valentino's to someone who will love it as much as my husband and I did. Believe me, I've had offers already, but not from buyers I'm convinced have this place's best interests at heart."

Ruby slid into a booth and took in the restaurant from the new angle. "I've previously run two successful bistros. I think I can continue to make a success of this place. In fact, I know I can. I'm not in this only to make a quick buck."

"Just as well. Anyone interested in making a quick buck ought to start somewhere other than the restaurant business." Natalie studied the younger woman. "I know you sold your bistros a number of years ago. What makes you want to get back into the restaurant world again?"

Ruby met her gaze. "It's a fair question. When I got married I sold my restaurants and that's something I've always regretted. I'm on my own again now and I want to do what I used to love doing, which is running a place like this. But I can't risk starting again with a brand-new venture. I have a nine-year-old son to support now. It makes sense for me to buy somewhere that's already successful and thriving."

Natalie thought about this. "You're looking for a fresh start."

"Yes, I am."

And wouldn't it just be perfect, Natalie thought, if her decision to sell Valentino's in order to begin her own fresh start might mean that the woman sitting in the booth found hers?

"It's been a long time since you ran a place like this," Natalie said. "Aren't you worried you'll be overstretched?"

"You said you have a good assistant manager. I'd hope to keep him on."

"Well, it's true that Paul is very good. However, I learned today that he's decided to use the opportunity of me moving on to shake things up in his own life. He's been offered a job as a restaurant manager elsewhere and has accepted, so he's currently working his notice."

Ruby looked disappointed. "I didn't want to have to hire any new people as soon as I took over, but if that's what has to be done, then …"

"There may be another option. Laura, my longest-serving waitress, is as close to assistant manager as you can get without the formal title. I suggest you offer her the job. In fact, I offered her the job before Paul joined us, but she said she enjoyed waitressing and was happy as she was. However, she was indispensable when I was recovering from the shock of losing my husband, and she may feel differently about things now. I feel sure she's ready for a change in life, and a new role might be exactly what she wants."

"Wonderful!" Ruby smiled and leaned back in the booth. "Listen, I know we still have details to work out. But there is one thing I want to talk about before our solicitors get involved."

"Go ahead, ask me anything you like."

"It's a little delicate," she began, kneading her hands together. "I know how drawn out the process can be when it comes to the commercial property market. But I'm happy with the due diligence so far and don't want to wait any longer than necessary to get started here. I wonder whether you'd be agreeable to finalising a sale as quickly as possible, maybe even within a few weeks?"

Natalie, caught by surprise at the idea of leaving Valentino's so quickly, found herself glancing around the restaurant. Her gaze settled on a little framed photograph that hung by the side of the bar. Just like the photos in her office, this one showed herself and Angelo, and in this particular shot, they stood beside the new coffee machine they'd just had installed, Angelo grinning as he pressed the buttons on the shiny contraption while Natalie laughed at his antics.

Smiling at the memory, and thinking of all the memories she'd made in this place with the man she'd chosen to spend her life with, Natalie felt something inside her finally let go.

"I can make that timeframe work," she said, turning back to the woman who would soon be Valentino's new owner and smiling when the younger woman clapped her hands together in delight.

"Fantastic!"

"You're going to be very happy here, I just know it. And if you are half as happy as Angelo and I were, you will be lucky indeed."

Ruby rose from the booth and began walking to the door. "So, what's next for you?"

And in that moment, Natalie felt a shift deep within her, and the sensation was like a baby bird softly beating its wings for the first time.

"A new beginning," she said.

KEITH REARRANGED the bottles of single malts on the glass shelves, stood back, and considered. Then he shifted things around some more and adjusted the dimmer on the built-in illumination system he'd just had installed.

But the bottles looked too lined up and regimented. Tinkering once more, he moved a few into clusters and groups.

When he stepped back again, he smiled. It was perfect, and just what he'd been aiming for.

Seeing the new whisky display finished and looking so good made it worth hanging around downstairs in the pub for so long after closing. Just that morning, the electrician had finally finished the lighting installation Keith had decided to invest in. There'd been no time during opening hours to begin stocking the new shelves. And Keith had been too excited to wait until morning.

But now as the clock rolled towards one, he admired

the new displays and was happy. Tomorrow once the pub was cleared and cleaned, he'd set out the new whisky menus on the tables and see how the customers reacted. Hopefully they'd pay to try something new, if only for novelty value. And once they realised what they were missing they'd come back for more.

That was the theory, at least.

He hoped the new whisky stock would make the pub some good money. Mostly though, he was looking forward to talking to the customers about the whiskies he'd chosen, just as he'd enjoyed writing the descriptions he'd penned for the menus. It had been fun. And there was nothing wrong with a little fun in life.

A knock at the locked pub doors had him looking up and frowning. Probably some drunken passer-by, seeing the lights still on inside and thinking the place was open.

"We're closed!"

"Keith, it's Natalie. I saw the lights were still on. Can I come in?"

He quickly unlocked and opened the door. "It's a bit late for you still to be up and about, Natalie. Is everything okay at the restaurant?"

"Everything's fine. But I have some news, and I wanted to tell you right away."

"Of course, come in."

Stepping into the pub, she spied the new whisky shelves. "Keith, that looks wonderful."

"It was more work than I thought it'd be. I thought the electrician would never get it finished. Trust a tradesman to take two weeks on a job that should've lasted half an afternoon. Anyway, it's done now, and I'm pleased with it."

"It's totally transformed the bar, Keith. Well done."

He watched her fidget as she stared at the whisky. "Would you like to try one?"

"Oh no, I think we've established that I'm not a whisky drinker."

"How about something else? You look like there's something on your mind, and I'm guessing a drink might help you say whatever it is you've come here to say."

She smiled. "You are very good at reading people."

"I'm a pub landlord. It's part of the job."

"In that case, I'll take a vodka tonic."

He poured her drink and selected a regular blended Scotch for himself. Tempting though it was to tear open the seals on one of those new single malts, he wanted to get some nice photographs of the display while everything still looked pristine.

He held out his glass, touched it to Natalie's, and waited. Although he already knew in his heart what she'd come over to tell him. Letting the silence spin between them, even for just a second, would delay, if never change, the inevitable.

"Keith, I've informally agreed terms to sell Valentino's," she finally said, swirling her drink. "I've rejected a couple of offers on the restaurant already because I want to make sure that Valentino's goes to the right person. I believe I've now found that person."

Keith nodded and then smiled. "I'm happy for you Natalie."

"That *For Sale* sign has been up for weeks now, but it didn't actually feel real until tonight, when I realised that this woman – Ruby Leighton – is the one I'm going to sell to. And once I realised, it felt right. I'd be lying if I said I hadn't had my doubts about what I was doing."

"It's only natural that you'd have doubts."

"But those all disappeared tonight. The new buyer is keen to move quickly and so, if our solicitors can also move quickly, it's likely that I'll be gone in just a few weeks."

Shocked surprise hit him, and he saw Natalie register the change in his expression.

"I thought there'd be more time before you left."

"In truth, so did I. But she's keen to take over. And I see no reason to delay things when I want to move on with my life."

He sipped his Scotch and thought about this. "Well in that case, we'll just have to make the most of the time we've got left."

But Natalie moved closer and laid a hand on his arm. "I can't, Keith. I can't see you any more. I know you're starting to feel things for me ..."

"Natalie—"

"... and the reason I know is because I'm starting to feel things for you too." She smiled softly. "But I know that there's no real future for me and you. If we continued seeing one another, we'd both have fun and I'd become very fond of you. But that's all it would ever be, fun and fondness."

"I could live with that, Natalie."

"I'd never allow that, because you deserve better. I'd hate myself for hurting you the way so many other women have hurt you."

"It wouldn't have to be like that."

"Yes, it would. My heart was broken when Angelo died, you know that. But I've loved every minute we've spent together these past few weeks. Being with you has helped me to believe that I can move on, and that I'm ready to move on. You showed me that, Keith. And it means a lot that you did. And all I hope now is that you can understand that."

He sipped more whisky and rubbed at his chin. He understood the weight of this moment and understood he could make it easy or hard, make their parting sweet or sour. The choice was his.

Walking around the bar, he refilled their glasses. "I need to stop falling in love with women so easily," he said and smiled.

She paused, before joining him in laughter. She held up her glass and they silently toasted one another.

"Keith, the perfect woman is out there for you."

"And if I keep going at my current rate, I might actually find her before I'm ninety."

Laughing, she drank more vodka. "Are we okay?"

"Of course we're okay."

"I'll miss you, Keith."

"You're not gone yet."

But she leaned over and took his hand across the bar. "I'll miss you," she repeated.

"Aye and I'll miss you." He drained his glass and set it down on the counter. "Come on, drink up and get yourself home. Do you need a taxi?"

"I'll call one from the restaurant."

At the door, they hugged, and Keith understood it would be for the last time. He'd see her again, of course.

But not like this. And so he held her while he could, before finally letting her go and watching as she crossed the road to her restaurant.

She gave him a small wave as she closed Valentino's doors behind her.

And that was that, he thought.

Turning, he picked up their empty glasses from the counter, and because the moment called for it, moved to refill his own. As he held it beneath the blended Scotch optic, he glanced at the pristine rows of single malts, waiting to be opened.

He'd wanted to wait and take a photograph of the new display in the morning, when the bar was clean and shining and before breaking any of the bottle seals. He'd wanted a photograph that caught it all in a perfect moment. But perfect, he knew, was just fiction.

And so he chose one of the best single malts from the new collection, tore open the seal, poured a generous measure, and raised a toast to Natalie in the silence of his empty pub.

CHAPTER 19

There was a surprising late August chill in the air, and inside Valentino's the customers were adapting by ordering hot minestrone and bowls of creamy pasta. Laura surveyed the restaurant for any signs that people were in need of service, but saw none. The lunch rush was over, the tables were cleared, and only a few people still lingered – the mother and her toddler who often came in to pass an hour together, a couple of workmen in fluorescent vests finishing their toasted sandwiches, and, by the window, Mr Davidson scowling into his soup.

Laura's shift was almost over, and she'd been uncharacteristically watching the clock for the last half hour. Today she was eager to return to her flat. Since hauling herself over the finish line in the ten-kilometre race, she'd been thinking about things in her life and had woken that morning to find she'd made a decision. A big decision. Now she wanted her shift to be finished so she could go and do something about it.

She was already mentally pulling off her apron when Natalie came through the restaurant doors and shrugged off her raincoat. When she spied Laura stacking cups and saucers by the coffee machine, she headed straight over.

"I know you must be due to finish, but do you have time for a quick coffee and a chat?"

"Sure."

"Grab one of those quiet booths in the corner, and I'll be back in a minute."

While Natalie headed to her office, Laura prepared Natalie's espresso and a cappuccino for herself. By the time she'd carried the tray to the corner booth, Natalie was waiting for her there.

"Looks like we've had our summer," Natalie said, nodding out of the window at the falling rain while Laura set their coffee cups down on the table.

"I'm already enjoying this fresher weather." Laura slid into the booth and stirred sugar into her cup. "I like autumn. Everything always feels so crisp, with the leaves turning and the colder mornings arriving."

Natalie sipped her espresso. "Angelo always loved autumn too. It was his favourite season. He said nowhere in the world could look as beautiful as Scotland in autumn. And I think he was right." Smiling at the memory, she waved a hand. "Anyway, I have some news."

As she once more picked up her spoon and needlessly stirred her espresso, Laura watched her. And realised that she knew what was coming next.

"You've found a buyer for Valentino's."

Natalie nodded. "Yes, I have. Her name is Ruby Leighton. She previously ran a couple of little bistros in the city. Last night, she visited after we closed to look around one last time before making her decision. Now, we've agreed the broad terms of a sale and it's in the hands of the solicitors. I wanted to tell you first, before I make the announcement to the rest of the staff."

Laura set down her coffee cup. It had been almost six weeks since Natalie had first told her about her plans to sell the restaurant. She thought about how crushed she'd been that day, and her desperation to find some way to prevent it happening. It was amazing how much things had changed since then. And amazing, too, how differently she now felt about everything.

Laying her hand on Natalie's, she smiled. "I'm happy for you."

Natalie arched an eyebrow. "You are?"

"I know this is what's best for you and I know it's what you want. And so I'm happy for you."

"I can't tell you how pleased I am to hear you say that, Laura. The truth is I was beginning to wonder if this place would sell after all. I love the restaurant so much that I expected people to be beating down my door to buy it. I'm a smart businesswoman, and I know things rarely work that way, but the heart still believed that's what would happen. Anyway I knew I just had to wait for the right buyer to come along. And she has."

"You like her?"

"Very much. She's passionate about the restaurant, and while naturally interested in making money, that's not the only thing that appears to drive her. She's going to be a good fit. I want you to know I've advised her to appoint you assistant manager."

"You have?"

"For goodness sake, Laura, of course I have. I only wish you'd accepted the offer when I made it years ago. Ruby appeared very open to my suggestion, and when she takes over, you should expect that offer to come your way."

"Thank you, Natalie."

Natalie studied her. "Please don't tell me you'd turn down such a wonderful offer yet again. You are a good waitress, but you have so much more to offer, and—"

Laura smiled and held up a hand. "I'm not turning anything down. I'll think about it. When will she take over?"

"Probably in a matter of weeks, so you have some time to consider what you want to do. Promise me you will consider it."

"I promise. But this isn't about me, this is about you, Natalie." She fidgeted for a moment. "What about Keith? You two have been seeing a lot of each other."

Natalie cleared her throat. "We've had a wonderful time together. But Keith and I were never going to end up in a relationship, not a serious one at least. And so I thought it best that we stopped things before they went any further."

"Natalie, I'm sorry I tried to—"

But it was Natalie's turn to hold up a hand. "Not another word. I had fun. Keith had fun. And now I need to move on. And Keith needs to find someone who's right for him. I am not that person."

"Still —"

"I said not another word on the matter, and I meant it."

Laura saw the kind smile Natalie gave her and nodded. "Okay, understood. So you must be excited, knowing you can start making your travel plans now. Where will you go to first?"

"Well I'd originally planned on Ireland to begin with, however—"

"Waitress! Waitress! Hello, does anyone actually work in this place?"

They turned to see Mr Davidson waving his soup spoon in the air from the other side of the restaurant.

"I'll see what the matter is," Laura said, and rose.

"No, I'll go and deal with the old goat. Off you go home, I'm sure you must have things to get on with."

As Natalie made her way over to Mr Davidson, Laura thought, *Yes, I do have things to get on with.*

And it was time to do just that.

LAURA STOOD in her little bedroom, staring at the array of certificates she'd pinned to the wall over the years. Each one meant something to her, and she treasured them, no matter whether the activities had been frivolous or challenging. Together, they depicted how she'd filled her days and filled her life.

But it was now time to take them down.

As she pulled out the pins and tucked the certificates into an empty folder, she felt like the tectonic plates beneath her life were beginning to shift. This one small act, of taking down the old to make way for the new, marked the end of one thing and the beginning of another.

Once the wall was cleared, she stood back and stared. A blank canvas, she thought, for a new beginning.

With that work done, she began emptying her

wardrobe, her chest of drawers, and the entire bedroom, and when she was finished she hauled everything into the big room that had once been Yvonne's.

It was time for this change. For ten years she'd had a flatmate across the hall, and she wondered what it would be like to have this big lovely bedroom for her own. When she found another renter, they would get the small bedroom and she'd adjust the rent accordingly. After a decade watching every penny like a hawk and squirreling money into her savings account for the rainy day she'd felt sure would one day come, there was enough money to keep her going. In fact, after she'd done her sums, she'd realised there was enough money to keep her going for rather a lot longer than she'd imagined.

As she moved the last of her things into the big bedroom, marvelling at how much space there was, she picked up a folder she'd kept separate from the rest of her boxes. It was the folder Bruce had knocked over that day he'd helped when she'd been ill and half-delirious thanks to the virus she'd caught.

Sitting on the edge of the bed, she opened it and removed the university files and paperwork she'd stored away.

It was difficult to remember the girl she'd been back then, an excited eighteen-year-old at the start of her university adventure. Her parents had helped her pack up and move into student halls, and when she'd waved them off she'd been jittery with anticipation. The first few weeks of lectures had passed in a blur, and by the time the Christmas break had come she'd begun to get a handle on the topics she was studying. She was no genius, but she was a hard worker and the hard work had paid off with good grades. When summer came she'd gone home to her parents' house, hauling a stack of history books from the library that she planned to read during the long summer. She'd devoured those books.

And then tragedy had struck.

She flicked through the old files and paperwork in the folder. There were enrolment forms, old essays she'd completed in her first year, module reading lists. She scanned the reading lists and remembered how excited she'd once been about buying copies of those books and diving into them. After her parents died, not only had her university progress come to a halt, but she'd stopped reading history books altogether too. Anytime she tried to read those books for pleasure, she'd only been reminded of the future she'd thought would one day be hers.

It had taken her a long time to realise just how much she missed the life she'd begun all those years ago, and how much she still ached for what she'd been working towards. She'd imagined burying herself in those history books, and writing a dissertation, and graduating from university, and one day teaching in the classroom. She'd imagined lesson plans, and school projects, and field trips. And yes, she'd known that being a high school teacher wouldn't all be sunshine and roses. But she'd known, too, that her passion would always keep her going.

That passion had been knocked out of her when her parents were killed. She'd put on hold the life she'd dreamt of, thinking the pause would only be temporary. When she'd stored away those files and pieces of paperwork, she assumed she'd return to them at some point in the future.

But it was a future she'd given up on long ago.

Looking now at the old university documents in her hands, she wondered if that future might still be within her grasp.

Picking up her phone, she decided it was time to find out.

CHAPTER 20

Laura was waiting in The Crooked Thistle for Bruce when he backed through the pub doors with a load of boxes balanced in his arms. The pub was quiet, with only Jimmy Pearson and Big Kev in their usual places.

"Hey, gorgeous, what brings you here?" Bruce said.

Walking over, Laura kissed his cheek and helped him by sliding one of the boxes from the pile. "Did you take a trip to the wholesaler?"

He nodded. "A bunch of lads came in to watch the football last night and cleared us out of salt-and-vinegar."

"Listen, I can't go into town this afternoon like we'd planned," Laura said. "Yvonne's got the day off and invited me over to see her new place. I hope you don't mind if we postpone?"

"Course not. But you could've just texted me, you didn't have to come over."

"I did text you actually, but got no reply."

Bruce frowned and reached into his jeans pockets and came out empty handed. "I don't know where my phone is, hang on a minute." He walked back out, and returned a minute later waving the phone in the air. "I must've forgotten to take it into the wholesalers. Anyway, no problem about today. What are you doing tomorrow?"

"I'm working until two, why?"

"I've got a pub viewing at four and wondered if you'd like to come."

"Sure, if you don't mind the company."

"Mind it? I need it. I need company, I need advice. I'm getting desperate."

Keith appeared in the bar. "Bruce, good, you're back. Go into the kitchen and take a look at those loose floor tiles, would you?"

"Sure." Bruce turned to Laura and kissed her. "Have a good time with Yvonne, and I'll see you tomorrow."

As Bruce disappeared from the bar, Jimmy Pearson and Big Kev looked up from their newspapers and made crooning sounds.

"Young love," Big Kev said.

"Aye, young love, that's right," Keith said. "You're too old and twisted to remember what that's like." He turned to Laura. "Just ignore these two old farts."

"I like your new whisky display, Keith," she said.

He turned and admired it. "Aye, I'm pleased with it. Even these two misers have already tried something new."

She took Keith's arm and pulled him gently to the end of the bar out of earshot. "Keith, I know that Natalie's found a buyer for the restaurant. And I know that the two of you won't be seeing each other any more. I want to say I'm sorry, because I was the one who got you both together in the first place."

But Keith waved a hand. "Natalie and I had a wonderful time together. You don't have anything to apologise for. In fact, I think you did both of us a favour."

She looked uncertain. "Really?"

"Natalie needed a bit of fun, now that she's finally beginning to move on after losing Angelo. And as for me, well, I needed to be reminded that there are good women out there, and that I should stop letting myself chase after the ones who are wrong for me."

"Hmm, well …"

"And the fact is that you and Bruce ended up together while you were cooking up this scheme to pair me off with Natalie. I couldn't be happier to see you two hit it off."

"That's sweet, Keith."

"Don't know about sweet. But it's true."

Bruce stuck his head around the kitchen door. "Uncle Keith, I could use a hand in here."

Once Keith walked off to help Bruce, Laura picked up her bag and was preparing to leave when she heard a pinging sound coming from the boxes she and Bruce had set down on the floor. Turning, she realised Bruce had again forgotten his phone, this time leaving it balanced on top of the boxes of crisps.

Shaking her head, she reached for the phone, knowing it would be safer on the bar counter rather than balanced on a stack of boxes.

She didn't mean to read the incoming message that popped up on the screen. It was simply there.

This is Heather, again. Stop ignoring me and pretending this isn't happening, Bruce. We need to talk.

Laura stared at the message, long and hard. A cold sensation skittered across her skin.

While the phone was still in her hand, another message arrived.

I'm outside the pub right now and just saw you walk through the doors. I'm coming in.

Stunned, Laura continued staring at the phone screen. Seconds later, the doors of the pub swung open and a woman walked inside.

Heather.

Laura watched the woman glance around the pub. She was beautiful. Long auburn hair, startling blue eyes, cheekbones any woman would kill for, and dressed immaculately in a stunning dress that flowed all the way over ...

... all the way over her bump.

Understanding hit Laura like a fist to the guts.

The woman was pregnant. Probably around seven months.

In a flash, she remembered that afternoon she'd met Bruce's sister-in-law, Claire, who'd almost said something about the divorce that she'd seemed to think Laura must already know.

And now Heather stood before her, resting a hand on her baby bump.

"Excuse me," Heather said to her. "Do you know Bruce McGraw? I saw him come in here as I pulled up outside."

But Laura couldn't speak. She could only stare.

"Um, hello? I'm looking for Bruce McGraw?"

Stop ignoring me and pretending this isn't happening, Heather's message had read.

Laura looked one more time at the woman's swollen belly before grabbing her bag and running for the door.

BRUCE WAS FINALLY MAKING progress with the loose tiles in the kitchen when he heard Jimmy Pearson calling his name.

"Bruce! You'd better get out here."

Laying down his tools, he pushed through the kitchen door, expecting to see a sudden rush of punters looking for their lunchtime pints.

Instead, he saw Heather.

"You've got a visitor," Jimmy Pearson said, his tone unusually sombre.

"Heather, what are you doing here?" Bruce attempted to walk over but found his feet wouldn't move.

Heather frowned and gave him a look he remembered only too well from the unhappier times in their marriage. "I've been texting you, Bruce. You haven't replied."

"Did you expect me to?"

She flinched at the steel in his voice. 'No, I guess not.'

Her hand moved to the baby bump and sadness swept her face. Bruce felt sudden remorse for the tone he'd used, although he didn't fully understand why.

His gaze moved to her bump. "Are you okay?"

She rubbed her stomach almost absent-mindedly and her expression softened. "I'm okay."

Keith emerged from the kitchen. "Bruce, we need to get these tiles glued back down before ... oh ... Heather."

"Hello, Keith. How are you?"

"Aye, fine."

No one seemed to know what to say next. The only sound was the fruit machine, quietly singing to itself in the corner. Not even Jimmy Pearson or Big Kev, Bruce noted, seemed willing to risk an ill-advised comment.

"Um ... so, what brings you here, Heather?" Keith finally said.

"I need to talk to Bruce."

"Aye, right. Bruce, why don't you take Heather upstairs and get some privacy."

Bruce pointed in the direction of the back stairs and showed Heather into the small living room. When he gestured to the sofa, Heather waved a hand.

"If I sit down, I'll never get back up again. This baby's destroying my centre of gravity." She turned and saw his expression. "Sorry, I know you don't want to know about that."

"Heather, why are you here?"

"Because you didn't reply to any of the messages I sent and you've refused to answer my calls."

"Can you blame me?"

"Not really."

"So, I'll ask again. Why are you here? What do you want?"

She sighed. "My painting, Bruce. I want my painting."

He frowned. "What?"

Throwing her arms wide, she gestured at him. "My painting! The one you took when you left. It's *my* painting, Bruce. You *gave* it to me as a gift. You had a no right to take it. I want it back."

He felt his eyebrows beetling as he took this in. "The *painting*? That ugly painting, that's what you came for?"

"If you thought it was so ugly, why did you take it?"

"You know why."

Her expression changed and the sadness returned. "Yeah, I know. Look, I understand why you'd rather just ignore me. But that painting is mine, and I'd like to have it back."

Bruce stared and then felt laughter roll through him. "All those texts you sent were about that *painting*?"

"Yes, of course. What did you think they were about?"

"You just kept saying we needed to talk and sort things out. I had no idea what you wanted."

He walked to the other side of the room and looked out the window.

"Actually, that's not true," he said. "I thought it might be a lot of things. I thought maybe you and Dan had split up, and that maybe you wanted us to ... well, that you maybe wanted us to get back together."

Turning, he saw a look of complete astonishment cross her face.

"No, Dan and I are great. We can't wait for this baby to come."

Seeing the love and excitement in Heather's face as she said this, he felt the strangest feeling as the last shards of resentment he'd held inside just crumbled away. Until that moment, he hadn't even realised they'd been there or how much hurt he was still carrying inside. During the weeks he'd spent with Laura, he'd believed he was finally moving on from the horror ending of his marriage, but now he knew that Laura could only ever have helped him so far.

He had to let go. He had to let go of the hurt and the anger and the embarrassment. And now that he saw

Heather, so obviously happy and blooming in the new life she'd chosen – in the new life she'd left him in order to live – he realised that he too not only could let go, but that he wanted to.

And so he did. And up it went, like a balloon floating away into the sky. It was instantaneous and miraculous.

"I'm glad you and Dan are happy," he found himself saying.

Her smile came quickly. "Thank you, that means a lot."

"Give me a minute, I'll be right back."

He stepped through to his bedroom and returned with the painting. Since taking it down from the wall, he'd wrapped it in special packaging and thick brown paper while he sorted out the shipping.

"I was about to courier it to you. I should've done it before now."

She ran her hand along the thick paper wrapping. "You were hurt, Bruce, and lashing out. I'm sorry I caused you to do that."

He nodded and gestured to the painting. "You didn't come all the way up from London just for this, did you?"

"I was visiting an old friend in Edinburgh before the baby comes and wanted to see if I could talk you into giving me this before I went home."

"Is your car downstairs? I'll put this in the back for you."

"Wait." She stepped forward and moved to touch his arm, but seemed to think better of it. Her hand dropped to her side. "I know I said this a million times already. But I *am* sorry, Bruce. I never wanted things to end the way they did. I fell in love with someone else, but that didn't mean I wanted to hurt you. And I know I did hurt you."

As he looked at his ex-wife, he thought of all the pain he'd been holding inside for so long. "For a while, I thought I'd never get over it, Heather. You broke my heart."

"Bruce, I'm sorry, and—"

He held up a hand and smiled as an image of Laura filled his mind. "But lately, it feels like it's starting to mend."

"Really?"

"Yeah."

"That makes me happy, Bruce. I only want you to be happy."

"Come on, I'll carry this downstairs."

At Heather's car, he packed the wrapped painting into the back and made sure it was secure. When he turned to her, he wondered what he ought to say.

He decided he ought to say what he truly felt.

"I hope you and Dan have a great life together, Heather. You're going to be wonderful parents."

And for the last time, Heather gave him that smile that had, once upon a time in another life, set his heart beating fast.

"Goodbye, Bruce."

"Bye, Heather."

Watching her pull out into the traffic and disappear forever, he could almost see their paths finally fork and separate.

He felt nothing but relief.

. . .

When Bruce walked back inside the pub, Jimmy Pearson and Big Kev gave him beady looks.

"Looks like you've got some fast talking to do," Big Kev said.

Bruce's eyes narrowed. "What are you talking about?"

"Well, that was your ex-wife, wasn't it?"

"Yes."

"Your pregnant ex-wife?"

Bruce sighed. "Sorry to spoil the gossiping, but it's not my baby."

"In that case, you might want to explain that to Wee Blondie."

Bruce's head snapped up. Keith, who'd been polishing the glass shelves of his new whisky display, turned around and stared at the two men on the barstools.

"What are you talking about?" Bruce said.

"The best we can work it out," Jimmy Pearson said, "you left your phone on those boxes of crisps, and when it pinged, Wee Blondie picked it up to put it on the counter. Her face turned white when she saw the message, didn't it, Kev?"

"White as a sheet."

Bruce, spying the phone on the bar counter, grabbed it and read the messages that Heather had sent while he'd been in the pub kitchen.

"Then your ex-wife walked in," Big Kev said. "Wee Blondie took one look at that bump of hers and sprinted out the door."

"Shit!" Bruce said. "She put two and two together and got a disaster."

"For God's sake," Keith said. "You have to set her straight."

Bruce dialled Laura's number but it went to the answer service. When he dialled again, the same thing happened.

"Did she say where she was going?" he asked Jimmy as he grabbed his keys.

"She didn't say anything, mate."

Bruce squeezed his eyes shut and tried to think. "She said she was going to see her friend, Yvonne."

"There you go," Keith said. "Find Yvonne and you find Laura."

"But I don't know where she lives. Damn it."

He dialled Laura's phone again. This time it went to the answer machine without even ringing.

"Okay, she's ignoring me. Of course she's ignoring me. I'm an idiot. Okay, okay. I'll try her flat, and if she's not there, I'll work out where Yvonne lives and track her down."

"Yvonne's a nurse, isn't she?" Keith said.

"Yes!" Bruce said, pointing at his uncle. "She's a nurse over at the Royal Infirmary. I'll go there and see if I can find out where she lives."

On their bar stools, Jimmy Pearson and Big Kev chortled.

"No one's going to give out address information about hospital staff, son."

Bruce paused halfway through the door, but only for a second. "I have to try. I have to find Laura. I have to put this right."

CHAPTER 21

Laura couldn't think straight. Her mind swam with one idea and one idea only: Bruce's ex-wife was pregnant.

He hadn't mentioned it, had never even so much as *hinted* at it, and she couldn't help but wonder if the reason was now obvious – the baby was his, and he'd wanted to keep it quiet.

A child would forever link him with his ex-wife. Laura thought it was something she could've grown used to. Plenty of people had children from previous relationships – it was no big deal.

But it was a big deal when the child was kept secret.

She thought of those phone messages he'd received and ignored and acted so oddly about afterwards. Oh God, had those been from Heather?

Of course they had. She'd been a fool not to realise it.

A bus pulled up at the nearby stop and Laura got on. She found a seat and sent Yvonne a message to say she couldn't come over after all.

But almost as soon as the message was sent, Laura's phone rang. Checking the screen, she sighed to see it was Yvonne.

"Laura, I've got prosecco chilling in the fridge for us. What's the problem?"

"Something's come up, and I need ... look, I just need to sort something out, okay?"

There was a pause before Yvonne responded. "Has something happened?"

"No ... look, I don't want to talk about it on the phone."

"Do it anyway."

Laura sighed and lowered her voice to avoid the nosy ears of other bus passengers. "Bruce's ex-wife came into the pub."

"His *ex-wife*?"

"Jeez, shout it a little louder, Yvonne, I don't think you quite managed to rupture my eardrum."

"What did she want?"

"I don't know. But she's pregnant."

"*What?*"

"Probably about seven months."

"And is the baby his?"

"Well, I guess it has to be."

"Why? Why does it have to be his? She had an affair, didn't she?"

Laura sat stunned, watching the world rush by outside the bus windows while she thought about this.

"You said she was about seven months pregnant, right?" Yvonne continued. "And you told me they split up, what, six months ago? Of course the baby isn't his."

Of course it wasn't, Laura thought. It couldn't be his baby. Could it?

"But if it's not his baby, why didn't he tell me anything about it? He's told me about how she had an affair and how it crushed him. Why wouldn't he tell me about a baby, too?"

"I guess you'd have to ask him. But my best guess is that he wouldn't tell you because men are idiots. No one really knows how their silly brains work or why they do the things they do."

"His sister-in-law almost let something slip when I visited them. It had to have been about the baby. She thought I knew. Oh God, maybe it *is* Bruce's baby, Yvonne, and Claire thought I knew."

"You're running in circles, Laura. The only way to find out is to ask him."

"I don't think I can. I'm too terrified in case it *is* his baby. And too confused about why, if it isn't his baby, he wouldn't tell me the whole story."

"Look, you're crazy about this guy. Anyone with eyes can see it, and anyone with eyes can see he's crazy about you too."

But Laura was shaking her head. "No, I need to take a step back. We've been moving too fast and this is a wake-up call. Even if that baby isn't his, I can't help but feel he's got feelings for her, Yvonne. What was I thinking, getting involved with someone barely a few months out of a separation and divorce?"

"Now you're just being silly. Look, come over here and we'll talk, and—"

"No, I'm just going to walk around for a while and have a think."

"Okay, but I'm here if you want to come over."

"I know."

"I love you."

"I love you too."

Laura ended the call and trudged off the bus. She began walking, heading in any direction, no direction.

The baby couldn't be Bruce's. Yvonne was right. Wasn't she?

But what if it *was* his baby? Remembering the text message that Heather had sent, Laura cringed.

Stop ignoring me and pretending this isn't happening.

Oh God, had Bruce been ignoring the fact his ex-wife was pregnant with their baby? That didn't seem like the Bruce she'd come to know – and come to love.

But after only a few short weeks together, maybe she was deluding herself about how much she actually *did* know.

"Laura, are you quite alright?"

Blinking, Laura looked up and stared in bafflement at Natalie, who had somehow appeared before her.

"I just came out of my solicitor's office across the street and saw you standing here," Natalie said. "Are you okay?"

Laura glanced around the busy street, where people rushed past and traffic zoomed along the road.

"I ... I was going to get a cup of coffee."

Natalie eyed her carefully. "I'll come with you, in that case. I need a coffee myself after spending an hour discussing the details of the Valentino's sale with my slippery solicitor."

Natalie steered her towards a nearby cafe, and once they'd ordered coffees and taken a seat by the window, she unwrapped her scarf and looked long and hard at Laura.

"What's the matter?"

Laura stirred her cappuccino. "It's a long story."

"I've got time."

She stirred the teaspoon some more before finally surrendering and summarising the events of the last half hour. When she'd finished talking, Natalie nodded and sipped her coffee.

"Well, it sounds to me like Yvonne is right," Natalie finally said. "I can't imagine that Bruce is the sort of man who would keep the imminent birth of his own child with his ex-wife a secret from a new girlfriend. However, I'm also aware that people can, and do, let us down. Keith certainly never mentioned anything about it to me, but then again why would he? I think Yvonne is right. You need to talk to Bruce."

"But he kept this from me."

"If it isn't his child, how has he kept it from you? If it isn't his child then there's nothing to tell."

Laura rubbed her eyes. "I haven't had many serious boyfriends, Natalie, you know that. And I opened up to Bruce about a lot of things in my life, and about stuff I find it hard to talk about. It hurts that he kept this from me. I know that doesn't make much sense."

"You're right, it doesn't."

"We've said we love one another. And I do love him. But there's too much about him I don't know."

"Laura, let me tell you something. You don't fall in love with someone because you already know everything there is to know about them. You fall in love with someone because you *want* to know everything there is to know about them. And if that love is real and the person you are in love with is basically good at heart, then there's very little you learn about them that could ever change how you feel."

"That's ... that's ... do you believe that?"

"I not only believe it, I lived it. Angelo and I were married within months of meeting each other. I didn't know all there was to know about him and he didn't know all there was to know about me. We learned as we went along, and not once did I ever have cause to doubt the love I felt for him."

Laura looked out at the street and shook her head. "Maybe I'm not capable of that."

Natalie set down her coffee cup. "Laura, during all these years I've known you, I've come to know one thing for sure. I've kept it to myself, but I'm going to say it now. You got scared after your parents died, and believe me I understand why and certainly don't judge you for it. You were only nineteen after all, of course you were scared. But you've gone on to become too cautious in life, because of what happened. In your job, you've stayed with me at the restaurant to avoid taking any real risks out there in the world. And in relationships, you've chosen men you're not really interested in so that when it ends, you won't get hurt too badly, if at all. At least that was true until Bruce came along and upended everything. And now, because something unexpected has happened, you're trying to run."

"Hang on—"

"We live in a complicated world filled with complicated

people, and there's no such thing as a safe bet. Don't find excuses to distance yourself from this man who's finally turning your world upside down, when that's exactly what your world happens to need."

Laura stared, confusion raking her mind as she tried to understand. "Are you saying I ignore the pregnant ex-wife?"

"I'm saying you ask questions about the pregnant ex-wife. If you don't like the answers, then decide what you want to do. But don't use the pregnant ex-wife as justification to creep back into your little shell and hide. You've been in there long enough, don't you think?"

Laura stared at her coffee. Moments ago things had seemed so hopeless. Now they seemed so simple. In her heart she knew what she had to do.

She pushed back her chair and smiled. "Thanks Natalie."

"I take it you're not going to eat that biscotti?"

"It's all yours," she said, running for the door.

After an hour of searching, Bruce hadn't found her.

He'd started at her flat, but got no answer at the door. At Valentino's, there was no sign of her and he was dismayed to find Natalie gone from the restaurant too. She might have been able to give him a lead.

And as for his idea of finding Yvonne, to whose home Laura had been heading, well, that was a dead end. Just as Jimmy Pearson and Big Kev had predicted, no one at the hospital where she worked would give him any information. All he got for his troubles at the reception counter was the attention of a burly security man who eventually told him to get lost.

In despair, Bruce drove around Mungo Park, because he knew Laura liked it there and thought she may have gone for a walk. But there was no sign of her.

When he returned to her flat, he planned to sit outside in his car if she wasn't yet back. But up on the second floor, he found the tall storm doors to her flat open. His heart skipping, he rang the doorbell.

Relief flooded through him when Laura answered.

"Laura," he began, hands out in front of him, "whatever you're thinking you saw earlier, you've got it wrong, because—"

"I know the baby isn't yours."

He paused. "You do?"

She opened the door wider and he stepped inside. He wanted to take her in his arms and hold her, but knew that this was a big moment and that more was needed than just an easy act of physical comfort.

"Did you really think I would've left London if that baby was mine, whether my marriage was over or not?"

She shook her head. "No, I don't. I jumped to conclusions. Not because I doubted you. But because I wanted to."

He frowned. "I don't know what you mean."

She walked to the living room and he followed. They sat, but almost immediately she got back up again and paced to the window.

"I've never got as close to a man as I've got to you," she said, rubbing her arms nervously. "At my age, I know that's crazy, but it's true. After my parents died, I had no one. No other family, at least none that were close. I was alone. But

I got through it alone. Natalie and Angelo were the only people I got close to, and then Natalie told me she was selling Valentino's. And I thought: *See this is what happens when you get too close. You get hurt.* But even with that warning ringing in my head, I fell for you."

Bruce said nothing. She needed to say what had to be said, and interrupting would only make it harder.

"It scares me," she continued. "It scares me how fast I've fallen for you. I'm totally, madly in love, and it scares me. When I saw your ex-wife walk into the pub and saw she was pregnant, I convinced myself in a split second that it proved how wrong I'd been to get close, how wrong I'd been to let myself feel these things that I feel for you. Because you never know what's coming next in life, and all you can do is bet on yourself, and when you take a chance on someone else, well, in waltzes their pregnant ex-wife to ruin your whole world."

She laughed sadly and shrugged. "I know that sounds stupid."

"It doesn't sound stupid. Don't you think I've felt the same way ever since my marriage ended? You're not the only one who's ever been so badly hurt that you decide it's easier never putting yourself out there at all. Don't tell yourself that there's something wrong with you for trying to keep from getting hurt again. Since I came back here to this city to start again, all I've been trying to do is get through each day. And then I met you. And you've changed everything."

Laura glanced out the window once more before turning back. "You told me a lot about what happened when your marriage ended. But you never mentioned a baby."

A long beat passed. "It hurt too much to talk about it."

He felt her gaze, and she moved across the room and sat beside him. "Can you talk about it now?"

He took her hand and kissed it. "After Heather and I got married, I wanted us to have kids right away. But she wanted to wait and kept saying the time wasn't right. Then we started having some trouble, and weren't getting along so good and ... well, soon we weren't sleeping together much, either. I thought we were just having a bad patch, most marriages have them, I supposed. Then one day, I found a pregnancy test in the bathroom bin. And it was positive. And this wave of happiness just rolled through me. We hadn't slept together for a while, but I figured that the last time we had, we'd somehow managed to make a baby even if we hadn't been trying to."

He raked his hand through his hair. "Anyway, that night I told her I'd found the test and that I was so happy. And that's when it all came out. Heather told me she'd been having an affair with this guy at work – Dan – and that the baby was his. She said the timings made it impossible for it to be mine. And she said she loved him and that she'd been trying to pluck up the courage to tell me she was leaving me to be with him and have the family they'd already started."

Laura squeezed his hand. "I'm sorry."

"Heather hadn't just had some silly fling. She was in love with this guy. At the time I didn't realise that was actually a good thing. I didn't realise it until today."

"How is it a good thing?"

"Because she didn't throw away our marriage for a meaningless affair. She actually fell out of love with me and in love with someone else. Until I saw her today, I didn't realise how happy she was. She's where she should be, and she's with who she should be with. I might have been that person once, but I'm not any more. And it was only today I realised she's gone from my life, and I can finally let go of everything that happened."

Laura looked away and he saw sadness in her face. "You still have feelings for her."

"No!" he said, holding her hand tighter to him. "Yes, I *had* feelings, but not feelings of love. I *hated* her for what she did. That's why I took that stupid painting of hers, because I wanted to hurt her. And that's why I was ignoring all the messages she'd sent these past weeks."

She glanced up. "I thought you'd been acting strangely. You told me it was nothing."

"What was I going to say? Oh, it's just a message from my ex-wife, but don't worry because I'm ignoring her? As it turns out I should've just talked to her. All she wanted was the damn painting."

"You thought she wanted something else?"

He shrugged. "I thought maybe things hadn't worked out with Dan and she was hoping we could get back together. I thought I wanted to reject her the way she'd rejected me, and I hated myself for wanting to hurt her like that. But that wasn't really what I wanted at all. Heather's made a new life for herself, without me. And now I want to make a new life for myself, with you."

She shifted on the sofa. "Bruce, we've only just started seeing each other, and—"

"I'm in love with you Laura. I didn't expect it. But it's what's happened. If you think what we have is just harmless fun that'll fizzle out in a few months, tell me now."

She said nothing.

"You don't think that's what's going on here, do you?" he said.

"No."

"Me neither. Today I finally closed the door on a sad and difficult part of my life. And all I want to do now is open the door that has you on the other side of it."

He saw her lips curve and his heart beat faster at the sight of her smile.

"Bruce, you make it hard for me not to fall in love with you even more than I already have."

Laughing, he touched his fingers to her face. "I don't know what the future holds any more than you do. But maybe we could find out together. What do you think?"

She moved her hands from his, laid them on his shirt and pulled him close. The kiss she gave him answered his question.

CHAPTER 22

"We're off the beaten track, but not by much, I promise."

The estate agent had been chattering all the way there, but Bruce didn't mind. He wasn't sure about this prospect – either in terms of the building or the location – but was willing to take a look. And the closer they got the more the surroundings reminded him of where his London pub had been, on the furthermost outskirts in a sweet, riverside location that belied the fact that ten million people lived nearby.

This place was a little like that, he thought. There was a village feel, even though the main road ran busy and uninterrupted six miles all the way back to the centre of the city. The location felt good, like it had potential.

Seeing Laura smiling in the passenger seat beside him as she looked around at the main street and the rows of old cottages and, beyond, the hills stretching off to the north, made it feel even better.

"There's a train station right here in the village," the

agent explained as they got out Bruce's car. "Regular buses run back into town. And as you can see, there's a sizeable car parking area that comes with the property"

He surveyed the building. "You said this place used to be a pub?"

The agent nodded. "Until about ten years ago, and I doubt you'd have trouble getting a new licence. The publican owned the building outright and when he died suddenly it was passed to a nephew, who decided the pub market wasn't right and turned it into a cafe. A lot of day trippers come here, what with the walking trail that starts near the river, and the big country park nearby. The nephew thought that a cafe was a better bet, but he wasn't much of a businessman, or so I'm told, and it didn't do well."

"When was the place last trading?" Bruce looked uncertainly at the rundown grounds and the boarded-up windows.

"Not for a few years. The current owner – the nephew of the previous publican – shut the place up when it didn't work out for him. The price reflects the current condition."

"Open it up," Bruce said. "We'll take a look around and I'll come back with questions."

The agent nodded and while she dealt with the ring of keys and the locks on the doors, Bruce walked over to Laura and the two of them stood taking the place in.

"It needs work," Laura said. "A lot of work. Are you up to this sort of challenge?"

"You should've seen the place I bought in London. It didn't look as bad as this, but it wasn't far off."

"Really?"

"Really."

"Then you are a glutton for punishment."

There was no doubt the property needed a massive project of works. Even if you could ignore the overgrown grounds and the frost-heaved paving and car park, the building had been allowed to languish for much too long, unloved and untended.

Once inside though, things improved. Bruce found himself liking the space and the high ceilings and big windows. The place probably worked better as a pub than as a cafe in terms of layout. It was too big and roomy for a cafe. But as a pub, he could see how it would have just the right blend of spaciousness and light, with enough nooks and crannies to provide cosy little snugs and booths to add character. Dismayed, he noticed that some clueless person had removed the original fireplaces and done a poor job patching up the empty spaces left behind. He found himself imagining how it would look with them reinstalled, and thought of cold winter days with flames flickering into the darkening afternoons while customers sat huddled at tables, eating hot lunches and drinking good wines and good beers.

And the space where the bar itself would go – now there was a lot of opportunity there, anyone could see that. Plenty of space for something really glorious, maybe using old reclaimed fittings, and you'd want a long, wooden countertop that would set the tone for the whole place, and …

"I've opened the back doors, Mr McGraw, if you'd like to take a look at the rear of the property," the agent called out.

"Thanks. Laura, want to come outside?"

"In a minute,' she called through. "I'm in one of the little bathrooms back here, and you should see these amazing old wall tiles."

"I'll take a look later. I want to see outside first."

He stepped through the double doors that led to the back and groaned when he saw the rear gardens were even more overgrown than those at the front. He'd have to hire a digger to fight through the shrubbery and think carefully about how to replant.

More cost. More than he'd imagined taking on.

Still, there was something about this place. Walking to the edge of the perimeter line, he could hear water running, and grinned in surprise when he found a little stream. It would make for an irresistible beer garden when the weather was fair. And the tall sycamore tree rising on one side made for good shade and an interesting feature, and—

Realisation hit with a jolt. He *knew* this place. He'd never been here before, but still he knew it.

This was the place he'd dreamt about. Dreamt about and longed to find.

Turning, he looked back towards the property and saw with amazement that if he'd sketched that vision from his dream and held it up to what he now looked at, they'd practically be carbon copies. There right in front of him was the red sandstone of the villa, which he'd barely noticed because his attention had been elsewhere. There were the slipped slates on the roof. There, too, were the buckled sections of guttering.

Standing beneath the sycamore tree as the stream

flowed gently behind him, he stared at the tumbledown building in stunned disbelief. He hadn't realised that dreams really could come true.

But a moment later he knew it for certain as Laura stepped through the doors, smiling as the sunlight caught her hair.

In that perfect moment he saw their future shimmering. He saw Laura beside him as he transformed all that stood here into something wonderful. He saw a summer wedding in the gardens. And he saw children, their children, running and laughing.

Filling with love as Laura drew near, he glimpsed what they would be together and the life they would have, and the gift of it made his heart soar.

"What do you think?" Laura said when she reached him.

Bruce looked at her and at the old building, as that vision shone in his mind. "What do *you* think?"

She looked around. "It's a mess. And it's gorgeous. You'd be crazy not to buy it."

Laughing, he slid an arm around her waist and felt the warmth of her, the life of her.

"I planned to live in the place I bought while I renovated it. That's not an option here. Another few months with my Uncle Keith are going to be tough to take."

She wrapped her arms around him and looked up into his eyes. "I happen to have a spare room."

He studied her, surprise and joy swirling. "Yeah?"

"Yeah."

"You're sure? I mean, it's a big decision and—"

"I'm sure."

The steady expression in her eyes told him she meant it.

Smiling, he kissed her head and pulled her closer. "What kind of rent would you want?"

"I'm open to negotiations. We could even consider bunking up together."

"I like the sound of bunking up."

"I can always kick you into the box room if I get tired of you."

"Fair enough."

"Good, that's settled. And as you're now officially my new flatmate, maybe you could tell me what you think about this idea I've had."

He leaned back and read the look on her face.

And thought he already knew what she was going to say.

CHAPTER 23

Natalie boxed up the last of the desk things in her office and ran tape across the top.

"It's strange to see all your stuff gone," Laura said, looking up from the pile of paperwork she was loading into a carton.

"Ruby will soon have it jammed with her own things, judging by the number of boxes she's already brought over." Natalie removed the last photograph of Angelo from the wall and looked at it before tucking it into a box.

"I can't believe it's already time for you to go."

"I'm happy it's come quickly. No lingering."

"How do you feel?"

Natalie considered the question. "I feel fine. I'm going to miss this place, but I don't have any doubts about going. That brings its own relief." She closed and taped the flaps on the box and looked at Laura. "I hope you feel the same way about the decision you've made."

Laura smiled. "I do."

"Good. In that case, as I'm all finished and ready to go,

it's time I gave you this."

Natalie reached below the desk and handed Laura a gift-wrapped box. Inside, was a framed photograph of Laura, Angelo and Natalie, smiling behind the counter at Valentino's. Natalie had found the photograph while clearing her office and known instantly it made the perfect gift.

"It's lovely, just lovely," Laura said. She stared at the framed image for a long time before she spoke again. "I got you something too."

"You didn't have to do that, Laura."

"Of course I did."

Laura handed her a box and Natalie opened it. She gasped in surprise when she saw the snow-globe that lay inside, and which held inside it a tiny model of Valentino's restaurant.

"How on earth did you find this?" Natalie said, shaking the snow inside the globe.

"I found this company online. You send them photographs of buildings or houses, and they make these little models to put inside the globes. I hoped you'd like it."

"I love it. I'm truly touched by this and I shall treasure it." Natalie shook the snow-globe once more, watched the snowflakes fall, and tucked it inside the box. It was a beautiful gift, and she found herself already thinking of a place at home where she'd display it. "If I don't go now, I'll start crying. And I absolutely will not cry as I leave this place."

She headed for the office door, but stopped and turned back to Laura. "Before I open this door, I want to make sure the staff haven't organised some foolish shindig out there for me."

"We haven't, you asked us not to."

"And I meant it. We had our farewell party and it was wonderful. I've said goodbye to the regular customers. But when I leave this place for the last time, I want to see it as it always is, as it always has been – busy and bustling. It's important that I remember it that way."

"We know that's what you want, and we know why you want it."

And when Natalie opened the office door and stepped into the restaurant and saw that it was indeed just as it always was – busy and bustling – relief swept through her. Although she wanted to move on, that didn't mean there was no emotion connected with doing it, and she knew she couldn't bear a huge scene as she stepped through Valentino's doors.

Still, there were fond waves as she passed through – a kiss from Paul, and another from Tanya, who rushed from the kitchen to embrace her. The new owner, Ruby Leighton, waited at the coffee machine and offered her own waves goodbye and kind words of farewell. Ruby's generous spirit boded well for the future of Valentino's, Natalie thought.

When she reached the door, she turned and looked around the restaurant one last time. A thousand memories flew through her head. And although she knew it was just her imagination, for a fleeting moment she felt Angelo's hand brush against hers.

Finally she turned and opened the door and stepped outside.

"Well," she said, sliding the boxes she'd carried into the back of her car before adding the ones that Laura had brought. She stood back and looked up at Valentino's. "Well, okay."

Laura smiled at her from the pavement, and Natalie saw tears in the young woman's eyes.

"Good luck, Natalie," Laura said. "Thanks for being a good friend. Thanks for everything."

"I hope you will go and live a wonderful life, Laura," she said, taking her into her arms. "You deserve it."

Natalie kissed her cheek and gave her arm one final squeeze.

"Happy travelling," Laura said. "Send me postcards."

"Will do. Now off you go before I cry and make a fool of myself."

As Natalie walked around to the driver's door, she glanced over at The Crooked Thistle.

Keith stood in the doorway. He raised his hand and waved. Natalie paused, waved back, and smiled.

And then got into her car and drove off towards the new life that she hoped was waiting for her out there.

BACK INSIDE VALENTINO'S, Laura found Ruby Leighton dabbing at her eyes beside the coffee machine.

"It's so sad to see Natalie leave. I know you must be upset right now Laura, but I wonder if we could have a quick chat?"

"Of course."

Laura followed her into the empty office and remembered the day when Natalie had called her in and broken the news about her plans to sell the restaurant. She'd been crushed at the news. Now, as she once more sat down in preparation for a talk with the boss, she thought about how much had changed in her life, and how quickly.

"Now, Laura," Ruby said. "You are a wonderful waitress, everybody says so. But I want more from you than that, which is why I'm offering you the job of assistant manager. The hours are longer, but you'll get a thirty per cent raise to account for the new responsibilities. I'm sure you must have lots of great ideas about what we can do to make this place even better than it already is, and I want to hear them. So what do you think?"

She looked at Ruby, who was gazing expectantly across the table. She had no doubt that the woman would be a good boss, and that Valentino's was in safe hands.

Smiling, Laura drew in a deep breath. "That's a wonderful offer, thank you. But I can't accept it."

Ruby's smile began to waver. "You're playing hardball. I suppose I can look again at the figures, see if I can increase the raise a little more, and—"

But Laura shook her head. "The offer's fantastic, that's not the problem. I've decided it's time for me to move on."

Ruby stared. "You're leaving?"

She nodded. "And I hope you don't mind, but another waitress wants to pick up my hours, which means I don't have to work my notice, if that's okay."

Leaning back in her chair, Ruby studied her. "Natalie spoke very highly of you, Laura. I'll be sorry to lose you. Have you found a job somewhere else?"

"Not another job, no. But it's time to finish something I've put off for too long."

"And this thing you've put off, it's important, is it?"

"Yes, very important."

"Well in that case, I'm disappointed, but I understand."

Laura rose and pulled off her apron.

"You're leaving *already*?" Ruby asked, her eyes wide with surprise.

"Natalie left today and I ought to leave too, before I lose my nerve and back out of doing this thing."

Ruby scrutinised her, long and hard. Laura thought she saw recognition in her expression, and not for the first time she wondered what had brought the woman to Valentino's. There was a story there, she thought, and she was sorry she wouldn't be around to hear it.

"Well in that case, of course you should go," Ruby said, smiling. "I hope you'll come back sometime and have coffee and tell us how you're doing and what you're up to?"

"Count on it," she said.

Once she'd left the office, Laura, like Natalie before her, looked around Valentino's, taking it all in. Ten years she'd spent in this place and now she was leaving. She felt the moment deep inside her.

"Waitress!"

Looking up, she saw Mr Davidson at a nearby table, pouting over a sandwich. Smiling, she walked over.

"This sandwich is disgusting!" Mr Davidson said, gesturing at it. "I said no tomato, and yet they've put tomato in it! I said no mustard, and yet they've put mustard in it! What are you going to do about this?"

Laura stared. Then smiled. Finally, she leaned down and planted a huge kiss on Mr Davidson's cheek. His expression turned from angry to stunned, before finally melting into a huge smile.

But Laura didn't see it. She was already gone.

CHAPTER 24

A few weeks later and summer was just a memory, replaced with the crisp scents of turning leaves and the chilled air of late September.

Bruce pulled into a free parking spot and turned off the car engine. From the passenger seat, Laura craned out of the windscreen and watched the hordes outside moving across the campus.

"Excited?" Bruce asked.

"Excited and nervous. They all look so young. I'll never fit in."

"Is that why you're here? To fit in?"

"No, but still. I'm geriatric compared to this lot."

"Get used to it. Once you're qualified and teaching secondary school, you're going to look completely ancient."

"Thanks."

Laughing, he squeezed her hand. "You're going to love it."

Laura pulled her backpack from the floor and checked one more time that she had everything she needed. Laptop.

Pens and pencils. Notepads. Timetable set up on her phone. Campus map folded in her pocket.

"It doesn't feel like ten years since I last did this," she said. "Time can be funny, I guess. I'm doing the right thing, aren't I?"

"You are absolutely doing the right thing. Given how many history textbooks you've read these past weeks, you could probably pass the exam right now."

Staring out the window – at the university, the students, and the journey she was about to begin – Laura shook her head in wonder.

"I never thought I'd do this. I never thought I'd go back and finish what I started."

Bruce reached over and ran a hand through her hair. "I'm proud of you, sweetheart. It takes guts to do what you're doing."

She smiled and squeezed his hand.

"And I don't want to upset you on your first day, but I want to say ... well, I want to say that your parents would've been proud of you too."

She felt a lump come to her throat. "Yeah."

"And if it turns out university isn't for you after all, I could always use a labourer over at the pub. We're pulling up floorboards next week."

"That sounds like a good reason for me to get to the library and start working."

He shrugged. "Worth a try."

She smiled and looked back out at the busy campus. It felt like everything was finally falling into place.

Glancing at her watch, she opened the car door. "Okay, wish me luck."

"Good luck. But you don't need it. Everything's going to be amazing."

Leaning over, she kissed him and thought: *Everything already is amazing.*

After Bruce drove off, Laura pulled her backpack over her shoulder and started walking towards her lecture theatre.

And towards the future and whatever it might hold.

THE READER'S CLUB

Join my Reader's Club and I'll send you a **FREE** Fairhill novella – ***A Little Romance*** – written exclusively for members. It's a lovely story to curl up with and I hope you'll enjoy it.

Reader's Club members also receive my newsletter every two weeks, including all the latest Fairhill gossip as well as bits and pieces about the books I'm working on and what I get up to when I'm not hunched over the keyboard tapping out stories. They're also the first to hear about future book release dates and special offers.

It's completely free to sign up, I'll never spam you, and you can opt out anytime. And don't worry, I won't constantly bombard you with emails asking you to buy my books - I hate that too.

I do hope you'll join my Reader's Club and claim your

FREE copy of the exclusive Fairhill novella ***A Little Romance***.

Sign up at my website: www.alixkelso.com

DID YOU ENJOY THIS BOOK? PLEASE LEAVE A REVIEW

I'm a new independent author, just starting out. This is very exciting! But I don't have the deep pockets of the big publishers or the ability to buy lots of advertising to promote my book (the petty cash fund barely covers tea bags right now).

Reviews from people who have enjoyed my book are incredibly important for finding new readers who might also like my stories. ***Every review*** really makes a ***big difference*** in helping me to continue publishing. And so I'd be hugely grateful if you'd consider leaving a review either at the online store where you purchased this book or at Goodreads if you prefer. Your review doesn't have to be long – just a few words saying why you liked it will be enough.

Thank you!

A MESSAGE FROM ALIX

The Perfect Moment began as a story about Laura and Bruce and how they found their way to happily-ever-after. But the characters of Natalie and Keith quickly resisted my attempts to 'use' them just to advance the main story, and I soon found myself drawn into their lives too.

Yet Natalie and Keith don't find their own resolutions at the end of the book. No matter how hard I tried to force them together, they were having none of it. After many sleepless nights, I decided to trust what the characters were trying to tell me. And I quickly realised that maybe I wasn't writing just one story, but a series of them. And that's how Fairhill was born.

And so the good news is that Keith's story will continue in the second Fairhill novel I'm working on right now, and Natalie's story will continue in the third novel. So if you want to know how things turn out for them, don't forget to join my Reader's Club and be the first to hear news about future release dates.

Finally, a word about Fairhill – it's an entirely fictional area of Glasgow that I dreamt up. Its essence can be found throughout the different parts of the real city, but because Fairhill is fictional I can mess around with the neighbourhood features to suit myself and the stories.

A few readers have asked how I came up with the name 'Fairhill'. In Glasgow, there are many areas with the -hill suffix, such as Govanhill and Maryhill. As for the 'Fair' part – well, the Glasgow Fair is a two-week holiday period in July that's been observed in the city for centuries. Until relatively recently, most businesses and trades would close down entirely for the Fair Fortnight, and many still do. As a kid I always found the idea of the Fair Fortnight magical, with its promise of the travelling fairgrounds which would arrive, yet another tradition that also has a long history in the city. And of course 'fair' also means lovely and bonny, which seemed perfect; after all in Gaelic, Glasgow means 'dear green place.'

Alix Kelso - Glasgow, 20 February 2019.

ABOUT THE AUTHOR

Alix Kelso is the author of the Fairhill novel series. She's happiest with her nose in a book and may lash out dangerously if disturbed while reading. Having previously worked as a shop assistant, waitress, hospital cleaner and dishwasher, she eventually became a university lecturer. Although she enjoyed the academic world of teaching and researching and helping her students, she always loved writing stories in her spare time and finally decided to pursue her dream of publishing a novel and becoming a full time writer.

Alix lives in her home city of Glasgow with her husband and their rescue dog. She enjoys pottering in the kitchen, walking in Glasgow's many lovely parks, and is a firm believer in the therapeutic benefits of a long lunch with a big glass of wine.

You can find out more about Alix and her books on her website: www.alixkelso.com

38451911R00193

Printed in Poland
by Amazon Fulfillment
Poland Sp. z o.o., Wrocław